MW01167317

CYRUS STONE:

HUNTER OF EVIL

ADAM CAGLEY

With contributions from Ari Stidham.

Cover design by Adam Cagley. Illustrations by Cosmic Blizzard,
Pixgrim Studio.

ISBN: 979-8-218-22158-4

For mom and dad.

CONTENTS

1

BEFORE

New Orleans. A city known for parties, music and their barter based beads-for-boobs economy. That's the way most people know it at least. Sure they know about the strong voodoo undercurrent the place has, but most of the practitioners are nothing more than smoke and mirrors. Of the dozens of witchdoctors and priestesses, there's only two I knew that could actually practice the craft and they were all but retired. The rest were nothing more than a tourist trap. Holiday Inn charlatans offering spells and potions and rituals for money, luck and love at a hundred bucks a pop. I knew the city differently. There was a side to it that only revealed itself when the moon was high and the parties had burned out. A face it hid from the tourists and the locals alike. It wasn't all jazz and Mardi Gras. It was vampires. A whole metric ass-load of them.

The city was lousy with them. Like everywhere you looked it was rather drunk tourists, guy with a trumpet or a god damn vampire. Figuring out which was which was always a massive pain in the ass. Covens from all over the country could trace their origins back to New Orleans, hiding amongst their prey and wearing their faces.

This particular coven had been at it for the better part of two weeks. They were still young. In their vampiric infancy really. At that precocious age where they think being undead is cool, before they learn how hard it actually sucks. They weren't locals. I'd been tracking them from somewhere up north. Some other city in Louisiana who's name I'd forgotten because who the hell cares about Louisiana cities that aren't New Orleans? Lafayette? Is that one?

I'd tracked them from somewhere up there! They moved down erratically, their path anything but direct on their way to the Vampire Mecca. Covering their tracks and hiding their corpses as they went. On rare occasions there was no corpse at all. If they were covering a lot of miles, they'd bring their victim with them and drain them slowly as they traveled. Road snacks. Litter on the side of the highway. And on even rarer occasions, they'd turn them. Add to their ranks. There were only two when I first caught their scent and plotted their path. But in New Orleans? There's no shortage of fresh food and new friends.

I have to work fast.

A trail of blood ran across the state and led right to an abandoned warehouse on the east side of town. Warm rain poured down as I hid in the shadows between street lights across the way from it. But it wasn't enough to wash the streets clean. Just enough to soak me through from hat to boots and make a cigarette impossible to light. Not for lack of trying though. I tucked into my soggy hat and damp coat and finally got one to spark. I took a long drag as I surveyed the battlefield.

Dilapidated. Rundown. In complete shambles. The warehouse was closer to a ruin than an actual building. These new age types like the grunge of old abandoned buildings. Hospitals, houses, factories. There were two classes of vampire: the Obscenely Rich and Unnecessarily Horny or the Shit Broke and Always Hungry. And you wouldn't catch this group at a demonic rave or some weird, sexy masquerade thing. They were the spiky hair and chain-wallet subset of vampiric culture. Sloppier, dirtier, slightly more annoying. Typical of younger vampires, the ones who hadn't aged into the money and power immortality brought or maybe just didn't have a master willing to show them the way.

The thirst burned hotter in vampires of that grade. The older, hornier ones had the confidence of knowing they could feed whenever they needed or wanted. They treated human blood like an event. Savoring it and hold-ing it in the same regard some mortals held fine wine. Their younger, unshowered kin were more like rabid coyotes. Desperate and feral with a less discerning taste, consuming anything they could cleanly get away with. They thought it made them edgy.

I blame Kiefer Sutherland.

Shadows danced across the cloudy, grimy windows of the long forgotten warehouse. The flicker of movement that usually points towards something moving with inhuman speed. With youth came the height of their new powers. Something they'd have to enjoy while they could. That's the thing they never tell you when you sign up for the vamp life. For the first handful of centuries it's all super strength, mind control and orgies but as you get older and creep closer to ancient you revert. Survive past 650 or 700 and it's the thirst and nothing more. I liked to think I was providing them with a service, a vampiric exit strategy. Putting them out of their misery before they outlived their abs.

I pulled my flask from the inside pocket of my jacket and took a deep drink. Irish whiskey. The old familiar burn let my body know it was time to go to work.

No one's dyin' in Nawlins tonight, baby. Not on my watch.

I flicked my cigarette into a puddle and started off across the street. From what I could tell there were two doors in or out of the warehouse, one in front and the other out back. A main entrance and a loading dock out of street view, once meant for trucks, crates and boxes, now used exclusively for the coven to bring their victims through. To be fair, I didn't really look that hard, but those doors were both unlocked and unguarded. In my line of work we call that a freebie.

I chose the loading dock. The heavy steel roll-up door was wide open. They didn't know any better yet, these kids. They knew how to keep police off their backs, if they were even looking for them in the first place. But that's not what they needed to be worrying about.

I walked through the wide open loading door. Blood trails on the ground told me which way they dragged their victims. The wild laughing and shouting and terrified screams coming from the main floor let me know exactly where they were in the cavernous darkness inside. I stuck to the shadows, moving silently and quickly like a ghost in the night around the shadows and shapes of old sorting equipment and boxes of old who-the-hell-knows-what. I reached for my belt and did a quick weapons check. On my right hip I felt my gun. A stainless steel six inch Colt Anaconda .44 Magnum sleeping peacefully in its leather holster and loaded with six silver bullets. On my left, an eighteen inch stake, sharpened to the finest point imaginable and made of the same high purity silver as my bullets. Hanging at my side was my satchel, loaded with garlic, holy water, enough extra ammo to put down a whole legion of undead and a wide assortment of other evil hunting tools and weapons, both otherworldly and thisworldly.

I saw them before they saw me. The sound of the heavy rain outside and on the windows masked my approach, even to their supernaturally sensitive hearing. In the center of the main warehouse floor, my four dancing partners were waiting for me. Two women and two men and a fifth with his hands bound in duct tape in the center of them. Four vampires and their evening meal. Which was good, their numbers hadn't ballooned as badly as they could've. Yet. New vampires usually want company but this group seemed to be pretty picky about who was cool enough to roll with them.

A lone light dangled above them, it's yellow bulb flickering and barely lighting up half the space. I was right about the hair. This group looked like they just came from some gross club seeing some gross band called like The Flaming Weasels or some dumb shit like that. They were never going to go for the more lavish vampire lifestyle. This coven was too punk for that.

Assholes.

I heard them call the biggest one Rocks. Rox? Who cares? Rocks. Probably because he was dumb as a pile of them. Yet he seemed to be the one in charge. A great lumbering fat fuck with a face full of piercings in a patch covered vest with a short mohawk.

We get it, you're edgy, calm down.

He must've been the first. Vampire hierarchy wasn't complicated. First through the door got the seat at the head of the table.

The small coven circled the duct tape guy like sharks. They were just trying to scare him, which of course he should've been. He looked like the type that had never even left the suburbs let alone been trapped by vampires in a shitty old warehouse. This was probably the farthest into the city he'd ever even been in his whole short, balding, middle aged existence. He definitely wasn't cool enough to make the cut and roll with them. I don't even think he was even tall enough to ride most roller coasters. He was dinner and nothing more.

Oh Jesus, he's crying. And begging. It'll be ok, little buddy, help is here.

I stepped out of the shadows and towards the group, a hand on my gun and a hand on my stake.

"Hey there, kids." I said, super calm and cool. "You don't know me but I think it's time we met."

Startled by my interloping, they tried the whole hissing and fangs bit. An intimidation tactic.

Come on.

"My name is Cyrus Stone. And I hunt evil."

The minions moved as one, thinking a second helping of man-blood had just wandered onto their plates. I whipped out my weapons and fired at the nearest vampire as they charged me. A short woman with a shaved head and way too many tattoos. The bullets ripped into her chest and her skin sizzled as she flew back to the floor, writhing in the agony that only something evil could feel when penetrated by high-purity silver. I fled back to the shadows. Their eyes could no doubt see me in the dark now that they knew what they're looking for. I had to be quick.

"Get that mother fucker! We're eatin' good tonight!" Rock or Rox or whatever yelled out to his remaining undead. In life, there's no way this dude was an alpha. There's no way he'd ever even seen his toes for that matter. He was enjoying his new position of unholy authority.

Sorry, bud, ride's over.

Two were on my back with the big asshole standing guard over the little man. And he looked hungry.

Will he wait for the others before he digs in?

I caught a glimpse of his foul tongue slobbering all over his big fat lips as I ducked behind a row of metal shelves.

Nope.

The two others - a guy with dreadlocks in a pair of ugly cargo shorts and a rail thin woman in combat boots - rounded the corner of the shelves and locked on to me.

I don't have time for this.

They were on me before I could move with that inhuman speed I'd been waiting for, nailing me in the chest with a shoulder check strong enough to send me flying back across the room. My gun slid away as I hit the ground but I kept a grip on my stake. Two biting and foaming mouths were on top of me before the warehouse could come back into focus. Have you ever had two hungry gutter punk vampires on top of you, gnashing their fangs and snapping at you

11

as you try to hold them up and away from your neck? Let me tell you, it sucks. It smells like shit. Like it's bad enough if you don't brush your teeth but when you add the scent of stale, old blood to the mix it becomes mind alteringly awful. Plus they were annoyingly strong. So it got tricky to keep them off of me for long. Luckily, my stake was up by the dreadlock guy's neck. Don't even get me started on the dreadlocks! Like having matted, furry trash snakes in my face.

I made a series of highly calculated, split-second decisions.

If I can maneuver my wrist just a few degrees to the left, I can press the silver into his neck, burn him and get him off of me.

In a flash, my wrist moved.

Shit! Too much.

The tip of the stake slid through his neck, ripping it completely open. Blood dumped down on to my face and into my open mouth as he screamed and recoiled. With all my strength I kicked the skinny boots lady off of me. She went soaring back into the shelves as I climbed back to my feet, her arm twisting around at an unnatural angle on impact.

Dreadlock guy gagged and growled, still un-alive.

It takes more than that to kill a vampire. Shoot them or stab them with silver, sure. Cut them with it and you'll just piss them off. Which I'd clearly done.

Neither of them looked particularly happy. Boot girl's arm crunched sickeningly as she twisted it back into its socket with a snarl. The vertebrae in her back snapped, crackled and popped as she stood up. I grabbed my gun and got the fuck out of there while the gettin' was good.

My boots slid on the smooth concrete under them as I rounded the corner back onto the main floor. There he was. That big fat tub of trying-too-hard they called a leader, drooling disgustingly over the little guy.

"Help me! Please!" The little guy begged.

That's what I'm here for.

"Workin' on it." I said as I raised my gun and got what's-his-name in my sights.

BOOM! I squeezed off a shot. He bent down to take a bite as the bullet flew

13

through the air. Blood sprayed out of the head vampire's (his name is stupid, I refuse to use it) shoulder, barely missing his neck.

"Damn it!" I'm usually a better shot than that, I swear.

He screamed, out of anger as much as pain. Even with his - we'll call it "plentiful" - size, he could still really move with the help of those younger vampire powers. He rammed his full weight into me, lifting me off my feet and sending me across the room like a wrecking ball.

I slide across the concrete as I touched down, a row of shelves stopped me as I crashed into them. A little dazed, I looked up. All three vampires were heading my way, doing that slow "we're evil and we're gonna fuck you up" walk. I hated that walk.

So damn cocky.

"Cyrus Stone?" Leader guy snorted. "You ain't shit."

The others laughed. Even the guy who was missing a good chunk of his throat. Blood spurted from his neck hole.

"You killed Spoon, you son of a bitch." The big one said as they continued their slow walk.

"Spoon?" I asked.

What the hell is he talking about - wait - no. Seriously?

"That dead one's name was Spoon?!" I asked as I got up off of my ass. "What, are normal names too mainstream, you posers?"

That pushed the right buttons. The skinny chick lunged for me, determined to avenge her pathetic fallen friend.

"Not yet, Ambrosia Salad!" The fatty barked at her as he grabbed her and pulled her back.

"Ok, come on, you're fucking with me now."

"We're gonna take it nice and slow with him." He seethed through slobber covered lips. "I wanna taste all that sweet, sweet pain."

"Calm down, chubs, it's blood. Not barbecue sauce."

I had a few choices there. I had killed their friend, wounded one of them and shot their boss. They knew I wasn't fucking around.

Shoot the big one in his face, the other two could run or, more likely, I could get pinned down by them again. Run for cover, have all three chase me. See if I can shoot the other two before the boss man can make a move. I'm fast but am I that fast? Feels like there's gotta be another play here.

They stopped a few yards away and stared me down, just waiting to see what my next move would be. I readjusted my grip on my gun and threw out my super badass catch-phrase as I brought it up.

"Let's dance, hot pants."

BOOM! One round off, dreadlocks went down.

Skinny stupid name boots girls was uncomfortably close by the time I got the second off. The silver payload burst into her gut as she knocked the gun from my hand. It skittered and slid across the floor. But at least I had drawn blood.

That evens the odds a little.

The leader joined the fray and the odds went right back down. Not great. But not undoable. He gripped me by the throat and lifted me from the ground, high over his lumpy mammoth head.

"Nice try." He snarled at me.

"Eat a damn vegetable." I spat back.

I reached into my satchel and pulled out a full clove of garlic. Before he knew what was happening, I buried it deep into his gullet. Half way down to the elbow. His fangs scratched my skin, the sleeve of my jacket barely keeping them from cutting. A few drops of blood down the hole wouldn't even register when the garlic started to do its work.

The big guy threw me to the ground in a rage as the garlic's effects started to become apparent. He wretched, trying to spit it up.

Good luck with that, asshat.

He heaved and gagged, his bulbous stomach lurching. A river of blood shot out of his gaping mouth as he projectile vomited across the room.

"Help! Somebody help me for the love of god please!" Short stack pleaded. I had damn near forgotten about him.

"Give me a second!" I yelled back as I got up. "God, so impatient."

Vampire supreme (that's a vampire with sour cream and cheese), wheeled around, clawing at his throat and tearing deep grooves into it. The torrent of blood just wouldn't quit. Not until he was completely empty. He sprayed it in every direction like an unattended firehouse. He was going to puke up everybody he'd eaten in the last few weeks and judging by the size of him, it was going to take awhile.

Boots was clutching her stomach a few feet away, the pain a belly full of silver brings becoming gradually more unbearable. I picked up my stake and made my way over to her.

Let's put her out of her misery.

In an instant, her hands changed. Her fingers grew unnaturally long. Her nails shot out like jagged barbs. She took a swipe at my face. I ducked back.

Too slow.

Another swipe came, then another and another. I stepped back with each one in an smooth tango of death.

"Someone's got some fight left in her!" I condescended.

The silver in her belly kept her slow. I took the lead and stabbed at her with my stake. She dodged it the way only a creature who just got their first taste of a silver wound and was desperately trying to avoid a second would. Frantic. Panicked. Scared. I hacked and slashed and stabbed through the air as she scrambled away from me.

One, two, stab, cha-cha. Three, four, die, cha-cha.

She didn't even realize that I was just pushing her back to where my gun sat. And like an idiot, she slipped on it. Stepped right on the handle and out went her legs. She fell back and landed flat. The gun slid right to my waiting boot, cocked up at an angle to catch it. I bent down and picked it up. She looked up at me with the worst kind of fear in her eyes. She thought she was going to live forever. She thought she would never have to pay the price for the deal she made. Now she realized, rack up a tab on Earth and Cyrus

Stone will send you back to Hell to settle up.

"Don't beat yourself up, kid, you're new at this."

BOOM! A crater formed in her face. Blood and rotted brains blasted the floor.

BOOM! One more for good measure and her head disintegrated entirely.

Now where did the "boss" go?

I didn't hear puking anymore. The lake of crimson on the floor told me that he must've been done. But I didn't see him.

Is he still—

"Ah shit, there you are."

His body was pale and shriveled. Like a man-sized raisin made out of skin, he'd completely dried out. His clothes hung from him, dangerously close to falling off completely. He'd lost almost all of his weight in a matter of minutes.

You're welcome.

He clutched the little guy close to his saggy, wrinkled body, gripping him by the throat, his hands still duct taped in front of him.

I swear if he kills this dude, I will full on lose my shit. I didn't go through all this effort for nothing.

"Let him go." I said. Hoping that would work for once but knowing better.

"My. . .my friends. . ." The vampire whimpered.

"Yeah. Well. They kinda had it coming. C'mon, Spoon? Ambrosia Salad?"

"And. . .and. . .Spank. . ." He barely said through a frustrated sob.

"No, don't. Do not! The guy with the dreads was not named Spank!"

"It doesn't matter." He said as he moved through the Five Stages and anger replaced his depression, his face taking on a new deadly seriousness. "Once I get my strength back, I'll make more. And you'll be first."

"I'm flattered, but I'll pass."

"You'll be my fucking lap dog for all time and forever! Eatin' whatever scraps I feel like givin' you!"

Time slowed down. His mouth opened wide. His fangs gleamed in the light as they bore down on the little guy's tender throat. I raised my gun.

21

One shot left. Gotta make it count.

The shot wasn't exactly clean but I could make it work. I took aim.

Gotta account for his movement this time. Lead him, don't chase him. Put the bullet where he's going to be, not where he is. Right between the eyes.

I squeezed the trigger.

CLICK!

Fuck! Out of ammo.

I dropped my gun and brought up my stake. With all my might, which is considerable, I threw it. It tumbled end over end through the air. His fangs came down on the little guy's neck.

I'm pretty sure he just pissed himself.

The stake made its way across the room just as the vampire's teeth make contact with that delicate neck skin. The point buried itself into the vampire's skull. He fell back and hit the ground with a thud as time returned to its normal pace. Dead.

Damn, I'm good.

The little guy trembled. I was right. He totally pissed himself. I wouldn't be giving him a ride home now, but at least he was safe.

"Th-thank you." He said trembling as I made my way over to him.

"Don't mention it."

I dug my stake out of the vampire's skull as he burst into flames. I looked around the room as the other dead monsters did the same. As suddenly as they started burning, the flames flickered out. Leaving behind piles of charred bone and skin turned to ash.

Nailed it.

"So do you like, have someone you can call or something? Someone to pick you up?"

The little guy nodded, terrified.

I ripped the duct tape from his hands as he let out a small yelp.

"I'll wait here with you." I said with a sigh.

And then I gotta get home.

2

DOWN, DOWN, DOWN

The dream was always the same. Desert surrounded me on both sides. A ring of crows circled something dead off in the distance. Some pour soul stuck hopelessly wandering the vast nothing until the crows could collect their meal. Ahead of me a mountain range shot up to the sky like an impenetrable wall of jagged teeth. Civilization was miles and miles and hours and hours from me now. Like that's something I'd ever even knew in the first place. Behind me there was nothing but clear blue sky.

I was always headed to the same place. There was only one road in our out, but somehow that was always enough. It sliced through the mountains, winding up and away through their pass, chewed up by their teeth and swallowed by whatever lurked past as a thick mist spewed out.

What I'd do there, on the other side, I never knew. But I could almost see it ahead of me in the face of those mountains. The blood. The horrors. The fucking abominations. I could practically taste the salt and sulfur in the air. A voice called out to me from the pass. It echoed out of the mountains and drifted carelessly over the desert. Taunting me. Like "HA HA you're never gonna get me! You suck! Nuuuuh!" Super annoying. I want to shut it up. With my fists. And my boots. And maybe, if I have the time, something stabby.

The differences were always subtle. A different face. A different name. A different evil. Always the same place. This time it was the car I noticed first. An older model Ford sedan. Not super old though. Maybe ten or fifteen years old. Not exactly recent, it didn't even have GPS. Not exactly comfortable, the AC gave out hours ago.

No time for luxury when you have work to do.

I reached into my jacket as the last of the desert passed by and the mountains loomed over me. Night came early around here. Like the sun had the good sense not to stay any longer than it needed to. And the moon came late like it never wanted to at all. Nothing survived here. And what did was pretty fucking far from friendly.

Old, dried trees worked their way up to the peaks like a horde of angry skeletons trying to climb over. I've actually seen that before! Not the most coordinated group, skeletons. No muscles. I pulled my flask from my jacket and took a long drink as the darkness of the mountains swallowed the car. My head swam for a second before the warmth spreading through my belly reminded me that I'm awake.

It's never a dream.

No matter how much I wished it was.

I polished off the rest of my flask and took a look around the car. I was in the backseat.

Why am I in the backseat?

A small pile of cigarette butts littered my boots and the floor. At least a pack's worth.

How long have I been here? Where did I get picked up? How far did I make it on my own first? Who the hell is driving?

Unopened bottles of water sat in the cup holder next to me. Two of them. A laminated sign hung from the driver's seat but I couldn't quite make it out. My night vision was better than most but the words were whiskey blurry.

"Are you sure this is the way?" The driver asked grimly.

I don't want to tell him, but I have to.

"Unfortunately, yes."

"Cool, cool, yeah." The driver replied. "And you'll remember to leave me a five star review"?

The words on the sign came into focus.

TIPS APPRECIATED!

Am I in the back of a fucking Uber?! I'm in the back of a fucking Uber! Why am in the back of a fucking Uber?! This is going to cost so much!

"Why?!"

"Well, I mean, I let you smoke in here. I drove you all the way from Jefferson. I—"

That's not what I was asking.

"Jefferson?! Jesus I must've been on one."

"Yeah, man, you were pretty drunk when I picked you up. I thought you were joking about this address but—"

"I don't even have a phone!"

"Oh yeah, you gave it to me."

The driver, just a kid really, no more than nineteen or twenty, passed a black cellphone back to me.

"You said I needed to keep it safe because it has all the pictures of your kids on it."

"I don't even have kids!" I argued as I snatched the phone from him.

You see, I had a post hunt ritual. I kill, I wash the blood off, I get as drunk as humanly possible. There's no way I'd ever sleep again otherwise. Knowing what I know. Seeing what I've seen. It's the price I pay for keeping the world safe. Normally I end up stealing a car to get back home. It's the price the world pays for me keeping it safe! This time it was just the phone.

Oh this guy is going to get a fat tip! I'm not paying for it, who cares?!

And hey, I got an Uber instead of driving!

Good job, Cyrus. Look at you being responsible.

I tossed the phone onto the seat next to me.

"Yeah, five stars and a thumbs up or whatever."

I looked out the window. Rocks and dead trees sped by me. The rocks were littered with the charred remains of trucks and their delivery or trade drivers that had tried to race their way to freedom. The mountains themselves seemed to be on a mission to close us in. The shadows moved in ways no shadows should, reaching and clawing at the car, like a child too slow to catch a Hot Wheel as it rolled down the driveway and into traffic.

I won't tell him about that. He'll be scared enough soon.

The road curved sharply, almost wrapping completely around the side of the mountain. I leaned to the side, practically falling over, as the kid took it too fast. It snuck up on him. Like many more would after that.

Hell they almost always sneak up on me when I do this drive. But he's sober, so what's his excuse?

The closer we got, the more the hairs on the back of my neck stood up. I could be blindfolded in the trunk and I would still know home wasn't far.

The pass opened up like the end of a tunnel. Miles down at their base, in the center of a sprawling valley of dirt and dust, I saw her.

Gulchy's Gulch. On the surface, it was small and quiet. A place that time forgot. Like *Cars*. That cool little town in *Cars*. But below was nothing but misery. Like *Cars 2*. Something was corrupting that backwater shit hole. It had been rotting down it's very soul for as long as I can remember.

The poor, unfortunate few that came across this nexus of evil never returned.

Except for one.

I always return.

With blood on my hands and death under my fingernails.

But, like, why? Why didn't they ever return? It's not like it was even that great! The town was as it was when it was built like a hundred and eighty-something years ago. The story goes that an old prospector named Gulchy E. Gulcherson came down out of the mountains and thought this valley was paradise. Like a dumbass. So he used the money he made pulling gold out of the rock to build the town. And they never bothered updating anything! Like "oh we got these new fangled e-lectric lights! That's good enough! Let's stop there, I tell ya what!" There was no logical reason why anyone in their right mind would ever want to stay. Had to be evil.

I should probably tell the Uber guy that.

"Is that it?" He asked, hoping I'd tell him we were lost instead of nearly there.

"Yep! Keep on going this way."

He'll be fine.

The lights from the town twinkled in the valley far below, like looking at a city from a plane window. The mountains enclosed it on all sides. A perfect ring of sharp rocks and jagged, stabbing peaks kept Gulchy's Gulch closed off from the rest of the world for all time, sealing it in like a dim jewel set deeply in a wicked crater. The dark heart of the beast that just swallowed us. The road we were on was the only entrance or exit and based on how pale he was, I'm guessing the kid realized that.

Sorry, bud. You're gonna have to come back through these mountains. If you leave the place at all. You might really like it or something, I don't know.

The road dropped into a steep descent. The car flew before the kid had a chance to put on the brakes. To get to Gulchy's Gulch we had to go down, down, down. The kid slammed on the brakes as he clutched the wheel for dear life. The car skidded to a stop. He gaped and awed at the valley below and the steep descent down to it.

"Sorry!" He spat out after a solid minute of me glaring at him.

Four stars.

He gently lifted his foot from the brake and we pressed on, rolling down as slowly as humanly possible without actually stopping.

At this rate, I'll be in town sometime next month.

I took the chance to survey the town from my high vantage point. As we inched closer and closer, I could make out more of the details. She was exactly as I left her. A small neighborhood was on the outside to the left. Houses that ran the spectrum from actual homes built on the sweat of their owners' backs to piles of wood in general house shapes. Outhouses were still a popular commodity for many of them. The rundown and long forgotten Gulchy Manor overlooked the houses of the commoners from a small hill behind them.

The town itself was split up into three rows of old buildings. The center was double-sided with storefronts and businesses facing out to the neighbors boxing them in on both sides, two streets keeping them separated. City hall, the post office (*Why? What are you mailing? Walk it across the street.*), the schoolhouse, the saloon, the general store, the doctor's office, the gunsmith, the saloon, it was all there.

A grouping of starving ranches and half-dead farms, modestly sized in their best years though those years were pretty well past, were tucked away in the back of the valley on the crater's far edge. Rain was a rare occurrence. The couple of times a year it would fall were treated like miracles. Every drop was collected, saved and stretched as far as it could go. They tried to pull whatever they could from that cursed dirt and somehow managed to keep the town more or less self-sufficient.

On the opposite side of town from the houses was the Gulchy's Gulch Cemetery. Everyone that had ever lived and died in the Gulch was buried there, going back generations to Gulchy himself. Standing in front of that, looking down on the rest of the town, was the church. Never had much use for that myself. I believed in a more hands-on approach to salvation.

After what felt like a year and a fucking half, we reached the bottom of the mountain. By now everyone and their mothers knew that someone was coming. Headlights weren't seen on the road very often and word traveled fast. I liked to think of it as a warning.

Cyrus Stone is back in town.

He gave it a little more gas as we hit the straight away through the valley's desert flatlands. Before long we passed the sign.

Welcome to Gulchy's Gulch!
Population: 166

The wood was barely hanging on, held together with a patchwork of nails and boards on the backside. Every time I drove through it, some jackass would just put it back together. It was a relic, hand painted who-the-fuck-knows how long ago. I don't think the population number had even changed since.

Someone dies. Someone farts out a kid. Circle of life.

The cartoony image of Gulchy we'd all come to accept was painted on the sign. His snow white hair shot out in clumps from under his straw hat. His long gray beard hung down over his red thermals and suspenders. His toothless grin and friendly wave welcomed anyone stupid enough to come here with a "Hawdy, folks!" written large above him.

I refuse to believe he actually looked like that.

The town grew larger as we got closer. Not like, actually bigger. The buildings were just closer up so they looked way bigger than they did from a few miles back. The Uber kid let up on the gas and slowed us again as the road led him past the neighborhood quarter of town. He looked around, taking it all in in anxious wonder.

I bet he feels like he just drove me to a ghost town.

There wasn't a single person on the streets. If it wasn't for the lights on in the houses, the bar and the church, the town would've looked completely abandoned.

The car rolled to a stop.

"Soooo is right here good or. . .?" The kid asked, too nervous to even look at me and refusing to loosen his deathgrip on the wheel.

"It's not exactly the address I gave you."

"Yeah. Yeah. I know."

I get it. He's afraid. He should be.

"Ugh, yeah."

I did a quick check.

Stake, satchel, gun, hat, cool.

And climbed out of the car.

"Don't forget about that five star review!" He called after me, anxiously hopeful.

"I'll do you one better. Keep the phone."

I headed off into town as the Uber turned and hauled ass back towards the mountains.

Drive safe, kid.

3

THE CHURCH OF THE SEVENTH SEAL

There was no one to greet me, but I could feel their eyes. Brazen binoculars from the houses, tops of fearful heads poking out from behind curtains and in windowsills. They were watching. The last time I was in town was ugly.

It always is.

Some son of a bitch grew an extra face! I don't even know what you'd call that! But if that wasn't evil then I don't know what is. People don't just go around growing extra faces! Plus he tried to eat me and kept moving after I had shot him in his original

38

face. I ended up having to cut his head off with a damn shovel before he went down.

Anyway, that's why no one liked me. They knew too much. They'd seen too much. Not as much as me! But still too much. That was the pain in the ass of it. Whenever I killed some fucked up creature out here and saved the town from being eaten in their sleep or mind controlled or wiped out entirely by a ravenous horde of things I couldn't identify, they'd get all pissed off. They didn't see the monsters, just the men and women they were and the monster that slaughtered them. Once upon a time Gulchy's Gulch was the kind of place a man could go to escape the rest of the world. Now a man retreats to the world just to escape it. The law would never follow me past those mountains. And the investigations on the other side would never find me.

I am a specter of righteous vengeance. A phantom of cold-blooded monster murder.

Nobody could take their eyes off of the mysterious and terrible Cyrus Stone.

Whatever. It's cool. I'll keep saving your asses, you'll keep being dicks to me. I'll get over it.

Everyone that wasn't watching me must've been at the church. The ones with nothing better to do flocked to it every night. Sitting for hours on end listening to ghost stories and making magic wishes and singing they're terrible fucking music. Not my scene. Never was, never will be. Magic wishes don't work most times. You need a lot of specialized knowledge to get results there! And the only thing those people had specialized knowledge in was being a bunch of fucking yokels.

Once it was realized that they were cut off from the world or once they decided they wanted to be, I was never sure which, they decided to keep Gulchy's Gulch insulated. Everything those people could ever need or want, they had right here in town. They lived and worked for each other. Like the Amish. But without the stupid neck beards.

There was a preacher man in this town. He fought like hell to save their souls.

But he was all bark, no bite. All talk, no action. All brain, no brawn. And me?

I'm all killer. No filler.

We'd never seen eye-to-eye, me and the preacher. Ever since the old Reverend Wright up and died a few years before and he blew in and set up shop in the church. He'd reformed it. Turned it into something different. Set up a new kind of religion to shove down the people's throats. Some kind of doomsday, end of the world bull-shit. The only religion anyone in this town had was the religion they were told to have so they bought it hook, line and sinker. The preacher, a man they called The Shepherd, had been gaining influence over the town ever since. Outsiders weren't usually welcomed too quickly in Gulchy's Gulch, but when he showed up they bought what he was selling right away, no receipts necessary, God fearing hicks that they were.

People loved their fire and brimstone until they actually had to deal with it.

It'd had a few different names over the years, the church. This most recent iteration was called The Church of the Seventh Seal.

Sounds pretty evil to me. I think I'll start there tonight.

It wasn't hard to find anything in Gulchy's Gulch. If it wasn't on the ends, maybe check the center of town. If it wasn't there, turn around and look behind you. Oh, there it is! There's that thing. The whole town took up maybe five hundred yards from end to end. So from the center of the Gulch I could see the top of the church's rickety spiring steeple reaching over the other rooftops. Always looking down it's nose at all the others.

I made my way past the center block on the far side, through the dark heart of the town.

Street lights. That's all I ask for.

Dirt crunched under my boots. In the Gulch's long history, they'd never even bothered to pave it. Or even name the "streets". For as long as I was aware of it'd always been "oh it's up the street." Or "did you check the other street?" I was heading up the other street. Or was it the street? I could never keep them straight. It always changed based on who you were talking to and which way you were facing. It was the street that doesn't have the saloon on it! If I started there I knew I wouldn't make it to the church tonight.

Look at you, Cyrus, being responsible again.

The moon emerged from behind the mountains. Just a sliver. Just a peek. Like the sharp curve at the top of a skull. Enough to give the valley a glow as I push on. The shades over all the windows had to be heavy. Once the moon got directly overhead, you could practically read in the center of town at midnight. Not that I would! I had better shit to do. But I could've! Is all I'm saying. If I felt like it!

I could hear their singing or chanting or whatever the hell it was they were doing, the people in the church, as I cleared the end of the street and the town. The Church of the Seventh Seal lied dead ahead, standing between the last few buildings and the cemetery like it was the only guard between the living and the dead. I took it in for a moment. Studying it. It was practically a ruin. The old wooden body, all the way up to the tip of the pointed steeple, was cracked and splintering. The handful of stairs leading to the front doors were tetanus or a law suit waiting to happen. Every few years the town slapped a fresh coat of white paint on it and it was due for one soon. It was hanging on to it's last hint of color, chipping and flaking, exposing the old rotten wood and layers of decaying paint underneath.

It looked like the Shepherd had knocked out the back wall and added an extension to support his growing congregation as more of the Gulchers bought the ticket and took the ride. A whole second building practically, that looked like it was haphazardly built by a rabble of mindless zombies. Then again, it very well might've been.

That wasn't here before.

The only new addition to Gulchy's Gulch in forever.

I cracked the doors just enough to peek an eyeball in. Inside, the room was nearly packed to capacity. I'm not good with fractions but I think at least six quarters of the town was there. Shoulder to shoulder in the creaky old pews. All crammed in like sheep in a pen, lit only by candles and lanterns. A real fire hazard.

The Shepherd stood on a small wooden stage before them, another of his upgrades to the church, next to a hastily constructed altar with an old brass goblet and whatever his chosen text was on top of it. He did the traditional priesty thing with his outfit. The black shirt and jacket, the black pants, the white collar. I just think he liked having a uniform. Not having to pick out his clothes in the morning probably left a lot of time for grooming his super manicured beard or perfecting his gentleman's ponytail. He paced the stage like a lion in a zoo, confident and predatory.

"There will be signs", he began. "In the sun and moon and stars and on the Earth. Distress and anguish among nations. In per-plexity at the roaring and tossing of the sea and waves. People fainting from fear and expectations of the things coming on the world, for the very power of the heavens will be shaken."

Is that from something?

"Friends, neighbors, kin," he brattled on, "these words do not frighten me."

They don't frighten me either, numb nuts. I don't know what they mean!

"Rather, they give me hope. For the Father has shown me the path to salvation. And you! You have chosen most wise. Through only the Father can the new world be attained. Through only him can your souls truly be freed. Look around! Look at what awaits just beyond our beloved Gulch! Decadence. Immortality. Sin."

Fuck off, nerd, those things are great.

"It permeates every fiber of every being outside this valley. And their time is coming. Or rather ours is. When mankind is gone, it is us who will stand! It is *us* who will inherit the New World left behind and remake it in the Father's name! We shall walk hand in hand into oblivion if only you'll trust your souls to the shelter of his salvation and serve him in the era to come."

He stepped back behind the altar and picked up his creepy-ass chalice.

"Some among you have yet to take the pact and form his covenant. Some in this very town still refuse to heed my words! And that's ok. Trepidation is to be expected by those who aren't ready to accept their destinies. You've taken the first step simply by being in this room with me tonight. But the wheels are turning rather you accept it or not and so I ask, as I always have, who among this congregation, who among my flock, is ready to join me at the Father's side in the New World?"

He pulled a large, curved ceremonial dagger from the altar.

That's a huge red flag!

Its curving blade, like a Scoliosis spine, shined at the end of an old black handle with something inlaid on it that had faded from full view long before this tool ever owned it. He slashed his palm open.

What the fuck?!

He held his bleeding hand over the chalice and dripped his blood straight into it.

What are you doing?! Stop it!

Steam rose from whatever else was sloshing around in here.

That's not good.

"Who is ready to become blood of the Father's blood? Who is ready to accept his gift and find their purpose in the New World?"

Two mildly anxious yet resolute Gulchers rose from their seats. An older couple I knew to be the owners of one of the small farms on the outskirts of the valley. A rounded man in overalls with hair seemingly everywhere except the top of his head and his wife who could've just as easily been one of his scarecrows and I never would've know the difference. I cracked the door open a little more to get a better view as the old farmers made their way to the Shepherd's altar.

"My friends!" He beamed, practically in tears. "What an excellent decision you've made!"

They laid the back of their hands flat on the altar as they reached it. The Shepherd held his blade and lightly swiped their palms in one smooth slice. Blood rose in solid stripes. He swooped up their hands before they could even feel it and squeezed over his cup. Their blood ran down into the brew as it sizzled even more violently.

"Do you trust me?" He asked.

"Yap." The farmers grunted in unison.

"With your lives?"

"Yap."

A smile teased at the corner of his mouth.

"And your faith?"

The farmers paused and debated the question for a beat.

"Berlongs ta the Father."

He raised the concoction up. In turn, they each drank a half, deep purple dribbled thickly down their chins. Their bodies immediately seized. Their muscles tightened and spasms as they doubled over. They coughed and spat like whatever they drank was choking the life out of them.

"Metamorphosis requires suffering." The Shepherd said to the others. "Never forget that. No matter how long or brief it is though, it will always be but a small price to pay for glory."

The farmers fits swelled as they grasped at their throats with their quaking hands before immediately stopping. Their bodies went limp as they slowly returned to their previous positions and postures and locked eyes with the Shepherd. He placed a hand on their shoulders and squeezed.

"Welcome to the New World. When the time comes, the master will let what he needs of you be known. Blood of my blood!"

"Blood of my blood!" The congregation chanted back at him.

Alright, enough dicking around. Time to make my entrance.

I kicked in the doors and stepped inside. The crowd flipped around and glared straight at me. An interruption would've been bad enough, but I was the last thing they wanted to see. The two farmers fell into defensive positions in front of the Shepherd.

I took a few steps down the space separating the rows of pews.

This place really does suck.

There was dust and cobwebs everywhere. A Leviathan Cross was sloppily carved into the wall behind Shep's altar.

It reeks of evil. But it'll take some keen detective work to suss it out.

"Hey, anybody know anything about any evil?! I'm looking to hunt some evil."

That should do it.

"Ah, Cyrus Stone, ladies and gentleman!" The Shepherd said to those judgey fuckers as he gently brushed his new wannabe body-guards to the side.

"You know me?" I asked back.

"We all know the murderer who took poor old Terry Kimberlin's head clean off not one month ago!"

The crowd started warming up as he riled them.

Terry Kimberlin? Which one was Terry Kimberlin?

I had filled quite a few of those graves out back.

"You're gonna have to be a little more specific than that!"

Terry Kimberlin...Terry Kimberlin...

"Oh wait! Was he that guy who grew an extra face?!"

"He was the handyman responsible for the upkeep of this sanctuary!" The Shepherd shouted at me, way too emotional over a dead janitor.

That explains it.

"Oh, right, him." I said as I made my way to the center of the room. "Was he doing a shit job before I killed him or was all...*this*...because of me?"

Seriously. It was gross in there.

"If this is because I killed the mutant handyman I might actually feel a little bad."

"He admits it!" Shep declared like a *Law and Order* guy.

"That two-faced freak had it coming!"

Go ahead. Ask me why. I dare you.

The crowd started to boo and shout whatever obscenities their podunk brains could generate.

"Yeller-bellied coward!"

"Burn in hey-ll!"

"He never even finished high school!"

And a whole host of other insults that ranged from mildly accurate to outright filthy lies.

"Sheriff Archer!" The Shepherd commanded from his alter.

The Sheriff stood up from his seat in the front row right on cue. An old Sam Elliot-looking piece of shit, complete with a big white mustache and a buzz cut. I swear he had been sheriff for the last three thousand years at least. Even before there was a Gulch, Sheriff Archer was probably running around, arresting cavemen for pissing in the street outside the saloon. I bet he even slept in that tired, old black and gray uniform and vest with his gun belt draped around his boney hips, clutching that cheap brass badge he had pinned to his chest.

"Arrest that man!"

Oh yeah, old man, no, take your time. Hike your pants up to your bellybutton before you take the handcuffs out, make sure you're good. I'm on your time here.

"So is that a no?" I asked the room. "Nobody wants to tell me about any evil?"

"The only evil in this room is you, Stone!" The Shepherd shouted over the dull roar of his crowd.

Real original.

The people turned hostile. Throwing trash and balled up papers and copies of their hymnals at my head.

"Ow!" Book to the face.

"Stop it!" Wad of paper to the ear.

"Knock it off, assholes!" Apple core to the side of the head.

Who brings snacks to church?!

They only hit me with like a twenty percent success rate so really all they were doing was throwing shit at each other. But still! It was annoying! I spied a gross old woman a few rows ahead of me. Like real old. Her skin was like leather pulled over a bag of old chicken bones.

"What about her?! She looks pretty fucked up! You sure she's not like a witch or something?!"

"Nothing more than a blood thirsty butcher!" The Shepherd labeled me in front of all those people.

"Uncool!"

Sheriff Archer crept forward like he thought he was going to sneak up on me.

"You know I see you there right?" I asked, not sure of what his game plan was there.

"Come quietly, Stone. We don't wanna make a mess in front of all these good people, do we?" He said like he was talking to a child.

I mean kinda.

"We will deal with you and all your kind in time, Stone!" The Shepherd threatened as he refused to step out from behind his alter like a bitch. "You and all the denizens and lowlifes that shelter you will face our righteous judgement."

Alright that's a bit much. I'm over it.

The Sheriff started to close in. I decided to help him out. I took a few steps towards him and in a flash of speed, strength and skill, kicked him square in the balls.

"HA-TCHAAA!" I cried out triumphantly as toe shattered testicle.

I turned and hightailed it out of the church.

4

LE COEUR SPECIAL RESERVE

For as simply as the town was laid out, finding a good hiding spot was never a problem if you knew where to look. And I always knew where to look. There was space between the buildings. I wouldn't call them alleys exactly, more like narrow passageways between buildings for trash and storage.

I ducked in between two buildings and hid behind leaky a trash can.

It's a glamorous life I lead.

But experience told me they'd never look for me there. For such a hard, callused people, Gulchers really knew how to give up. "Is he on the street? No? Well did you check the other street? Damn it, he must be gone!"

I could hear the rabble spilling out of the church and taking to the streets. Sheriff Archer was already forming his posse. Assembling whatever he considered to be the able-bodied out of the Shepherd's congregation to hunt me down. If they could've taken up torches and pitchforks, I'm sure they would've. Instead they just had guns. And knives. I was lucky it was just trash they threw at me in the church.

What's their plan here?

Was due process out the window? Was it just straight up mob justice they were after? Or did they think their pistols and hunting knives would help them bring me in? That I would see them, shit my pants and just surrender.

Try harder. Do better.

The moon was high overhead, lighting up the town with an eerie gray glow. That was all the light they needed to hunt the hunter.

"He couldn't have gotten far! Someone check the street!" Archer commanded from the steps of the church.

"Whata 'bout the other street?!" One of the other dumb rednecks asked him.

"Good idea, Johnson! Take your people up the other street!"

Sure, divide and conquer. Eye roll.

The group split off, pouring out into the streets. The two-faced janitor a few months back, the werewolf mail man before him, the succubus secretary a couple years ago, the undead tailor a few years before that. They had plenty of reason to want me in chains or worse. Only because they never really understood. And as I watched them shuffle through the streets on both sides of my hiding spot with nothing but blind hate in their eyes, I started to doubt they ever would.

"You can't hide for long, Stone!" Archer yelled out as he made his way out from the church.

Wanna bet?

I pulled my jacket close and my hat down low as I tucked into the shadows of the alley. Nature's camouflage. Slowly, they surrounded me on all sides. This storm would pass sooner or later, like all the others before it. But until then all I could do was watch and wait. Every time I came home we went through the same song and dance. And every time I'd hide in the exact same spot.

I watched as they popped their heads into windows and tried every door to see if I had kicked it in or magically unlocked it. Which, of course, both were always options. But it's a little obvious.

As a man that's been face to face with moaning hordes of the undead before, I can tell you that this was pretty damn close. Their groans and threats and general bolstering combined with their shuffles, stomps, drags and scuffles into a general mash of nonsense noises. Flooding the streets and drifting through the alleys. They could no doubt hear it in the neighborhood. More would be joining their ranks soon enough. Their numbers would swell with even more brainless, angry townsfolk chasing down their boogeyman as he crouched behind a trash can that was leaking some kind of nasty, sticky sludge onto his jacket.

A flashlight landed on the ground at the edge of my alley. My butthole promptly puckered. The only person in that mob even remotely smart enough to have finally realized what a solid hiding spot that was would've had to have been...

"Give yourself up, Cyrus. Enough of this. It's time you answer for your sins, boy." Archer said tauntingly as he stood at the opening to the alley.

Please don't look over here, please don't look over here, please don't look over here.

I couldn't help but feel like this was a little personal for the old Sheriff. He'd had it out for me ever since I was a precocious teenaged orphan living off of handouts on the mean streets of the Gulch. He stacked my warrants high even before I had hunted my first evil. And for everything he could possibly think to lock me up for.

Drunk and disorderly conduct.

Who hasn't?!

Petty theft.

I wanted snacks!

Misrepresenting the weight of livestock.

That's an exaggeration.

Lewd acts in a government building.

Alright yeah, that was me.

Add to the mix the fact that the succubus secretary was kinda his wife and he developed a real issue with leaving me the hell alone. I did him a favor that he definitely didn't deserve! Like, dude, you knew who she was you met her, that's not on me. And yet to Archy, I was the one that continued to get away. His cuffs had never once touched my strong, hero/outlaw wrists and I aimed to keep it that way.

I watched as the elderly bastard stood at the end of the alley, shining his flashlight in every direction except the one that mattered. He was close and he knew it. The rest of his merry band of dumbasses had dispersed through the streets, scattering out and casting a wide net. But it was strangely like Archer could smell me on the air. Slowly, he turned towards me. My breath froze in my chest. I hugged as tightly to the gooey trashcan as I possibly could as his flashlight ran over me. The beam past right over my head and scanned the wooden walls on both sides with predatory patience.

Shit. The jig is up. The alleys are burned.

Archer stared down the alley with a snarl and a growl like a wolf closing in on a camper, but yet he stayed in place with a hand on his gun. Did he know? Was he catching on? Was he about to discover his prize hiding amongst the feed store's recycling?

"Johnson!" He barked into the air.

"Who's that?!" Johnson, whoever the hell he was, yelled back almost startled.

"Sheriff Archer!" The Sheriff hollered, half through an impatient groan.

"Oh! Wha's up, Sheriff?!" Johnson shouted, a few dozen yards away on the other street.

"Anything yet?!"

Johnson didn't immediately reply. He was taking his time, choosing his words carefully.

"Nope!" He called out.

"Well did you check the saloon?!"

Does he know?

"No, sir, not yet!"

"Well get on it! I'll meet you over there!"

Jesus, invest in walkie talkies!

And with that Sheriff Archer moved off. His flashlight leading him away from the alley. My butthole released as I breathed a slow sigh of relief. If there had been a lump of coal up there, I would've turned it into a diamond.

Wait, not the saloon!

I had to book it. If they got there before I did, my whole night would be shot to shit. They'd camp it out and wait for me and I'd never get in. All they knew about the saloon and I was my fondness for getting drunk and starting fights there. And I aimed to keep it that way. I mean, that was big part of the draw for me, sure, but not the total appeal. I would need to distract them. Draw them off the scent.

Time to go to work.

I rose and brushed the dirt from my legs. Across from me was a small wooden ladder, haphazardly attached to the wall. Step by step I climbed to the roof of the neighboring building. And step by step I waited for the old wood of the ladder or the rusted nails to break away and send me plummeting back to that gross leaky goo can. How they didn't hear the creaking and whining of my weight on the failing ladder, I will never know.

To the group who saw me first as I crested the roof, I must've looked like some dark and angry spirit rising up out of the night to unleash my terrors throughout the town. I locked eyes with them from a story up as they froze in place.

"Come and get me, mother fuckers!" I challenged to anyone who could hear.

"Sheriff!" One of them screamed in a desperate panic.

The dispersed pockets of angry mob went into a frenzy, turning in circles and running in all directions to see where my voice and their buddy's scream had come from. Like an ant hill after a good swift kick, they scurried around wildly searching for the threat. Fear overrode most of their higher brain function, if they had any to start with. Had I struck again? Was I right behind them?! Down in the fray, Archer struggled to maintain order.

"The roof! The roof, you morons!" He shouted out to them. "The feed store!"

No one was listening. They thought every shadow and critter that ran by past them was me, sneaking around for my next kill. Archer's eyes darted right at me. They locked on with the laser focus a man his age usually reserved for a bowl of bread pudding or an early bird buffet. Before I know it, his gun was out of its holster and I was dodging bullets.

Pretty sly for an old guy.

His rounds tore into the wood, sending jagged shrapnel splinters exploding into the air. I took off across the roof. Running straight for the edge and with the speed and majesty of a loping antelope, I leaped over the edge and onto the next roof. Bullets struck at my feet and whizzed over my head as the Sheriff followed from below.

The rest of the posse soon caught on. Their guns all trained on me in sequence. At least a dozen, now aimed with murderous intent. Due process had well and truly fucked off. The edges of the roofs burst like fireworks of wood and hot lead. They were terrible shots, the Gulchers.

Their guns didn't see much action beyond the regular target competitions to fend off boredom or occasional hunting trips to kill whatever was clinging to life at the base of the mountains. They were mostly decorative, hanging from their hips as they walked around town, and had almost never been fired at moving, human targets. It was a miracle they didn't accidentally shoot each other as they tried to get a bead on me while giving chase. But Sheriff Archer was a pro. He knew what he was doing. Each round was getting just a little bit closer to finding home. He always was a good shot.

But never this good.

I barely kept ahead of the bullets, splinters of the roof biting at my ankles and bullets getting just close enough to warm my skin as they flew past. I looked back over my shoulder. Not only was Archer keeping up with me, he was gaining with savage, animalistic speed. Navigating around the others with an agility I didn't know he had left in him. Never once breaking his stride or his gaze, his gun never lowering for a second.

What the fuck?

I laid down the throttle as the edge of the far row of buildings drew near.

Archer's gun dropped. His haunches flexed as he lowered himself at top speed.

He can't be serious.

Archer leapt with a hungry look in his eyes I had never seen on him before. His arms out in front of him, clawed and clutched. No doubt intended for my chiseled and rugged face. He flew through the air straight for me, on a path straight for the roof's edge. For a second, I could've sworn he would've made it. I ducked in anticipation.

BANG! THUMP!

He missed. By like three feet. Slamming into the side of the building instead and falling to the ground in a heap. I was relieved but:

For a second I could've sworn...

I jumped from the roof down to the dirt below.

Tuck and roll!

And sprang to my feet like a super good gymnast guy. Perfect score for the man out of Gulchy's Gulch.

I dusted myself off and walked to the edge of the street next to me. The posse closed in from both sides of the block, cutting off my path back into town. The mountains and the neighborhood were at my six. The angry Gulchers multiplied as more filed out of their houses, guns in hand. No doubt shaken out of their dreams about horses and dirt by the hail of gunfire I had just managed to escape.

Archer made his way to the front of the group without even a hitch in his step, gun drawn.

"Enough! It's done! No holding cell this time, we're taking you straight to the gallows!" He sneered at me.

"Yeah, sure, hey! Did you think you were gonna make that jump? Because for a second I kinda thought you would." I asked, really wanting to know.

"I said enough!" Archer yelled, officially out of patience.

"I mean, I'm not even mad. I'm kinda impressed! That would've been cool. You kept up with me for a bit there too, that's not easy!" I told him, as surprised as I was confused.

"Keep your guns on him, boys!" He ordered to the posse as he approached with his cuffs, more determined than he had been in the church.

"Are there no women in this unruly mob?" I asked, genuinely curious.

"I got you, you son of a bitch." He growled with glee.

"Leave my parents out of this, you geriatric fuck!"

I dug a hand into my satchel.

"Don't you move!" He snapped as he cautiously froze.

From deep within the bowels of my bag, I pulled out two small purple balls. Himalayan Vanishing powder. Creates a fog so dense and so thick that even the mostly sharply eyed creature of the night couldn't see through it. I sure as Hell couldn't.

Before Archer could reach me, before the posse could get a shot off, I threw them at my feet.

POOF!

Fog burst out and enveloped us like a low hanging cloud of swirling maroon and burgundy. Shots rang off and voices bellowed through the confusion. We were completely blind.

"Don't lose him!" I heard the Sheriff yell desperately.

Sucks to suck, bro.

I bolted through the fog, just hoping I wouldn't crash into anyone as I made my way to its edge. I could hear them all around me. Shooting and yelling and wrestling with whoever they thought might've been me.

"I got 'em!"

"He's on top 'o' me!"

"He's ovar here!"

No I wasn't. I had emerged from the fog and left them to their mayhem.

They'll be at it all night now.

The fog would clear, of course, in like an hour tops. And when it did they would start searching the neighborhood and mountains. If they could even see straight. Himalayan Vanishing Powder had a mildly hallucinogenic effect. I liked to use it sparingly. It's hard as fuck to get for starters but it's also just like, really cool to have on hand for a chill Saturday night. Nobody had any real idea which way I had actually gone. By the time the fog cleared their pursuit of me would probably look more like "Is that him?! Is he that lizard now?! Hey, did anybody notice how pretty these tumbleweeds are?!".

Time for a drink.

In the center of the far block of the Gulch lied my favorite place in the whole wide world. The Blood Moon Saloon. The only place in town I was glad had never really changed. Even then, the few times it had just made it better. Thick, heavy steel doors kept the good times in and the bad times out. At one point in their history they had been those flappy, wooden half-door things. Now they were three inches of solid metal. The large glass windows were triple layered and bulletproof, an upgrade born out of necessity twenty-something years ago. At one point they let you see everything that was happening inside, but now dark tint prevented that. A faint glow behind them was the only proof that the building was even occupied. The hand painted sign over the door was simple and unchanged. A crimson moon with the black silhouette of a beer stein against it. The paint was always fresh. It was the most well maintained building in all of Gulchy's Gulch. The owners saw to that. Good people, the Le Coeur family. Never once cut me off.

My hand gripped the cold steel handle of the securely latched door. No, not steel. Silver.

It's the little things.

I gave it a good hard turn and pushed my way inside. It was empty. It almost always was these days. When I was younger you could always count on a full bar, at least two fights and maybe someone popping a titty out. Nowadays people seemed to be more content spending their time at home or in the church than in the company of fine, upstanding drunks and scoundrels.

My boots clunked heavily against the floor as I crossed the room. Dim lights hung over the bar to my left, creating small circles of yellow and orange on the lacquered wood and cracked leather arm rest. There was a healthy supply of old oil lanterns scattered around the room, but their glass was so cloudy they struggled to light up much at all. Bright moonlight shined in the windows behind me, diluted heavily by their tint. The long bar stretched from one end of the room to the other with a break towards the far wall that led to the back kitchen. Not that many people ever chose to eat at the Blood Moon. It only ever offered the same two dishes it served at its grand opening three or four generations ago, well done steak and whatever the hell a hog maw was. Tables and chairs were scattered around with a player piano in the far corner. Neither of them looked like they had been touched in a hot minute and it didn't seem likely that would change any time soon. There wasn't a soul in sight, but I knew he was around. He was reliable like that. A glorious wall of that sweet, sweet elixir of life stood behind the bar, accompanied by a few taps for the handful of beers that he kept on draft. I took a seat in the middle of the bar and waited.

He'll be around.

Right on cue, the bartender rounded the corner from the kitchen and made his way over to me behind the bar, polishing a pint glass as he walked. Barnaby Le Coeur. The latest in the long line of Le Coeurs to own and operate the Blood Moon Saloon. He was getting on in age. His limp wasn't new but it was certainly getting worse. When I first met him, his tight, short afro wasn't quite doing the salt and pepper thing it had developed into and his face didn't have nearly as many wrinkles and lines. He looked older than he actually was though. He had an important job, running the Blood Moon was a big role to fill in Gulchy's Gulch. Even if the people had forgotten that or had never even knew to start with. And stress can do a lot to a man.

His pressed white shirt and black apron were pristine. Evidence that the night had been dead. In the busier days, around this time, that shirt would be wrinkled all to hell and the apron would be spotted by splashes of liquor and beer. His hair would've been going wild and sweat would be catching in the crease at his brow. But tonight he looked like he hadn't served a single drink.

Why is he polishing that glass?

"What can I do ya for, traveler?" He asked me.

"Come on, man." I groaned.

"Can't read minds, friend!"

"Seriously? Every time?"

"Got a good mezcal up from Jalisco! Real artisan shit. Worth a sip if you're feelin' squirrely."

"Barnaby. You know for a fact that I'm feelin' squirrely!"

He stared at me blankly as he kept on polishing that pointless pint.

God damn it. Fine!

"Good evening, barkeep. Three fingers of Le Coeur, neat, on the dead man's tab." I said, reciting the same damn thing he made me say every single fucking time I sat at his bar.

"There it is!" He said, a little proud that he got me to buckle. Again.

Barnaby grabbed a dusty old bottle off of the top shelf. Le Coeur Special Reserve. The wax around it's cork had never even been scratched let alone peeled off. It's contents were one mystery I always wanted to solve but likely never would. He gave it a lift and the wall of bottles shook. The sound of heavy gears grinding and clanking and motors straining to turn filled the room. I squinted against the strip of bright white light that shot out at me and stretched across the floor as the wall parted, widening as the doorway appeared.

"Welcome home, Cyrus Stone." Barnaby said as he disappeared into the light.

5

DOOR NUMBER TWO

I stepped through the doorway and into the Le Coeur Inner Sanctum. It was the safest, most well protected place in the whole of Gulchy's Gulch and as big as the bar itself, if not somehow bigger. Shelves reached up to the ceilings and took up most of the walls to the left and right and around the door. They were stuffed with books, artifacts, weapons and ammunition and the makings for all kinds of alchemical potions and brews to suit a wide variety of needs, magical and otherwise.

It was hallowed ground. Along the far wall, running its length, was the Le Coeur Family Crypt. Every Le Coeur to ever serve

Gulchy's Gulch was interred behind heavy rectangular plates of gradually oxidizing silver, their names and important dates etched into them, each one a little more dilapidated and discolored than the one after it. There were only four name plates on the wall, four final resting places currently occupied. But empty spaces allowed for four more. Apparently Barnaby's family didn't expect to get past number eight. Or figured some future baby would figure out a better place to keep their honored dead than in the secret room behind a bar.

At the foot of it, below the names and empty spaces, was the great and titillating Le Coeur Box of Mystery. Not its official designation, just something I had taken to calling it since Barnaby promised to show me what was inside some day but in nearly thirty years, had only left me high and dry. No matter how much I harassed him about it.

"You ain't ready for that shit!" He'd yell every time I'd ask or try to steal it. It's old, blackened, riveted steel and gargantuan padlock called to me.

A work bench was tucked between the shelves to my right. Tools and an assortment of parts were hanging from a peg board and scattered around it as well as blueprints and sketches; experimental prototype weapons in different stages of R&D. Cots and bed rolls were at home in each of the corners, just in case. Need be this room could've served as an infirmary, a weaponry, a library, a doomsday shelter and our graves.

Barnaby limped ahead of me into the center of the Sanctum. A small chandelier hung over him, giving the room an orange tint like that time I got my head stuck in a pumpkin. Trunks and chests full of whatever Barnaby deemed important or dangerous enough to be locked away took up a good amount of the available floorspace. He stepped around them carefully, nursing his bad leg as he went.

"Every time?" I asked as I followed him in.

"We can't be too careful. Not these days." He told me, sounding a little more paranoid than usual.

I knew that, but still. The whole secret passphrase thing was a little overdone.

"How's the knee?" I was actually curious!

"Were you followed?" Barnaby answered with an embarrassed glance down to his old war wound. Straight to business.

"I took an Uber. Can I get that mezcal or...?"

"Why were you gone so long?"

Good to see you too, bud.

"I've been busy!" I explained as I tossed my hat onto the workbench.

"I hope you have been!" He spat back.

"You should've seen the mess in New Orleans!"

"You haven't seen what's been happening around here!" A voice from the far side of the room called out.

An old leather armchair and a large mahogany desk sat nestled in between the shelves of books and artifacts to the left. In the chair was Barnaby's sister Charlotte. A beautiful young woman (by twenty years at least, I never asked for details there) with a long mane of curly brown hair tied back into a ponytail behind her. Her rounded, golden reading glasses made her look like someone who would've been more at home in a college library with the other kids who didn't get invited to the cool parties than she was posted up in the Sanctum, entwined in the fight against evil. She would've been better off trying to save the world through campus protests against GMOs or something equally obnoxious. Not our way.

"Don't you have other friends?" I was actually curious again.

"Good to see you too, Cy." She said with a sly little smile.

"Please don't call me that."

"The wolves wear sheeps faces!" Barnaby interjected.

"Like, literally?"

That would be kinda cool.

"The eyes! They deceive." He offered me as a clarification.

"Sure, whatever that means. So the mezcal —"

"Enough, man, c'mon! There's bigger things to deal with here."

"Fine! So what's the deal? What's goin' on?" I groaned.

Barnaby didn't call me home for just anything. So when he reached out right before I hit New Orleans, I knew it had to be something serious and potentially cataclysmic. But that doesn't mean you can tempt a man with a beverage and then just deny him that! Super uncool.

"That's the problem." Charlotte said from her chair.

"No, don't get up, it's fine."

"We're not entirely sure." Barnaby continued. "But you can feel it out there, Cyrus. Something's come over these folks. The Gulch has always been rotten but it's like something has taken what little soul it had left."

"I know. I paid a visit to the church. Asked a few questions but they didn't give up very much."

"Exactly!" Barnaby exclaimed. "Those people wouldn't say shit if they were neck deep in it! And believe me, they are."

"Gross!" I said because it was.

"They won't do anything the Shepherd doesn't sign off on." Charlotte said.

"I noticed. They got a real boner for him now, huh?"

"You have no idea."

"I really don't! That's why I'm here." I said with a shrug.

"Ten years!" Barnaby said in a burst of anger. "Ten years I've been asking the Mayor for the permits to put in a patio! He shows up out of nowhere she just gave him a big thumbs up for his extension to the church without even thinkin' about it!"

"It looks like shit if it makes you feel any better." I told him.

Barnaby sat, easing down on top of a trunk with an exasperated sigh.

"His influence, their devotion, it's not natural." He said as his frustration grew, his voice full of spite and venom. "We're already looking into it."

"I mean, should I go kick his ass or something?"

Barnaby gave his eyes a rub. He took a breath before continuing.

"He's a poison, yeah, but he could be a symptom of a much bigger sickness." Barnaby added as he shook his head. "We need you, Cyrus."

I took a moment. The Shepherd was the least of my worries.

They should know. This could be a thing.

"I had a run in with Sheriff Archer tonight." His near roof-reaching jump still fresh on my mind.

"Of course you did." Charlotte said.

"Who invited you?!"

"What happened?" Barnaby probed.

"He chased me across town. Like actually chased me. Kept up with me even! Maybe gained on me a little." I didn't want to say the next part. It sounded stupid. But then again, in our line of work, the things that sounded stupid usually meant something bad. "He jumped at me. And almost made it up onto one of the roofs in a single leap. Is that something?"

Silence from the two Le Coeurs. They looked as confused as I felt, but with a dash of something else. Something grim. They glanced over at each other and shared a thought I wasn't privy to.

"Are you sure that's what happened?" Barnaby finally asked.

"Pretty sure, yeah. What does it mean?"

"I don't wanna pull the trigger here and call it a five-alarm fire. We have to be sure here. But we'll hit the books and dig into

84

to it a bit more." The elder Le Coeur offered.

"Tomorrow is Gulchy Day!" The younger said with a little too much enthusiasm.

Gulchy Day, the annual festival celebrating Gulchy and the founding of the Gulch. It always felt a little dick-sucky to me. The whole town would gather at the edge of town next to the cemetery and praise the old prospector with a feast and games and shitty folk music and stupid-ass dancing. My timing couldn't have been worse. I usually tried to stay away from the Gulch on Gulchy Day. Or as I liked to call it White People Eating Cold Ham Hocks in the Dirt Day.

"Right." I groaned.

"Keep an eye on it." Barnaby ordered. "Watch for the three of them. But don't do anything! Don't get involved! Observe them but keep your distance! If we're right, everyone there could get caught in the crossfire of a shitstorm you can't even imagine! We'll get you more info as we have it."

"I've got someone I could outsource some of the book work to. You two focus on the big picture, I'll bring in backup for the Archer thing." I offered kinda willingly.

"You sure?" Barnaby asked with a cocked eyebrow. "I thought you liked to keep her out of Gulch business."

"Yeah, it's fine. Sounds like we could use the help." Something in the Gulch was making them nervous, it was written all over their faces.

"Well, we'll take it. Oh!" Barnaby said as he got up off his trunk with a small groan he didn't think I'd notice. "You bring in your outside help, I'll give you mine."

He crossed the Sanctum to his shelves of antiquities and artifacts.

"A new toy?!" I couldn't really hide my excitement so why bother trying?

"You know it!" Barnaby said with a wink.

He meticulously dug through his collection of weird looking old...things. Barnaby always had the coolest gear for me. One time he gave me a walkie-talkie that could talk to poltergeists. But it was only good for one use and I had butt-dialed it so when I needed it it didn't work for shit. That was a bad example! But usually he gave me something pretty solid.

"Here we go!" He finally said after what felt like a small eternity.

Barnaby pulled a necklace off of the shelf. An old stone amulet with something carved into it that I couldn't really make out with a leather cord threaded through it.

"The Amulet of Tortoises!" He said proudly.

I took a moment to admire it in the light. Ancient amulets like this were always conduits for untold power and the secrets of time itself. Slowly, I put it on. The leather pulled against my neck as the amulet's weight took it down. It was lighter than the hockey puck of stone would've implied. The best magic amulets were always like that.

"I'm sorry what?" I asked as I realized what he said and my excitement shot all the way back down to fucking zero.

"The Amulet of Tortoises. Any tortoise, anywhere. It'll let you tap into their minds and see and hear what they do."

"What? Why would I? Does it at least work on turtles too?!"

"Nope! Just tortoises!" Charlotte exclaimed like that was suppose to be a good thing.

"So this kinda sucks."

"Don't overlook the tortoise, Cyrus Stone." Barnaby said as he leaned in closely. "Don't make everyone else's mistake."

"Right. The tortoises." I said as I picked up my hat.

"You just put it on and—" Charlotte started.

"I know how to work an amulet!" I threw over my shoulder at her as I headed for the door.

"Let's get to work. Keep me posted."

Barnaby headed straight for the bookshelves. Charlotte (*finally*) got up and joined him. They began pouring over the cracked and faded spines of the different grimoires and volumes of ancient knowledge that had been both collected and written over the course of the generations. The light of the sanctum faded and the darkness of the bar beckoned as I stepped through.

"And I'm taking the mezcal!"

6

BE IT EVER SO HAUNTED

I hit the street with the bottle of mezcal stashed securely in my satchel. The town had fallen into a quiet stupor. The horde of hallucinating Gulchers and the Sheriff dispersed on their own individual Vanishing Powder trips. A couple of them were way out in the flatlands, a few were past out in the street and even more aimlessly were wandering aimlessly around their houses, their eyes glued to their feet. The rest were around somewhere and based on the banshee wails (not literal banshees) I could hear calling in the distance, they were having a pretty damn good time. They'd all have to be up and at it early in the morning to do their share of setting up for Gulchy Day. The whole town was always just as involved in the setup and teardown as they were the actual celebration. But the fortunate few spending their night in the gentle psychedelic embrace of Himalayan Vanishing Powder would be moving a little slower than the rest.

The moon was already beginning to hide back behind the mountains, leaving the town in near total darkness again. The last remnants of its light hugged close to the outside of the church and the headstones in the cemetery. This was the only way I'd ever walk to my place. When the odds of anyone seeing me do it were at their lowest. It was late. Even the nosier, more vigilant Gulchers had long since packed it in.

I don't do well with neighbors. That's partly why I never bothered looking into a house in that part of the Gulch. I lived in one once, a long time ago, but there wasn't much left of it now. Labeled "CONDEMNED" by order of the Sheriff, it had nearly burned to the ground the night my parents died. It's bones were left to the dirt. Walking through the neighborhood was never a solid idea for me, but walking by the old Stone house was an even worse one.

I kept myself low as I moved past the edge of town and to the outskirts of the neighborhood, staying as tight to the houses and their ramshackle fences as I could. The occasional dog would bark at me from a porch or a yard, but none of them ever kicked up quite enough racket to wake their masters. And they certainly didn't care enough to come after me. I always wondered if it's because they knew I was the good guy, that they could sense on some deeper level that I was there to help. I liked to think it was.

Most of the houses of Gulchy's Gulch showed more signs of regular maintenance than the town itself. Not much more, but more. They were largely generational. Occasionally someone would start talking about building a brand new one, more room for grubby little kids or whatever other dumbass idea had crept into their heads. But then someone else would die and a house would be passed down or sold off and the circle of life would keep on spinning.

Looming over them like a low-hanging cloud was Gulchy Manor. The old plantation house that at one time would've easily outshined any of the others on their best days. Now it stood dark, silent and empty at the top of its short hill, a rotting corpse of its past self. No one ever went near it, both out of respect and the rumor that it was extremely haunted.

I should look into that eventually.

Tonight wasn't the night for that though. I turned my coat up and peered around the edge of town. Nobody was there to see me. And if they were then I couldn't tell, which meant they probably deserved to get a shot at me anyway. There was nothing to separate me from home but a short sprint across the flats.

At the foot of the mountains on the neighborhood side of the Gulch was a dense thicket of dead trees. Not quite a forest, but enough to give the idea of one. The leaves and green were long gone from them but they were packed together tightly enough to block out most of the light when the sun or moon was overhead like a canopy of sun-bleached bones. And at their end, pressed directly up against the mountain was an old log hunting cabin. For years, whenever the locals would try their hand at hunting out here, this was where they'd stop.

Hunters in the Gulch had an unspoken shared responsibility to the cabin their forefathers built. "Leave it purdee, strong and sturdee." But now they stayed clear of it entirely and it had been years since it was purdee. Two broken windows flanked the front door, which barely held on by a single hinge. The roof was caving in in places. The chimney was a pile of bricks thrown at the feet of the trees. The mountain itself threatened to drop her boulders and bury the whole damn thing at any given moment, mercy flushing it out of existence.

Like Gulchy Manor, the cabin had a reputation for being super haunted. Screams in the night. Lanterns that lit on their own. Scratching sounds in the dark that led to deep claw marks on the splintered walls. Unholy cries and moans like some twisted soul was searching for a prize it'd never have. A laugh of pure madness would erupt out from behind a door that refused to open, rattling the windows and shaking the decrepit foundation.

I Kevin McCallister'd the bejesus out of the place to keep people away! The lanterns were on timers that were triggered by the front door. The screams and cries were a motion sensor and a speaker from an old Halloween decoration I hid under the floorboards. The claw marks were usually me personally, dragging my stake into the walls when I was drunk or bored. The laughs came from my bedroom and were also me, if I thought of something super funny late at night like that video of the monkey smelling his own shit. Keep the change, ya filthy animals.

Be it ever so humble.

I pushed the door open and stepped inside my haunted abode. The smell of mold and dust rushed my nostrils in a warm welcome. The lanterns lit, right on cue. They lit the cabin just enough for it to be spooky as fuck. Just the way I like it. I unhooked one from the wall.

The cabin wasn't complicated. It was just two rooms. A living room with a wood stove and a door to the only bedroom. It was a practical place, meant for function rather than form. I stepped into the living room and tripped the screams and cries.

Most people have doorbells.

The two broken front windows were the only windows the place had. I broke them out myself to give it a more lived-in-by-ghosts-or-vagrants kinda feel. The Gulch hunters went to literally any other side of the valley to try their luck now, I could finally take my boots off and relax. And as I pushed open the door to the bedroom, the one that only locked from the inside, I did just that.

I kicked my boots across the room. They hit the wall and bounced to the floor with a clatter next to my bed. I use the term "bed" lightly, of course. In the far corner was an old twin-sized that was more spring than mattress, covered in stains I hoped to never properly identify. And that was it. Outside of the cobwebs and squirrel turds, the bed was all the master's sleeping quarters held. I tossed my hat and jacket onto the foot of it as I sat, dropped my satchel onto the floor and set the lantern down next to it.

Underneath the rusted springs of the mattress and it's frame, under a loose floorboard, I pried free my bed roll. Over the years I'd thought about bringing it with me on my travels, but I liked having something familiar to come home to. Something that existed at home and only at home. Plus, I didn't really have room for it in my satchel and traveling light was a pretty big deal.

I gave it a shake and spread it out over what was left of the mattress. Staring back at me, with those intense eyes that I recognized every time I looked at my own reflection, those eyes that held a certain level of world weariness and bitter rage, was Raphael. My favorite Ninja Turtle. Nobody understood him quite the way I did.

His grimace of teenage mutant attitude was calling my name. It wasn't until we were staring back at each other that I realized just how sore and tired I actually was. Every toned and sculpted muscle in my body begged for the cool comfort of my Ninja Turtle sleeping bag. I could let my guard down, if only a little. I could relax, as much as a person like me was allowed to. Everything would be alright if just for the night. Raph was on lookout. But as I pushed myself up and over to the door, I remembered that there was still work left to be done before I could sleep.

I closed the door and pulled the rusted bar latch across it with a grunt. A scrape and a clang secured the room. The Shepherd, Archer and the Mayor flashed through my mind. The look of worry and paranoia on Barnaby's face was hard to shake. If he was willing to let me involve an outsider in Gulch affairs, whatever was happening here had to be next level bad.

I sat back on the bed as I unbuttoned my shirt a little. A whiff of pungent man-musk wafted up at me as I grabbed my satchel from the floor. There was a call that still needed to be made. I gave my hat-hair a tussle so that it had that sexy/disheveled thing going for it and opened my shirt one more button. I would have to look good.

In the bottom of my satchel was a hand-mirror. My fingers wrapped gently around the cool silver of the handle. That thing was old. Like older than old old. From what I was told it went all the way back to sometime around the Salem Witch Trials. It had traveled a long way and seen a lot of evil just to get to me. This was one of the occasions where I saw fit to use it.

I pulled it from the bag and looked deep at my reflection. I was totally right. The shirt open, the hair, the few days of scruff I had growing, I was getting lost in my own eyes when the reflection began to ripple. The faded glass rolled like waves were passing through it, down to the shores of the handle. The whole mirror glowed a dull white. My image shifted and distorted, giving way to a new one entirely.

And there she was. Staring back at me. Katrina Pomerance. Her high cheek bones, jet black hair and piercing gray eyes reflected back at me. It's not that I didn't want to involve her exactly. I just didn't want her to call me "clingy" again.

"Cyrus Stone." She said with a glimmer that was rather white hot passion or white hot annoyance. "You look like shit."

She didn't mean that. She was totally flirting.

"How long's it been since you've showered?"

That's a damn good question.

"Yesterday!" I lied.

Katrina was a witch. But not the evil Bette Midler kind, more of the dance-naked-at-the-solstice kind. That distinction didn't do her much good in 1693. She was burned alive in her house by a rabble of angry Puritans all the same. We had a ton in common.

With her dying breath she bound her soul to her hand-mirror. It was found in the ash by a like-minded woman from her coven (who was way better at hiding her witchiness than Katrina was apparently) and held on to for a whole bunch of years. It was eventually found in a trunk after *her* death sometime in the mid 1700s. From there it passed between antiquities traders and collectors for the next couple centuries, or so the story went, until eventually I stole it from some Goth anime nerd who bought it on eBay. I didn't even know what it was!

Barnaby filled me in on that. I just saw this kid in a mall talking into a hand-mirror and bragging to his Edgar Allen Douchebag friends about how it could summon a witch. So I punched him in the side of his stupid head and ran off with it before he could do any evil. I was standing in line for a Cinnabon when my satchel started talking.

"It's been a few weeks." She said clearly annoyed.

She can't smell me through this, can she?

"How could you tell?" I asked.

"Since you last bothered me!"

It took me awhile, but I had to teach her to talk normal. I'd try to tell her all about my day, whatever I was hunting or had just murdered, and she'd start in with all the "thou art ye dothest, Cyrus Stone!"

"Oh right. Sorry! Been killing some monsters, some vampires, you know. Just busy being the secret protector of mankind."

"Of course." She said with the most disgusted and adorable little eye roll. "What do you require, oh secret protector of mankind?"

"I need help identifying something."

"You have a man for that."

"I need a witch's touch."

"I enjoy my solitude, Cyrus Stone."

"Look, I'm sorry. You know I wouldn't ask if we didn't really need the assist. Barnaby actually looked a little freaked out about it, Katrina."

"*He* did?!" She asked in disbelief.

"Yes! I saw actual nerves on that man tonight!"

"Damn."

"So I need you to help figure something out so he can keep his ear to the ground on this one. Will you help me?"

"What is it?"

"Let's say, hypothetically, that a sixty or seventy year old man ran almost as fast as me. Maybe even a little faster."

"I'd say you're getting slow."

"Ok, sure, sure. But let's also say, hypothetically, that there was a preacher with a weird amount of influence over the town and this particular old dude was like his buddy and could also almost jump over a one story building. Like a full revitalization of his strength and then some."

"Interesting." She paused.

"The preacher guy, he makes his people drink from a cup with some kinda sizzling drink made from his blood too."

She said nothing.

"What is that? Like some kind of Polyjuice Potion or something?"

"No." She finally replied. "That sounds like a strong blood oath."

"Oh shit! That's gross!"

"We learned about this briefly in my time. Be careful, Cyrus Stone. Blood magic like that is usually as dark and old as it gets."

"Isn't it always?"

"This isn't some werewolf or warlock! Powerful blood oaths tie to a powerful master."

A lesser man might've been scared by this, but I lived to blast holes in powerful masters.

"I'll pass that along." I said with a chuckle. "Thanks."

"Wait!" She snapped, her eyes settling around my chest. "Is that an amulet?"

"Oh yeah!" I had completely forgotten I was even wearing it.

"The Amulet of fucking Tortoises." I said with a sneer as I took it off and tossed it onto the floor.

"That's strong magic, Cyrus!"

"Oh yeah, as long as I've got a head of lettuce nearby I'll be good to go!"

"You know my specialty was earth magic, right?"

I had completely forgotten that too.

"Of course! I remember!"

"Don't discount earth magic! Or that amulet."

"No! Never!"

C'mon.

THUMP!

Something heavy rammed into my bedroom door. Something big. In a flash, I was on my feet with a hand on my gun. THUMP! The door shook in its frame. Someone was here.

"Katrina, I'll call you back!" I whispered quickly as I tossed the mirror onto the bed.

I drew my gun and slowly approached the door. Whatever had made it that far into the trees and past all my spooky defenses and deterrents must've had nerves of steel.

Well guess what, bud? My nerves are steelier.

I gripped the latch as the thump hit again, harder this time, more determined and forceful. Whatever was on the other side didn't just want to get inside, it wanted to go through the door in the process. Had one of the Gulchers stumbled upon the place? Was the Vanishing Powder keeping them blinded from reality enough to dull their fear? Or had Archer managed to see through it and track me down all the same?

I cocked my gun as I slowly ground the latch back.

THUMP! It was angry now. Whatever it was had come to dance.

Let's see who's making a house call.

I ripped open the door and thrust my gun forward into the dark cabin interior. But the barrel didn't stab into an eye socket or into a mouth as I expected it to. It was met with nothing but empty space and dead air. There was no one there.

Oh shit, is this place actually haunted now?

Something sharp scratched at my ankle.

"OHJESUSFUCK!" I yelled, not startled at all.

I looked down, half expecting to find some townsperson at the end of their trip, clawing their way towards me like a raver looking for water. What I saw instead, was a *fucking tortoise*.

His leathery little head poked at me, his dusty shell bumped the doorframe, his claw feet/hand things pawed at my ankle. I looked over to the bed with a smirk. The mirror's glow dimmed to nothing as I heard Katrina's satisfied laugh fade away on the other end.

7

GULCHY DAY

All over the Gulch people were preparing for a day that to them was Christmas and the Super Bowl rolled into one. It would've been a good time, a real party for the ages, if it wasn't all so god damn folksy. They rolled out their carts to peddle their *crap*, they fired up their ovens and grills to cook their *slop*, they broke out their finest suits and dresses and made their way through the streets to the designated patch of dirt next to the cemetery. All revved up with no place to go.

A thirty or forty-something-foot tall statue of Gulchy was constructed at the center of it all. A towering wooden figure of the super cartoony image of Gulchy we had all decided was historically accurate. Where the hell they kept it the other three-hundred and sixty-four days out of the year, I had no fucking idea. It was a leftover from the very first Gulchy Day, all those decades ago. And somehow it had survived in almost perfect condition.

An intricate working of tightly wound clockwork gears and cogs in his guts and limbs allowed him to wave his hand constantly throughout the day and bellow out an unnecessarily goofy and loud "HAWDY, FOLKS!" every few minutes. For the rest of the day. Like the world's most obnoxious cuckoo clock. It bounced off the mountains and echoed across the valley, letting the Gulchers know that Gulchy Day was in fact here at last. Like any of them could've possibly forgotten. My headache was already setting in.

The hour drew near. And before long the town would be filled with the sounds of children laughing and playing games, their parents eating and drinking to ear-assaulting torture of fucking *banjos*. Their merriment sickened me. But there'd be no better chance to gauge the temperature of the town all at once and suss out exactly which ass needed kicking most. Intuition told me it would probably be a toss-up.

From my vantage point high up on the road in and out of town, I had a bird's eye view of it all. I pulled a pair of binoculars from my satchel and watched. Watched as the Gulchers hugged and shook hands and embraced each other in brotherly love and neighborly camaraderie like they didn't all just see each other the day before. Or the day before that. Or the day before that! I don't know if it was them or the mezcal hangover I was nursing but I threw up in my mouth a little.

At the head of it all, the festival's entertainment for the day was loading onto a lengthy plank board stage. A tall, beige canvas banner with "Happy Gulchy Day" lovingly scribbled in bright red paint hung down behind it from beams easily twenty feet overhead. It ran all the way down to the ground and across the stage's entire length like a curtain. The day's entertainment had set up their instruments in front of it. Alright, look, when I say "entertainment" what I really mean is "four guys who were already drunk with their banj-a, gee-tars and worsh-burds". And once they started, the dirt dance floor ahead of them would become a dust storm of shuffling, two-stepping hillbillies.

They wouldn't be the only ones to take the stage today though. There was always a customary Gulchy Day speech to kick off and close out the celebration. Even though it would continue long after that. But as far as I could see, the Mayor, the Sheriff and the Shepherd hadn't shown their faces yet.

I scanned the festival from top to bottom, soup to nuts. Waves of people were pouring in, but none of the ones I wanted to see. To be fair, I didn't really want to see any of them. I would've rather still been in bed. But there I was regardless. The town itself was emptying and the festival was reaching critical mass. Yet there were no signs of movement from the church, city hall or the Sheriff's office.

The sea of people grew dense and chaotic. Children bounced from the candy vendors to the games and back again. Adults bounced from the booze wagons to the meat carts and back again. Families staked out their picnic spots. Have you ever poured beer on a beehive? It looked a lot like that. Distinguishing individuals from the swarming masses was becoming harder by the second and I knew as soon as the (Ugh) band started, once they were all kicked up into an even greater frenzy, it would become impossible.

I kept my gaze fixed on the stage. At least I knew where the Mayor would land in it all. But I had bigger fish to sizzle.

Come on, show yourself, you grumpy old bitch. I know you're here.

"What, are you and the Doomsday Kid catching an early-bird special at the Dickhead Buffett or something?"

Hunts require recon. And recon was not my strong suit. The longer I sat there, crouched in the dirt on the cusp of the spooky, shadowy mountains with bugs crawling up my ass, the more annoyed I got. And nobody wants a pissed off Hunter of Evil.

"Where are you?!" I growled impatiently to no one, my furious rage bubbling up inside me like a— "Oh shit, there you are."

The three of them emerged from behind the curtain/banner thing. Archer, the Shepherd and Mayor Delilah Craine. Walking shoulder to shoulder, all laughing and fawning like a bachelorette party on the Vegas Strip. And like a bachelorette party on the Vegas Strip, I could tell that there was something darker at play.

These suck!

I crammed my binoculars back into my satchel. They were too far out. I could see them, but I couldn't really make out anything important or even particularly telling. They seemed all happy and buddy-buddy, but so did every other idiot at the festival. That told me nothing. I would have to get closer. Especially if I wanted to hear the Mayor's speech. I knew what I had to do. But it was stupid so I didn't wanna do it.

I let out the single longest sigh in the history of sighs.

"Fine!"

And out came the Amulet of Uselessness from deep within the bowels of my shirt. The stone of the amulet was warm from the natural heat of my manliness, close proximity to which was prone to cause rising temperatures and even burns. I turned it over in my hand a few times with another super long groan.

"Pretty sure there are like coyotes and chupacabras and shit out here." I grumbled, still trying to wrap my head around the fact that I was about to control a god damn turtle.

Standard magic amulet operating procedure. I needed a drop of blood to awaken it's so-called power and bond it to me.

I know I've got a scab around here somewhere.

I hiked up my pant leg, revealing the old, crusty black leftover of a perfectly skinned knee. Rather a reminder of some mighty battle versus the forces of darkness, still in the process of healing, or the remnant of that night I did Irish Car Bombs and tried to jump a scooter over a parking meter. Definitely one or the other.

I picked at the scab delicately. The smallest drop of crimson leaked out from underneath it. I held the amulet below the blood and let it trickle. As the drop oozed its way down to the stone, the amulet began to hum and vibrate in my hand. It was awakening, eager to meet its new master.

The blood drop rolled down to the amulet, followed quickly by another. The amulet snatched it up like it had a thirst for the stuff. It's gray face turned red as the blood spread out over it. Two small drops stretched out to cover the stone as it vibrated more aggressively in my hand like it was letting me know my table at Chili's was ready.

The greedy and thirsty amulet drank the small current of blood. It soaked it all up like a sponge as its face began to glow. My eyes involuntarily snapped shut. For the briefest moment there was only darkness. A calm, still, black moment of peace where the only thing that existed was my thoughts.

I'm hungry.

And then a bright flash of light. My eyes fluttered open, but they weren't my own. I was staring at the coarse, hard dirt that I knew marked the edge of the cemetery.

I'm close.

Thoughts entered my mind that I knew didn't originate there.

Man, I'd really like to burrow right now.

I looked down to my feet. I'd recognize those claws anywhere. They scratched the shit out of my ankle when I opened my bedroom door. And again in the middle of the night when the tortoise needed to go out to poop or whatever it was he was doing outside all night.

My name...is Benicio. What? No it's not. It's Cyrus Stone. Hold up. Did someone name this tortoise Benicio? Did he name himself Benicio? Why is his name Benicio? I am Benicio?

I bookmarked all of that to ask Katrina once I had hands again. It was time to move. As I moved my turtley head up I could see the festival a few yards away. The grounds were abuzz with the excitement that I knew meant the proper start was fast approaching.

I'll give the amulet this, I could see everything way better from here. Mayor Craine made her way up a small set of steps on the far side and took the stage with a wave to the legion of eager Gulchers. Her fiery red hair was turning white in places, but I was willing to bet that wasn't from the stress of her office. Her short, plump frame scooted its way to center stage with a sort of youthful exuberance well beyond a woman in her mid-fifties. She was like a school girl on her way to the big dance, unaware that Cyrus Stone was just waiting to piss in the punchbowl.

"Howdy, y'all!" She shouted exuberantly to the crowd.

"HAWDY, FOLKS!" The giant Gulchy bellowed back with a wave.

"Howdy, Mayor!" The crowd cheered back in perfect unison.

Kill me. Please.

I wanted a better view. As the Mayor began her speech, I inched myself closer to the festival. Like literally *inched*.

Is this seriously as fast as I can go?

I gave my little tortoise legs a push, really laid down the throttle and went from inching to inch-and-a-halfing. Slowly making my way to the side of the stage.

"Today we come together as we always have." Mayor Craine began. "Like our daddies did and their daddies before them, to celebrate our beloved founder Gulchy E. Gulcherson."

The crowd went nuts over that for some reason.

"But more than good ol' Gulchy, we come together to celebrate what he did. What he made. His legacy! The absolute triumph that is our dear Gulch and the ties that bind us all together in the name of community. No one, absolutely no one could've had the vision, the foresight and compassion to turn this valley into a home for so many generations. But Gulchy? Gulchy did. Gulchy burst his way out of these mountains with sweat on his brow and a vision of the future."

Alright, that's a little much.

"HAWDY, FOLKS!" The statue roared like it was agreeing with Craine.

"He saw what we were, what we are and most importantly what we could become!"

What, inbred?

The crowd cheered again.

"And so today we share our love for the Gulch and our appreciation and admiration for Gulchy! We are truly here because of and for him." She proclaimed with a tear in her eyes.

The mayor's lady-boner for Gulchy was a little extreme, even by normal Gulch standards. The crowd applauded regardless.

Nothing but sheep, every last one of them.

Speaking of which:

"I'd also like to talk about someone who's still fairly new to Gulchy's Gulch. A man who many of us have found a mentor, a teacher and great deal of comfort and confidence in." Craine said as she wiped away her Gulchy tears away.

The Shepherd ascended the steps to the stage with the smug smile of someone who knew he was about to get his dick viciously and sloppily sucked. That responsibility appeared to fall on Mayor Craine.

"Shepherd," she said as he put his arm around her. She looked up at him like Superman had just caught her mid-air and dropped her on that stage. "We didn't know what to think when you first came to us. New faces don't come down our road very often and when they do, we usually don't get the chance to get to know them. But when you did, you were determined to make the Gulch your home and us your family. You were determined to show us the way and the warmth of the Father's light. And anyone with the wisdom to have joined your flock is all the better for it. Our eyes and hearts are open for the first time in a long time."

Most of the crowd cheered. A little more than half from what my leathery tortoise eyes could see. It seemed some still had the good sense to stick to their own convictions rather that have him tell them what they were. But the other half? The larger half? The half that cheered? You'd think they'd all just been told that bathtub moonshine was the cure for stupid.

"We thank you, Shepherd." Craine gushed on. "For everything you've done and everything you continue to do. The addition to the church! The first new development in Gulchy's Gulch in decades!"

The crowd went nuts.

"HAWDY, FOLKS!"

"For revitalizing the faith of our little town after Reverend Wright had let it lapse so severely!"

They cheered again.

"For offering a place of sanctuary for anyone open and willing enough to seek it. And for being such a beacon of hope in a world grown so dark, we thank you, Shepherd."

The Shepherd was grinning ear to ear as the applause died down. He took his arm off of the Mayor and opened them wide to the crowd.

"My friends, my neighbors, my kin, blood of my blood," he started. "It is *I* who should thank you. It is *I* who should praise and admire *you*! I know you were trepidatious of the stranger who appeared out of nowhere, preaching a new kind of belief, but you've all grown so warm and so kind to me. For all his faults, the boozing and the womanizing, we must also remember the good Reverend Wright did. He presided over the church for decades before his untimely demise. When I arrived I feared it was too soon. That you'd never embrace me or trust the Father. I knew no one could ever truly fill the shoes he once wore."

Wait, is he..? That son of a bitch is actually wearing his shoes! I'd recognize those old penny loafers anywhere. They're way too small on him.

"In my heart it is clear though. Reverend Wright's greatest accomplishment, it seems, was leading you to me. You've welcomed me into your lives and communities and I couldn't be prouder to call Gulchy's Gulch home. My message remains the same today as it did when I first came down that road. The darkness is coming. We must embrace oblivion, in our lives as we do in the end. Only the Father will guide us through it into the New World. There are some in the Gulch who have not taken my words to heart and to you I say: my door is always open. Whenever you're ready, I will show you what you need to know. I will show you the Father's true face, speak his name and give you the gift of his vision. Until then, please enjoy my gift to you."

He gestured dramatically to the food vendors.

"All food and drink today has been paid for. Whatever your tabs may be at the end of the festival, the Church of the Seventh Seal will cover it!"

The crowd went absolutely ape shit. Of course they did. You buy my drinks and I'll probably listen to whatever apocalyptic nonsense you're spewing too.

"It comes with a warning though, fellow Gulchers." He continued. "Know that time is short. The great and terrible darkness is coming to this world. I know it might not feel like it today, and I don't for a single second want to take an ounce of joy from our celebrations, but know that it is coming all the same. The Father has seen it. When you're ready, we will walk hand in hand, all of us, brothers and sister of the New World. If life in Gulchy's Gulch has taught us anything it's that only together can we hope to thrive."

His faithful cheered. The nonbelievers were excited just to get drunk on somebody else's dime. And some simply clapped. He was too charismatic and they were too susceptible for them not to be at least a little sold on his bullshit.

I turned Benicio's head to get a look at Archer. He stood at the foot of the stairs, waiting for the Shepherd like a dog waits for pets. Tears flowed down his cheeks and soaked his mustache like Tommy Lee Jones had just given him a hug and told him he was his real dad all along. Powerful blood oath or powerful man-crush? I sincerely had no idea.

The Shepherd left the stage and joined his dog as the cheers and applause died down. Mayor Craine followed closely behind him. He had the biggest, widest, most self-righteous and pompous grin I had ever seen on a man of the clothe. The three of them walked side by side by side back behind the banner/curtain as the band took the stage and started up their first noisy, twanging song of the day.

They were too close, those three. There was nothing inherently evil about it but there was not *not* nothing inherently evil about it either! Barnaby was right. The

Shepherd had Craine wrapped tightly around his finger.

Could they both be under the same blood oath? Craine and Archer?

I pushed my stubby little tortoise legs to follow them. I needed more information. I needed something to bring back to Barnaby and Charlotte beyond "I don't know, maybe it's a throuple?" I needed to see them when they thought no one else was watching. As I cleared the side of the stage, I really wished I hadn't.

Craine had collapsed face down in the dirt. Her body convulsed violently, sending small dust clouds out from under her. I could barely make out what her gentleman companions said as they rushed to her side over the soul-crushing racket of the band.

Come on, Benicio, we gotta get a little closer!

I pushed the dusty old tortoise body to its absolute limit. A voice responded from somewhere deep in my skull.

Aurrrrg!

I know, buddy, you just gotta give it a little more! I have to hear this!

I could speak tortoise now apparently.

Huh.

I'd have to deal with that later. As I got closer to the Shepherd, Archer and facedown Mayor, I could hear them a little more clearly.

"We're losing her." The Shepherd snapped, all the charm sucked out of his voice and replaced with nothing but malice.

Archer lifted her wrist and checked her vitals.

"She's still alive." He said like he was helping.

"Of course she is! Look at her!" Shep snarled back.

Craine shook and shuttered as her body flopped over like a trout on a boat deck.

"What do we do?" Archer asked, a hint of fear in his voice.

"What's happening?!" Craine finally cried out, wild terror in her wide eyes. "Shepherd?! Archer?! What are you doing?!"

I could see it all over her face. She was in pain. Like every nerve ending in her body was on fire. More than that, she looked lost. Genuinely so. She had no idea how she ended up in the dirt.

Did she hit her head?

"Hush now, my child." The Shepherd said as he placed a hand on her forehead. "The Father sees all, the Father sees all!"

"Get your hands off of me!" She shouted at him.

If it weren't for the band and the sounds of general frivolity, the whole town would've heard quite the commotion and no doubt come to watch this scene un-fold.

"HUSH! I said!" The Shepherd barked at her.

Craine started to cry as her body con-tinued to lurch. I moved a little closer, towing the line between obvious and just a tortoise. The Shepherd forced her head back down to the ground as it shot up to-wards his chest.

"You're more resilient than you seem, aren't you, Delilah?" He seethed.

"What do we do?!" Archer asked with ab-solute panic spread across his face, the first time I had ever seen it on him.

"She's rebelling against her gift. We need to get her back to church." The Shepherd growled back. "I can't do this properly here."

In a split second, Craine's body went from dying fish to completely stiff. Her arms locked in to her sides, her head snapped back, her shoes clicked as her legs sprang together. And then she was still. If only for a moment. Archer stared on in shock. The Shepherd backed away cautiously. Craine's frozen body rose up into the air, her bright red hair hanging down desperately, her back still to the ground. She hovered there, a few feet off the ground as her eyes rolled to the back of her head, revealing their now bloodshot whites.

"Help...me..." Craine whimpered as a tear rolled off her cheek.

It plunged down and crashed into the dirt, leaving the tiniest pool of mud. Her mouth cracked open, her jaws moving farther away from each other than should've been possible, even when dislocated. A deep, inhuman howl came out of her. Something unearthly. More like a fog horn than anything our vocal chords were capable of. I glanced back over to the festival. The Gulchers were still none the wiser.

Of course.

The howl stopped as suddenly as it started. Delilah Craine's head twisted from side to side, her neck cracking and snapping, her mouth still wide open. And out came a voice.

"Blood." It belched through Craine's unmoving lips, raspy and deep. "Of my blood."

Her body dropped to the ground in a heap. Dust shot out around her. Archer took a bewildered, if not outright frightened, step back. The Shepherd rubbed his temples, thoroughly over it.

"Go. Get her back to the church. Now!" He ordered Archer. "Make sure no one sees."

"But how—"

"I don't care! Figure it out! I need to make the preparations." The Shepherd threw over his shoulder as he stormed off, leaving Archer alone to deal with the mess. Whatever it was.

He charged straight for me in a huff, his irritated scowl set on the church.

Oh shit, oh shit, what do I do? Think turtle thoughts!

"Auuurg!"

The Shepherd's foot snagged my shell as he passed. He stumbled a bit and glared back at me.

"Fucking desert." He muttered venomously.

My eyes snapped open. *My* eyes. I was crouched on the road overlooking the town and Benicio was down in the shit. I looked down to the festival. My eyes narrowed in a determined scowl. Just like that I had something more to bring to Barnaby and Charlotte. The Mayor was possessed. And I was going to bring her to the only two Gulchers that could help.

8

KID-NERPIN' THE MAY-ER

Possessions were the nastiest kind of work. Two souls fighting over one sack of flesh and blood. One with little to no concern for the damage it caused to it and the other too helpless to stop it. That's the thing the movies and stories never really prepare you for. The human is still inside. Always. They're not cast down into the pits of Hell or lost in some spiritual void, they're riding shotgun in their own body, prisoner to the thoughts and actions of whatever entity is at the wheel. Powerless to do anything about it or even really try. The people that come out of it, the ones that are saved, are never quite the same. They never trust a single one of their thoughts or actions for the rest of their days. The very best case scenarios never sleep again, too haunted by what they assume were dreams in the first place. And then there's the knowledge they come back with. Finding out through first hand experience that demons exist and that they can take your body for a joy ride with the slightest encouragement and a ridiculous amount of ease isn't something most people recover from. They fight it with all their mental might and if they're lucky, the worst case scenarios usually end up totally and completely insane.

I wasn't very handy when it came to evicting demons. I always tried, I swear! But my method usually ended up with a dead demon and an equally dead human host. It's delicate work and a dangerous balancing act. I was not a delicate man and might've had some kind of inner ear problem. I don't know, I never looked into it. Barnaby though! He and Charlotte were Mayor Craine's best hope of coming out of this alive and with a tiny sliver of sanity left. More so, what had she seen? What did she know? If the Shepherd was somehow responsible for her current...affliction, and he almost definitely was, then she probably had something useful for us.

I raced down the hill and onto the flatlands at breakneck speed. The desert passed by me in a blur as I ran straight for the festival. If there was one thing I hated, it was killing someone's buzz and ruining a good party. No matter how stupid that party was. And with literally every gun, knife and makeshift implement of pain in attendance I couldn't risk an open confrontation. Stop the Sheriff, save the Mayor, skip the gunfight. That was the new order of the day.

The festival and the colossal Gulchy grew ahead of me until I was in his shadow and smelling their sweat. Thankfully, the Gulchers were all enjoying themselves way too much already to notice the boogeyman coming down out of the mountains. Mid-afternoon wasn't exactly my preferred operating time, but you work with what you get. If even one of them had seen me, discretion would've gone right the fuck out the window. Their happy, stupid, smiling faces, both drunk and otherwise, let me know that I was good to go. That and the fact that no one was screaming or shooting at me yet.

"HAWDY, FOLKS!"

Shut. The fuck. Up!

I stopped at the edge of the party and ducked behind a meat cart. What kind of meat? I had no idea and neither did they. To the Gulchers, there was no chicken, pork or beef, just meat. And all alcohol was classified as booze. They weren't a discerning people. Which always made me wonder why Barnaby tried so hard to keep the saloon stocked with such a wide array of obscure liquor. They didn't know. They didn't care.

On either side of me were more meat carts and a few booze wagons. The band continued to assault the ears of the Gulchers, to their delight and my torment. They danced and ate and drank and socialized like a bunch of happy assholes. Completely unaware of what had just happened a few yards

away on the other side of the stage. I
scanned the crowd. Archer was nowhere to be
seen, which could've meant one of two things.
He had rather already moved her or was still
figuring out how to. My money was on the
ladder.

Keeping low, I moved from meat cart to
booze wagon, booze wagon to meat cart,
creeping along the edge of the festival
and using them as cover. In a flash I
leaped to the hastily assembled structure
next to the last booze wagon. With a tuck
and roll I hid behind the back wall of the
kids' shooting gallery. Children with
firearms and easily accessible, unregulated
alcohol. Always a winning combination. I
couldn't hear much over racket of the band
and the sporadic "HAWDY, FOLKS!", but small
puffs of dust from the backside of the wood
signaled children missing their quarter-
load shots.

From the shooting gallery I darted over
to its neighbor, a small half-booth with
no back wall. Lucky for me, the guy
running it had his back turned and the
kids playing were face first in buckets of

water fishing for apples that were god only knows how old. I ran past as quickly as I could. Only two structures separated me from the gap to the stage. The lame bottle ring toss thing that's been at every carnival since the dawn of fucking man and a tent that from the smell of it I was guessing served some kind of sugary baked shit.

I dropped low and crawled on my stomach like the stealthiest stealth commando past the ring toss. A plastic ring bounced off of it's target and over the edge of the booth. It landed square on my back and halted my crawl.

Oh shit.

Someone was going to have to get that. If my memory of playing this game at the festival as a kid served me right, there were only like ten rings total and they had to be shared by every player. No backups. But then I remembered the most important detail of Gulchy Day. The food carts, booze wagons and games had all been operated by the same people year after year after fucking year. The old man who built the ring toss, the game's creator I believe, didn't care enough to collect the overshot rings. Once they were in the dirt, they stayed there until they ran out. Game over, go home. I crawled on.

I got to my feet behind the baked whatever tent. Even through the thick canvas walls I could see tiny silhouetted shadows devouring pounds of dough and sugar like rats on a carcass. I could've honestly walked straight through this spot and nobody would've noticed me. I'm not made of carbs so the kids wouldn't have cared, and the adults running it would've been too busy keeping the sticky swarm satisfied. There'd be no quarter for them if they couldn't.

Nothing separated me from the side of the stage now but five or six yards of open space. Slowly, I peeked my head around the corner. The Gulchers that weren't currently eating or drinking or wrangling their crotch goblins were in front of the stage dancing in the dirt. It was a considerable amount of people and the dust coming off of their dance floor was forming into a small cloud as they boot scootin' boogied. With no cover, I had to rely on my speed, my agility and a small amount of luck to get by them unnoticed. I took a deep breath and ran as fast as I could past them, holding my hat to keep it from blowing off in the face of my awesome speed.

I ducked down and pressed my back flat against the side of the stage. All I had to do now was slide my way past the stairs and to the edge without being seen and hope I wasn't too late to rescue the Mayor. A tiny, familiar head poked around the corner at the back of the stage. Benicio stared at right at me. I couldn't explain it, but I swear it felt like he was gazing straight into my soul. We were bonded now, I guess. And I'm not sure how I felt about that. The look he gave me was all the intel I needed. I could tell that dry, scaly face was trying to say "She's still here. You made it in time." I gave him a nod of thanks as he turned around and headed back behind the stage. Inch by inch I scooted my way over to the stairs. That's when I heard something that usually would've made be incredibly happy, but in this moment was not very welcome at all. The music stopped.

"A'ight, y'all!" The band leader said to the crowd as they clapped for him and his equally untalented friends. "Wur gon tek a lil' break. Hit up those thar booze corts and be bek in five!"

Seriously? You just started.

I squeezed into the corner made by the stairs meeting the stage and tucked myself into the smallest ball I could. The band staggered down past me one by one and settled at the foot of the stairs. They stood, not three feet away from me, their heads swiveling and scanning in different directions. Did they forget something on stage? Their dignity or self respect maybe? Could they tell I was here? If they turned around, I'd have no choice but to take the loud route. Push my way through them, make a run for the Mayor and figure out how to get her back to the saloon with the whole god damn town on my ass.

"Over they-er!" The leader declared as he pointed to the booze carts.

Oh right.

It was a little past mid-day. The stage was littered with empty cups and bottles they had rather brought with them or had been offered by the Gulchers in lieu of payment. They were too drunk to even *find* the booze by now let alone drink any more. Not that I was judging. They stumbled off as fast as their legs could carry them in the direction I came as I breathed a sigh of relief.

I moved to the end of the stage and carefully, peered around the corner. Archer was on the move, carrying a very unconscious Delilah Craine over his shoulder and wrapped in his coat and a blanket to conceal her identity. Benicio was in "hot" pursuit as they made their way towards the church.

Time to move.

I burst out from the side of the stage and sprinted for the Sheriff, my gun drawn. I quickly closed the gap between us. As I got within striking distance, he turned to face me. His own pistol aimed squarely at my gut.

"Hold it, Stone." He said as I skidded to a halt and aimed right for his mustache. "Drop the gun."

"Drop the Mayor." I replied as I thumbed back the hammer.

"This Mayor?" He said with a smug grin as he turned his revolver to the mass of fabric covering her head.

I took a step closer.

"Not so fast! You stay right there or I blow her brains all over the desert." He growled.

"You won't do that." I said with a smirk as I holstered my gun. I wouldn't be needing it after all.

"You wanna bet?! I could put a bullet in her right now and just say it was you! Who wouldn't believe that?"

I took another step towards him. Then another. And another. Archer cocked his gun.

"Don't test me, boy! You have no idea what's at stake here!"

"No. No, I do not. Not yet anyway! But what I do know is that you won't kill her."

"You don't think I have the balls?!"

He buried the barrel of his pistol deeper into the fabric and the skull underneath.

"I don't really care about your balls. But you won't kill her."

I was practically on top of him now. I could smell whatever lotions or oils he used to keep his mustache tamed.

"Because Daddy wouldn't like that very much, now would he?"

I grabbed the barrel of his gun and jerked it away from the Mayor's head. A shot popped off and a bullet sailed past my shoulder, barely missing it. The blanket and Archer's jacket unwrapped Craine as she fell to the dirt and we grappled over the gun. He was strong. Stronger than he should've been. I expected him to put up a good fight, but the dark magic at work here was helping him give me a real run for my money. It took all my strength to keep him from turning the business end of the gun to my gut. Four hands wrapped around one gun. One finger on the trigger. Another round fired, tearing right through the side of my jacket.

"Mother fucker!" I yelled.

That was close, yeah, but this jacket was super hard to find! And expensive as fuck to get fixed! Archer groaned in pain. For a second I thought the damage to my favorite jacket wounded him as badly as it had me. Until I glanced down and saw Benicio burying those claws of his right into the toe of Archer's boot. They couldn't have done too

140

much damage, just enough to throw the Sheriff off his groove. I took advantage regardless, pushing the gun up with all my strength. It slammed into the bridge of his nose with a crack. Blood shot down his face and stained his mustache as he fell back, as unconscious as the Mayor.

"Thanks, buddy." I said to Benicio. "Think you can get up to the church? Keep an eye on things for me?"

"Auuurg!"

I would've known that was a confirmation even if Benicio hadn't started inching off towards the church. I knelt down next to Craine and checked her pulse. It was faint, but she was still there. Carefully, borderline gingerly, I took her up into my arms. As I looked up to my escape route, the opposite side of the festival from the way I came, the most direct path between where I was and the Blood Moon, I couldn't help but notice the *giant fucking crowd* that had gathered. Every Gulcher, including the band, was standing around the far side of the stage watching me with mouths wide with horror like a school of fucking carp.

"HAWDY, FOLKS!"

Oh right, gunshots make noise. Noise attracts people.

I would need a tongue as silver as the stake on my belt to get out of this.

"Uhhhh..."

"Cyrus Stone is kid-nerpin' the may-er!" The leader of the band shouted.

"Fuck."

With my exit blocked, I made a run for it back the way I came.

"I'm only trying to help!" I yelled over my shoulder as the crowd turned from shocked onlookers to blood thirsty mob. Gulchers were pretty good at making that transition. They could do it pretty seamlessly. All dopey and slow one minute, fire and fury the next.

Like in the church but worse, the crowd started shouting their cornfed insults at me mixed with cries of disbelief and Kentucky Fried Outrage. I could hear the gentle chorus of dozens of guns cocking, blades unsheathing and bottles breaking. How do you escape an angry mob while carrying a fully grown and super unconscious woman? A lesser man might panic in that situation, but this wasn't my first rodeo. As I rounded the corner of the stage into the now empty festival grounds, I pulled my gun. Faster than you could blink, I shot out the two metal rings holding up the banner behind the stage. I heard even more cries of anger, confusion and frustration as it drifted down onto the unruly Gulchers. Gunshots popped as bullets poked holes in the canvas. They were more likely to hurt themselves in there than they were me, which is something I probably should've felt bad about but this was a real "greater good" kind of situation.

I bolted straight up the center of the emptied festival and towards the town proper. Even the kids were missing from the places they had been before which led me to believe they had joined the mob. Which then made me wonder what kind of fucking parents let their children join an armed mob.

Not my pig, not my farm.

I glanced over my shoulder as I cleared the entrance of the festival and saw the people who had managed to rather escape the falling shroud of canvas or avoid it altogether stampeding out from behind the stage. Their voices thundered after me, mashing together into a nonsense battle cry that sounded something like "RABRABARABAAAAH!" But I had a decent lead on them. If I could make it to the saloon before they could see me go in, I could disappear into Barnaby's Sanctum before they even knew I was there. If I was already running full steam ahead, then I pushed myself even full steamier, sprinting forward as fast as I could while carrying the Mayor's stocky and limp weight.

I hit the stretch of road and block of buildings that led to the Blood Moon. From here I could see her thick windows and heavy door, the crimson sign over it call-ing to me like a finish line. The rumble of feet shook the ground behind me. A voice broke through the noise, roaring over the crowd. I slowed for the briefest second as Archer shouted from deep in his gut:

"STONE! GET BACK HERE, YOU SON OF A BITCH!"

He was up. He was on his feet. His mustache was matted with blood, his nose was shattered and holy hell was he pissed.

Shit shit shit shit shit!

I couldn't take the chance. I broke away from my straight line to safety and down the other street. Archer and the mob followed. No Vanishing Powder this time. It seemed kinda fucked up to leave the entire town tripping for a night. Especially since there were probably kids in the mix. And honestly I just didn't have enough. But as I scanned the buildings ahead of me I knew what I had to do. There was only one place in the middle block of Gulchy's Gulch that had a backdoor. It didn't make sense for most of them to, seeing as their back walls were shared with the buildings on the other side of them. But the doctor's office did. It was separated from its rear neighbor by a space just big enough to wheel the dead through and out into the alley perpendicular to it. The common practice being you enter through the front and hope you don't have to leave through the back. I paused at the front of the office, long enough to fling the Mayor over my shoulder and pull my gun. Archer and the crowd appeared at the edge of town, closing in fast.

Good. Watch this.

I shot out the window of the doctor's office. One of those big custom jobs, like waist high and running from the door to the corner of the building with "Oxy Sold Here" hand-painted in big block letters across it. I couldn't help but feel a twinge of regret. There was no beef between Doc Torrance and I. Except for that one time he told me I needed to stop drinking and smoking if I wanted to live to see fifty. Who needs that kind of pessimism? Especially when townsfolk and monsters try to kill you on a regular basis. Like let me live my life, man, damn.

I climbed through the empty frame and over the shattered glass into the office after I was good and sure Archer at the very least had seen what I had done. The office was empty, of course. Doc was probably somewhere in the tidal wave of Gulchers heading my way or still stuck under the banner. Cutting through his exam room, past the supply closets and the pair of rooms reserved for patients that needed to hang out for awhile, I hit the back door. I was careful not to smash my way through it, despite how much I wanted to. It wasn't even locked. And a smashed door just screams "Hey, he went this way!" I opened it like a normal person and rushed through, closing it again behind me.

I held on for a moment, waiting until I heard it.

"He's in here!" Archer yelled from the other side of the broken window.

Fuck yeah.

I made my way through the dead exit and crossed the alley back onto Barnaby's street. I could hear the nonsense battle cry of the mob filling the office behind me. I checked the street, just to be safe. Clear to the left, clear to the right, I was good to go.

I raced down the street to the saloon, bursting through the door with the Mayor on my shoulder and kicking it shut behind me. Barnaby was waiting for me at the bar, no doubt having heard the trouble coming his way, the door to the Sanctum already opened.

"I thought I told you not to get involved!" He scolded.

"Hate to let you down, bud, but it had to be done."

"Is that the Mayor?!"

"Kinda."

I rushed through the white light of the Sanctum door as Barnaby closed it behind us.

9

TORTOISE RECON

The Shepherd stood at his alter as the town outside his church quieted down and the afternoon sun dipped low, edging the Gulch closer to its premature night. He furiously tore through the pages of his book, studying whatever arcane text it contained intensely. His knuckles turned white as he clutched the stem of his spooky goblet of steaming evil drink. Benicio pushed his way through the slightly open front door and hid himself between the wall and pews. The scraping of his claws on the rough wooden floor, or the sight of a big-ass tortoise pushing his way inside for that matter, might've been a dead give away if Shep hadn't already been so distracted.

The Church of the Seventh Seal had clearly been a hot bed of activity since the festival abruptly ended. But not for its usual spewing of half-baked promises and apocalyptic rants for the most wide-eyed and easily sold Gulchers. I'm sure that after his speech earlier today, there would've been even more people than on any other given night, but tonight they used the church to organize.

Maps of the Gulch were spread out and tacked onto the walls, divided into search grids. Why? Why did they need maps? Why did they need search grids?! Were they planning on getting lost in the town that's just a bunch of *straight fucking lines*?! They were taking their day way too seriously now. Which was honestly under-standable. In their eyes, Cyrus Stone had just knocked the shit out of the Sheriff and run off with the Mayor. But the eyes, they deceive.

The Shepherd closed his book with an exasperated sigh. He turned to the Leviathan

Cross carved into the walls and dropped to his knees. His head bowed deeply to his chest and his hands came to rest on top of his thighs. His eyes rolled to the back of his head as they fluttered closed. There he sat, in silent...prayer? Meditation? One or the other, for sure. There he sat! Communing with whatever deity he called his "Father", whatever being he was in service of. But who? There's too many faceless gods to name in the world, too many opposing forces at work. Who did the Shepherd belong to?

The doors flew open behind him like a fierce wind had hit them. Archer stormed in, on a mission.

"Sorry to interrupt, Shepherd." He said as he made his way to the alter, apprehensive about intruding on Daddy's private time but unfortunately having to do it anyway.

The Shepherd's eyes shot open.

"Give me strength." He whispered to someone, no one, before he stood to face his lackey.

The Shepherd must've known that what Archer had to say couldn't have been what he wanted to hear. His brow furrowed as the Sheriff approached him. Archer paused a moment, building the courage to break it to him.

"Bad news." He said through his breath.

"I had a feeling." Shep replied calmly.

"We checked every house short of the Manor, searched every crevice of the town. He must've taken her up into the mountains."

"He's a coward. Cowards hide."

"We're gonna regroup. I'm taking every available gun up there to flush him out."

"No need, Archer." The Shepherd said with a devious grin.

Archer's eyes narrowed with a cold focus.

"We'll be waiting then." He grunted sternly.

The Shepherd let out a small chuckle. Whatever made this man laugh couldn't be very positive for me. He made his way back behind his alter and picked up that damned chalice.

"I owe you my apologies, Sheriff."

Archer cocked an eyebrow, confused.

"I was short with you earlier. I shouldn't have been. I am sorry."

"Not necessary, Shepherd." Archer said like a good little dog.

"It is though." The Shepherd told him almost empathetically as he swirled whatever concoction was filling the chalice. "The pressure I'm under, it gets to me sometime!"

"I understand. Being Sheriff—"

"No." The Shepherd interjected forcefully. "Don't give me that. You really don't. Protecting the people is vastly different than what I'm trying to do here, Archer."

"Of course. Saving their souls is a heavy burden."

"Trust me, their souls are never far from my thoughts. They're always lurking right on the edge of my mind. Crying out for what I have to offer. Practically begging for it."

Was he starting to drool a little? Gross.

"Regardless!" He continued. "You've been a faithful servant. And a good friend. And such loyalty should be rewarded. Always. In the New World same as the old."

"There's no need. Really." Archer said with a small blush. "I don't do it for reward. I do it because I believe in you."

"You do?" Shep asked like the nerdy kid who just found out the homecoming queen has the hots for him.

"More than I've ever believed in any-thing."

"And you trust me?"

Archer considered this for a moment. He took a deep breath before giving an answer I don't think he would've even given to his succubus wife if she had asked.

"With my life."

The Shepherd grinned widely and gleefully.

"With your soul?"

Archer nodded dutifully. It was the truth. If asked to, he would lay down his life for this man. The evidence of a blood oath was mounting.

"And your faith?"

"Belongs to the Father."

"Then the time has come!" The Shepherd exclaimed with a giddy enthusiasm.

"For what, Shepherd?" Archer asked, eagerly awaiting whatever was in store for him.

"For you to receive your gift from the Father. He gave you his strength, but now you're ready for his purpose." He beamed proudly at his goon. "Cyrus Stone is a legitimate threat to the Father and to this valley, is he not?"

"I can handle him."

"And you will!" The Shepherd said confidently as he gripped the chalice tighter. "I haven't seen much of his handiwork in person. Beyond poor old Terry Kimberlin, of course. And the events of today! But I've known men like him and I've heard the stories, the atrocities he's committed against our people. How many of those graves out there are his doing?!"

He pointed towards the graveyard with the chalice. A deep black splashed out of it and ran down to his hand.

"Too many." Archer replied, his gaze growing distant and his thoughts drifting.

"Your wife."

Archer's fists clenched tightly. Drops of blood squeezed their way out of his palm and wrapped around his fingertips.

"He took the Mayor."

Archer nodded as the anger swelled in him.

"We need the Mayor."

The Sheriff's eyes returned to his master.

"I'll find her." He snarled.

"I know you will." The Shepherd said as he came around the alter and placed his free hand comfortingly on Archer's shoulder. "But first we deal with Stone. He's a predator. One which can't be allowed to stalk my flock."

He held the chalice out to Archer.

"But I've already—" Archer began as he stared down into the dark brew.

The Shepherd snatched up Archer's bleeding hand. He squeezed tightly as the Sheriff winced in pain. Drops of blood splashed down into the chalice. It was different this time. No steam. No sizzle. Whatever was in the cup began to glow and swirl into a tiny whirlpool. The dark light outlining their faces.

"To stop a predator, we need an even greater one."

Archer's eyes moved from the chalice back to the Shepherd, a hint of fear within them.

"Drink." The Shepherd commanded firmly. "And be made whole."

Archer looked back to the concoction, sweat forming on his brow, before doing as he was told. In three big gulps, he drained the entire chalice. Black ran down his face and soaked through his already filthy mustache like ink as he panted, breathless from the drink. The Shepherd stepped away from him with a sinister smile.

"I won't lie to you, my friend." He said as he took a seat on a front row pew. "This next part won't be particularly pleasant."

The Shepherd threw his arms up akimbo on the back of the pew and crossed his legs in the standard super chill relaxation posture. Archer dropped the chalice. It bounced across the floor, loudly clanging and nearly drowning out the Sheriff's gasps. He clutched his chest and collapsed to the floor, a look of pure, unadulterated anguish set on his face. Archer screamed. So loudly and so deeply that the Shepherd's scattered flock could hear it clear across the Gulch, not knowing what torment was being inflicted. He rolled onto his stomach as he frantically ripped his shirt and vest off. The sweat soaked clothes stuck to the floor as he wailed on.

The Shepherd began to laugh. A low, sinister, maniacal laugh that built up until it drowned out Archer's screams as he looked to his master with pleading, desperate eyes. The Sheriff's back began to pop and crack, his vertebra separating from each other by inches. His torso stretched as his spine elongated one foot, two feet, three. Two large masses formed at his shoulder blades like squirming cysts, pressing against the skin and testing its resilience as they writhed and ballooned grotesquely. His arms shot away from his chest as his face hit the floor. The muscles in them surged and twitched like he was hooked up to some kind of electrode. His legs followed. The bones snapped and crunched as his extremities grew to support his stretching torso. His boots and pants ripped away from him in shreds. The muscles popped and bulged with a series of sickeningly wet spurts and slaps. His feet grew at the toes, stretching out and out and out until his heels essentially served as a new set of knees, facing backwards and supporting large, wide, taloned feet. The nails on his hands fell off in a bloody heap as his fingers twisted into widely set claws. Sharp, thick, black nails shot out of his fingertips.

Archer struggled against his new body as he climbed to his knees. His teeth dangled by bloody threads, the force from his scream launched them from his mouth. Sharp, pristine fangs grew in their place like shards of broken glass. He had been through a gauntlet of pain and metamorphosis. I could almost respect it, a lesser man might've succumbed and dropped dead on the spot. The worst was yet to come for him though as his skull began to change shape. His screams were deafening, drowning out the Shepherd's raucous and clearly evil laughter. Archer's head grew wider as the bone split and crunched away in halves, his eyes moving away from each other as their sockets grew large enough to hold baseballs. The whites of his eyes expanded to fill the space, consuming all their color and leaving two pearly orbs in their place. His jaws spread until his mouth was large enough to easily fit a human head inside. The nose and ears melted from his face, leaving small lumps of wet flesh on the floor and bloody holes where they had once been. Thick, dark horns ripped their way free from his forehead, curving up and arcing away from his face as they wrapped around his misshapen head. The skin on his back finally gave out, splitting and tearing as the masses underneath pushed their way free. Massive, black wings erupted from him, kicking up a powerful gust with their first energized flaps as they tasted the fresh air. A tail like a tree trunk exploded from his tailbone. The black-stained hair of his mustache exploded across his body, leaving the fresh creature coated in a matted, dark fur.

A gargoyle, made from a man. The imposing creature stood. His new body as sleek and powerful as it was tall. To Benicio, he might as well have been a furry mountain with wings. A powerful blood oath indeed. He snarled as he took his first steps on his new legs and feet. The Shepherd beamed with pride as he approached his upgraded minion.

"Archer?" He asked.

The gargoyle, Archer, whipped his head to look down at his master, the bones in his neck cracking as it craned.

"Yes...Shepherd..." He replied. But the voice was no longer his own. It sounded less like a man and more like a clogged garbage disposal.

"How do you feel?" The Shepherd asked as he examined his monster's new body with a satisfied awe.

"Ready." The Gargoyle Sheriff snarled.

"Good. Good! Take those wings of yours out for a test drive. Find Stone and—" The Shepherd stopped short.

Benicio's claws scratched the floor as he scurried his little ass out of there as fast as he could. Archer and the Shepherd turned to see him inching his way to the door.

"I know that turtle!"

"It's a tortoise, master." Archer growled.

"What the fuck ever!" The Shepherd snapped. "He nearly tripped me at the festival!"

"He stabbed my foot. And Stone knocked me out."

"A spy! I can smell him all over that sad little beast!" The Shepherd shouted, sounding just a little paranoid.

Archer growled in agreement, his mouth full of fresh fangs on full display.

"Don't let him escape!"

Archer lunged at Benicio faster than I've ever seen a creature move. Which felt wildly unnecessary given the speed my new little buddy moved with. In a blur of coarse black fur and teeth, he had Benicio off the ground and wrapped in his claws. Everything went black.

10

EVEN GREATER NONSENSE

Silence filled the Sanctum as Barnaby, Charlotte and I stood in the center of the room. They stared in a puzzled shock at their feet and the still unconscious Mayor laying at them as I smoked a cigarette on the other side of her. Nobody had spoken since I delivered Craine into the Sanctum and gently dumped her on the floor. Frustration radiated off of Barnaby like a space heater. Confusion and concern drove out any other thought Charlotte could've possibly had.

I could seriously go for some nachos right now.

And it was Charlotte who finally spoke, clearing her throat with a small, nervous cough as if the words were choking her.

"That's the Mayor."

"Kinda." I replied.

"That's the Mayor!" She exclaimed as if saying it louder would make the whole situation go away.

"Kinda!"

"I told you to *watch!*" Barnaby scolded.

"I did!" I said in my defense. "Until I couldn't anymore."

"You kidnapped the Mayor!" He shouted at me with an accusing tone I really didn't appreciate.

"Kinda!"

"Do you know how much heat this is gonna bring down?!" He asked through a scowl.

"That is the *Mayor, Cyrus!*" Charlotte cried.

"Kinda!"

"Why do you keep saying that?!" She asked, doing her sincere best not to panic under the weight of it all.

"I mean," I said with a shrug, "she's not *really* the Mayor."

"Just because you didn't vote for her—" Barnaby started.

"She's possessed." I corrected him.

"What?!" The two Le Coeurs asked in shocked unison.

"I saw it. She dropped to the ground, flailed around a bit, then fucking *levitated*, said something in a spooky demon voice, fell back down and has been like this ever since."

"Lead with that next time." Barnaby said as he tried to rub the tension out of his neck.

"I rescued her."

"I'm sure the Gulchers saw it that way too." Was Charlotte's unnecessarily snarky response.

"You were right, Barnaby." I started. "She was in deep with the Shepherd and it's definitely not Delilah Craine at the wheel right now."

"That checks out." Barnaby said as he crossed over to the desk and the open collection of books strewn on and around it. A thick, heavy volume bound in brown leather sat on top of the others. It's pages were crinkled and discolored like old coffee filters. "Everything we read—"

"I talked to Katrina last night." I interjected. There were gaps in his knowledge that needed to be filled in before he could give me whatever hypothesis the two of them had worked out.

Barnaby stopped. Brown leather book in hand, he spun with wide eyes to face me.

"What did she say?!" He asked excitedly.

"Blood oath." I answered with a shrug.

"A blood oath?" Charlotte asked rather in disbelief or unsure of what that was. I split the difference and answered for both options.

"Yeah. A blood oath! Powerful magic that bonds together oath-taker and oath-giver. And based on *this*," I said as I lifted the Mayor's limp hand. "That's probably exactly what it is."

"I know what a blood oath is, but they don't usually involve possessions." She shot back smugly.

"They do when those are the terms of the agreement." Barnaby chimed in. "Everything we read points to the involvement of something pretty ancient like this."

"Great!" I said even though it probably wasn't.

"But what's the play here? Control the Mayor, control his followers, Archer gets new strength, for what? To rule over the Gulch?" Charlotte questioned, doing her best Nancy Drew impression.

"Play stupid games, win stupid prizes." I said as I pulled another smoke from my jacket and gave it a light.

Barnaby's gaze fell to the floor. But it wasn't the floor he was staring at, he was miles away in that moment.

"Or worse." He said grimly.

"If she was tight with him..." Charlotte started.

"Or if whoever's currently occupying her was." I added.

"Then maybe they can confirm a few things for us." Barnaby finished.

"Hey, good job, Cyrus! Maybe it wasn't such a stupid idea bringing her here." They were going to say it at some point, I just said it for them.

I took a drag from my cigarette as I crossed over to a cot in the back corner against the crypt and took a seat. I was determined to enjoy it, the smoke filling my lungs, and relax in the few moments of quiet I'd have left before the day devolved into even greater nonsense. More than anything I knew that I needed to be out of Barnaby's way until he needed me.

"We can't be too careful." Barnaby said as he watched me.

"I'm sayin'!"

"You know what we have to do."

I groaned. I knew indeed.

"That's why she's here."

With a signaling nod to Charlotte, Barnaby went to work in a flurry of determination and grit, bouncing between his workbench and the shelves grabbing everything we'd need. Various balms and tonics, a book of incantations written in Latin or some equally dead language, a silver serving platter so shiny I could see the rest of the Sanctum reflected in it as he criss-crossed the room. Barnaby dumped it all in the middle of the room with the Mayor, freeing his hands for the heavy work. In a locked chest underneath the workbench, he produced four heavy chains made of the finest blend of hardened tungsten and just enough silver to severely annoy anything evil. He split them between himself and Charlotte, tossing her a set and wordlessly instructing her on what to do.

A deep crease formed above Charlotte's nose as her brow furrowed. She knew it was only a matter of time until she'd have to get her hands dirty. She just didn't expect that time to come so soon. This would be her first exorcism. A nasty, dirty, ugly sort of business that, up until then, she had only ever read about. As ready as she was for this moment, as much as she had studied and tried to prepare herself for the very real evils the world contained, nothing would ever quite look the same to her after this. It would be the first of many tests for her. And you never really forget your first.

Barnaby, on the other hand, was an old pro. He knew exactly what we needed and where we needed it, moving with the efficiency and accuracy of someone that could've performed this ritual blindfolded. That didn't make him any more excited about it than Charlotte though. He knew what the task at hand really meant. The sights, the sounds and worst of all the smells. That's another thing most movies don't tell you about exorcisms! The stink of sulfur and death sinks into your nostrils and stays there for days after. It's a huge pain in the ass. You sit there wondering "Is that me? Ohhhhh no, wait, exorcism. That's right." Say goodbye to your weekend.

Silently they slid the desk chair into the center of the room, hoisted the Mayor up into it and cuffed the manacled ends of the chains to the her wrists and ankles. The pair wrapped the chains around her body and the chair as many times as they could before linking them together with a heavy padlock. She wasn't going anywhere, possessed or not. The Sanctum had been set up for this kind of procedure long before Barnaby and he had always hoped he'd never need this particular feature, but sadly that hand't been the case. Mayor Delilah Craine would be the fourth exorcism performed in this sacred space. The first being a farmer who turned out not to be possessed at all, just an asshole who took a sick amount of joy in the slaughter of livestock. No real loss there I suppose. The second was the town librarian who had stumbled upon the wrong book, read the wrong passage and never recovered. She might not have survived the ritual, but the book was now safely locked in a box over by the crypt. I didn't tell you that! Don't go looking for it! The third was none other than Eleanor Archer, the Sheriff's wife. Only too late had we realized that the beast wasn't using a human body, but masquerading as one.

Barnaby took Charlotte by the shoulders and stared deep into her soul as she breathed fast and heavy. Nerves were setting in. And nerves were no good to anybody here.

"Stay strong." He told her as her face hardened. "No matter what. You're a Le Coeur!"

Barnaby had faith in her and that was enough for me. But he also had doubts. As we all did.

"Let's do this." He said with a nod to me.

I stood with a sigh and went back to the Mayor. She was like some kind of heathen queen, drunk and unconscious on her throne, wrapped tightly in a silky blanket of silver and metal. Taking one last puff of my smoke, I knelt down and snuffed it out on the floor at her feet. She stirred as I exhaled a plume of tobacco and nicotine into her face. It was going to take a little more than that and I knew it. I gave her a few light slaps to the face, like Barnaby had given me too many times when he'd find me passed out in here. Still nothing.

"Hey! Mayor lady!" I screamed in her face.

Her eyelids fluttered. I was getting through to something, but what? The Mayor or the Undesignated Driver?

"Hey! Demon bitch!"

Her eyes shot open, bloodshot and red, like mine all the times Barnaby had found me passed out in here! There's a lot of similarity between waking up a dude who's been on a solid three day bender and someone that needs a good exorcising. Her glassy gaze darted around, scanning the un-expected new environment. First landing on the chains that bound her, then to Charlotte, who took a small, cautious step back. They moved to Barnaby, standing firm a few feet away. His arms folded across his chest with the stern focus his battle-hardened nerves had produced. Finally to me. A subtle change occurred, one you could only see if you were as close as I was. There was a hatred within those eyes. Like a prisoner who thought they had escaped but instead woke up in the warden's office.

"Cyrus...Stone..." she hissed.

"Hello there." I said coldly from under the brim of my hat.

"Cyrus Stone!" She wailed as a nearly human terror took over. "What am I doing here?! Why am I chained to this chair?!"

She looked back to Barnaby.

"Le Coeur?! What is this?! Is this about your patio?!"

Barnaby stroked his chin with silent contemplation and deep concentration as he stared on. And then the thought slammed into the Mayor's head like an eighteen wheeler on ice.

"Oh god you're going to kill me!" She shrieked as she began to sob. "Please! No! I have a family!"

"I'm sure they have a few questions for you too." I growled in her ear.

"Please! Let me go!" The Mayor pleaded as she struggled to look to Charlotte. "You seem like such a reasonable young lady! Please! Don't throw in with their lot! Nothing has happened here that I can't forgive or forget!"

"Um, Cyrus?" Charlotte said as she took a step forward.

Barnaby immediately waved her back, wordlessly commanding her to stay where she was.

Hold the line, kid.

"Whatever this is about, we can figure it out! Please! I have children!" She begged as tears rolled down her plump cheeks.

"This is how it starts." I reminded Charlotte, catching her as she took another step forward. Somewhere inside her, past her abundance of humanity, she knew that. She just had to hang tough and remember.

"Barnaby, he could've been wrong!" She speculated.

Oh yeah, super tough.

"Not now, Char." Barnaby shot at his sister.

She recoiled, knowing better than to get in the way, but persisted none the less.

"Everything I've read about exorcism—" She started, in full mid-exorcism lecture mode.

"Doesn't mean a damn thing right now." I finished, in full get-your-shit-together mode.

"Please! Please! Charlotte, is it?! Please don't let them kill me!" The Mayor continued, her face a sopping wet mess of tears.

This was just how demons operated. They'd do anything to stay in their stolen body and in our realm. Targeting the weakest in the room and praying on their sympathy, their empathy, their fears, whatever human emotions they made the mistake of carrying in with them. For Charlotte it was all of the above. Whatever was inside the Mayor could smell it all over her.

Can't say we didn't see it coming.

"Give me the tray!" I barked a little sadistically.

If there's one thing I loved most, it was pissing off evil. And the tray was highly effective at just that.

"No! What's that?! Don't let them hurt me, child, please!"

Out of necessity, it was Barnaby who delivered it to me.

"Let's see who you really are." I growled in the Mayor's ear.

Barnaby smeared a mix of herbs and anointing oils on her forehead in a greasy arc. I never asked what that particular mud was, but it smelled like garlic sautéed buttholes. It was effective regardless. It drew the demon forward while protecting the host from the shock of seeing what lurked inside. It also happened to be one of the steps I consistently forgot when I'd do solo exorcisms, but that's neither here nor there.

The shining silver of the tray reflected the being's true form as I held it inches from Craine's face. Like a skeleton made of melting jet black ink and oozing candle wax with a crown of small horns around its skull. A lower demon. A henchman of Hell. It snarled and gnashed its mouth full of daggers at the human form in front of the tray.

"Have a look, Charlotte." I instructed her.

She inched over to the center of the room, frightened of what she might see. When she finally laid eyes on the shining tray, the reflected demon lunged and snapped at her from within the silver. The tray jumped from my hands and crashed to the floor. But Charlotte stood strong. The fear and nerves vanished from her in an instant, along without the doubts as she realized what was really pulling the Mayor's strings, but the sympathy remained.

"We need to save her." She said with a cold resolve that mirrored her brother's.

Good job, kid.

The beast inside the Mayor realized it was in trouble, thrashing and pulling against the chains as hard as it could, rocking the chair as it threw Craine's full weight into it. Her head was on a spring, seemingly flailing and jerking in all directions at once. That horrible, guttural, grating voice returned, pouring from the Mayor's mouth in a tormented moan as I took a step back. Her head snapped up at me abruptly in a hard, sharp angle no neck should bend.

"You are expected, Cyrus Stone." It growled. "Hell awaits you."

"Am I supposed to be surprised by that?" I asked, genuinely curious, as her head cracked its way back into a more natural posture.

"Your soul will be *ours* for all time. He's waiting for you like he waited for all the others that came before." The being said as it writhed against the chains. The pain of being bound and reflected with silver becoming gradually insufferable to its damned spirit.

Barnaby and Charlotte glanced to each other, the concern writ large and boldly all over their faces. Not for the wellbeing of the creature, but for what it said. Something about the threat it made sent a cold rush down their spines that my spine was apparently immune to.

"Let's go to work." Barnaby instructed Charlotte. "Follow my lead." He added as they approached the demon and the collection of exorcism paraphernalia he had left on the floor next to it.

I backed off as I picked up the tray, holding it up to the demon to make sure it got a good long look at itself. Demons always had a tendency to get a little too comfortable in their hijacked bodies. The truth of this one's actual appearance was doing its job and working the internal infernal into a frenzy. The handles jumped in my hands as the tray shook from the violent entity it reflected. A horrible noise somewhere between a dry heave and a growl spilled from the Mayor's mouth.

Barnaby and Charlotte worked fast. Spreading oils and herbs all over her body. Smearing her with every natural purifier known to man and several man hadn't really caught on to yet. They emptied vial after vial of elixirs, tonics and holy water, splashing and soaking the floor, offering small incantational rites as they went. The wording had to be exact every single time or the soul rescued could end up in a kind of limbo within their own bodies, in the driver seat but unable to reach the wheel or the pedals. I was a solid seven out of ten when it came to this. But the next part? It was one of my specialties.

"Tell us what we wanna know, you piece of shit!" I roared down to the creature behind Craine's eyes.

"You will all die screaming!" It shrieked to the room as it started screaming. While the human body wouldn't be damaged by Barnaby and Charlotte's handiwork, the lower demon would've felt like it was steadily dissolving. Which was always fun to watch.

It's cries and moans filled the room, drowning out every other sound. I pressed the tray a little closer, forcing it to take an even harder look at itself.

"Tell us what we wanna know! I won't say it again!" I shouted over the screams.

"I don't know what you wanna know!" It cried helplessly.

"You *do* know what we wanna know and we wanna know it!"

"I do not!"

"Do too!"

"Do not!" It wailed.

"Who are you working for?!"

"Release me and I'll tell you!"

"No fucking chance!" Charlotte spat at the entity.

"What she said!" I added, the worse cop to Charlotte's bad cop.

I dropped the reflection and grabbed the Mayor's face, pulling myself in close. I could smell the faint odor coming off of her breath, and it wasn't the festival food.

"Then maybe we pull you out here for a little face-to-face."

The creature laughed through the Mayor's mouth. A sickly, cackle sounding thing.

"I'd like to see you try." It sneered, arrogant and unaware.

"Barnaby," I said with a grin, "let's do this proper."

"It would be our pleasure." He said as he waved Charlotte over to him. "Remember, strong will, stronger spirit." Teacher told pupil as they reached their hands out towards the possessed's face.

Immediately they fell into a sort of trance. Their eyes rolling to the backs of their heads as they chanted all the necessary spells, rites and incantations. The main one I could make out in the sea of Latin gibberish was "vilis culus daemonium". It was another part of exorcisms I kinda sucked at. All the "semper fidelis tyrannosaurus" shit. But I always remembered that last line! So give me a little credit. They shouted the words at the Mayor in an unrelenting barrage, increasing in intensity and volume with every repetition, their hands slowly drifting towards her face.

"Vilis culus daemonium!" They chanted.

"Fuck off!" The demon seethed.

"Vilis culus daemonium!"

"What's the Shepherd planning?!" I screamed at the demon, my awesome voice nearly shaking the Sanctum walls.

"Vilis culus daemonium!"

The demon convulsed aggressively while lashing out against its bonds and us, its howls of agony telling us that the ritual was working.

"Vilis culus daemonium!"

"The Shepherd...", it struggled to say, "...Is not...The Shepherd...is not—"

Every muscle in the Mayor's body tensed, rigid and motionless as a statue. Her jaws snapped opened at that impossible width I had seen at the festival what felt like days ago. The same gut-wrenching howl/horn poured out of her mouth. Barnaby and Charlotte held their ground.

"Vilis culus daemonium!" They did their best to shout over the noise. "Vilis culus daemonium!"

I gripped the tray tightly, my palms starting to sweat a little. Through the bellowing howl I could hear a voice like escaping steam, faint, whispered, barely even there at all.

"Cyrussss Stoooooone..." It beckoned to me.

I took a cautionary step back, knowing what would inevitably happen now. A thick black bile erupted from the Mayor's mouth like the flood gates inside her had been broken, pouring down her face and neck and soaking into her nice, neat Gulchy Day blouse. A pair of skeletal hands, as black as a moonless night, wriggled their way out past her lips, reaching and feeling until they hooked themselves around her cheeks.

"Vilis culus daemonium!"

BOOOOOOORRRRRR, the howl persisted.

The black skeletal hands gave way to a pair of black matching arms as the entity pulled its way out of the Mayor's mouth. Her jaws stretched to an impossible width. The top of its skull impossibly revealed itself as a set of shoulders came twitching and crunching out. The demon's face stayed aimed at the floor as it forced its way through its perverse self-birth. It switched from pulling to pushing as its body slinked out Craine's face. Down past the ribcage and heading towards the pelvis, all of its wretched bones dripping and oozing with the same black tar bile. It's head snapped up to look at its reflection, its ooze splattered across the tray and up to the ceiling. The demon paused and for a second it seemed to be admiring its reflection, like it was lost in its own eye sockets. What I knew to be a kind of confused look though. Seeing yourself is one thing, watching your birth through a middle-aged woman's mouth is something completely different.

Works every time.

I jumped at the opportunity. The silver tray wasn't exclusively meant for showing the demon its only ugly-ass face, it was our patented sneak attack. I reared the tray back, high over my head and in a flash brought it back down as hard as I could onto the top of that inky, waxy skull. The impact sent a ringing tremor up my arms and clear into shoulders, yet somehow the tray remained unscathed.

Magic flatware, bitch.

"Vilis culus daemonium!"

The demon's entire body slid straight out of the Mayor's mouth like a bad piece of calamari, splattering and smearing black filth all over the floor. Before it could get its bearings and collect itself, I smacked it hard against the side of the head with the silver tray. The demon tumbled over, sprawling out and leaving smeared black trails behind wherever it touched.

And then came the god damn smell! Rotting eggs and equally rotting flesh. Barnaby turned his nose away as he got out of the line of fire and let me operate. Charlotte gagged as she rushed to the unconscious and now unoccupied Mayor.

"Leave her!" Barnaby instructed as Charlotte began to unlock the chains. "It could still go back in. Give him space."

The two of them fell back to separate corners of the Sanctum, trusting me to handle it from there.

"You wanna try that again? The Shepherd is not what?!" I called down to the demon as I kicked it over onto its back.

The demon cackled, black goo flying out of its toothy mouth like spittle.

"Kill me...and you'll never know!" It taunted.

The tray rattled as I dropped it onto the demon's ribs but the sound was quickly cut off as I gave it a good hard stomp. The bones crackled like burning timber as small streams of smoke snaked out from beneath the tray.

"No, really, finish what you were gonna say." I taunted back as I leaned down in the demon's face. "I'm all ears."

The demon bit and gnashed at the air, trying to get a piece of me, throwing all of its weight against mine as I pressed the tray down on its chest.

"The Shepherd..." It fought through its suffering to say. "The Shepherd..."

None of us were paying enough attention to its legs apparently. Because as it thrashed beneath me, one of them managed to fly up and kick me square in the ass. I fell forward with a roll. The demon leapt to its feet, all snarling and growling scary and evil now that I wasn't practically standing on it.

Pussy.

Its eye sockets fixed on Charlotte as the black essence of whatever the hell that thing was made of dripped down them onto its high cheek bones. It let out a piercing battle cry and charged straight for her. Barnaby was on it first, naturally, sprinting across the room to intercept. Without missing a step, the demon batted him away effortlessly with one swipe of its boney arm, sending him flying back the way he came. Barnaby hit the crypt and dropped to the ground with a thud and thump, nearly landing on the Box of Mystery. The demon was almost on top of Charlotte before she screamed. A scream that was cut short with a deafening:

BOOM!

The demon's skull exploded into shards of dried out charcoal. The rest of its body lost its oozy sheen and crumbled into dust on the spot. I stood on the far side of the Sanctum. Directly behind where the demon last stood. Arm raised and gun still smoking. I gave it a good cowboy spin before dropping it back into its holster.

"Interrogation's over."

Mayor Delilah Craine gasped as she woke up and breathed her first free breaths in what I'm sure was a long while. Charlotte ran to her side as Barnaby got to his feet and did the same.

"Mayor Craine!" Charlotte began. "Mayor Craine, can you hear me?"

The Mayor quickly, anxiously nodded her head as her eyes bounced around the Sanctum. Barnaby unlocked the chains and manacles. Charlotte set out to unwrap them as she continued.

"Mayor Craine, it's Charlotte Le Coeur and my brother Barnaby."

"Mayor." Barnaby said with a courteous nod as he helped loosen the chains around her chest and waist.

"You're inside the Blood Moon Saloon right now. Do you know where that is?"

"Th-the other street?" Craine answered, in shock.

"Good, that's good. We're here to help, ok?"

The Mayor gave another rapid volley of nods.

"Do you remember anything of what you've just been through?" Barnaby asked urgently.

The Mayor stammered and muttered, her ability to speak coming and going in waves of post-traumatic stress.

"Charlotte, grab the big red one." Barnaby told her as he nodded to his shelf of potions.

I plopped my ass down on a cot and lit another smoke as Charlotte hurried past me. The last thing the Mayor needed to see was my murderous mug.

Best to give her time to find her footing again before we lay that surprise on her.

Charlotte returned to Barnaby with a bright red crystal bottle with a neck longer than it's body and an old cork shoved down the mouth.

"This one?" She asked Barnaby.

"That's the fella." Barnaby confirmed as he took it from her.

He yanked the cork out with his teeth and spat it away before offering the bottle to the Mayor. Charlotte went right back to finishing off the last of the chains around her legs. Even with her hands and body now free, Craine shook her head and recoiled from the bottle.

"It's ok, you can trust us. This will help. Not like the last thing someone made you drink." Barnaby said softly. This was where he really shined. His bedside manner was second to none. I'd been through enough mind-meltingly brutal hangovers and catastrophically devastating injuries with Barnaby at my side to know that firsthand.

Craine slowly, nervously, took the bottle. She sniffed at the mouth first, when she was convinced she didn't smell anything out of the ordinary, she took a long drink. Her cheeks turned pink and a spark of life sprung to her. She broke her lips away from the bottle and took a deep breath in.

"Thank you, Mr. Le Coeur." She said as she caught her breath. "Ms. Le Coeur." She added with a nod to Charlotte.

"What's in that one?" Charlotte asked Barnaby.

"Everclear." He responded plainly.

"I'm in the bar?" Craine asked as she poured over her surroundings. From within the Sanctum walls that could be pretty hard to buy. The weapons, the potions, the books, it was all a bit much to take in for the uninitiated.

"Yes." Charlotte said as she fetched an old bar rag to wipe the black bile from the Mayor's face. "Consider this an add on."

"That we didn't have a permit for." Barnaby added with the most subtle undercurrent of bitterness.

"Wh-what happened?" Craine asked as she took another drink.

"You tell us." Barnaby said.

Craine poured through every thought, every memory she could access.

"Start simple." Barnaby instructed, knowing exactly what she was doing. "Where do the dark spots start?"

"What day is it?"

"Gulchy Day." Charlotte said as she handed her the rag to wipe her face.

"Gulchy Day?!"

"Gulchy Day." Barnaby confirmed.

"How long have I been asleep?!" Panic and confusion began having their way with her. Typical of someone who just had a demon crawl out their mouth. "Where's my family?"

Barnaby looked to me.

I stamped my smoke out on the heel of my boot.

"If they're not currently tracking me down," I sighed as I got up. "Then they're probably at home I guess."

Craine whipped her head to me, her eyes wide with fear.

"Cy-Cyrus Stone?!"

"It's ok, Mayor." Charlotte said with a comforting hand to her shoulder. "He's with us. He's one of the good guys."

"I rescued you, Craine." I said as I stood in front of her and waited for my thanks.

"From what?! Where's my family?! What the hell is going on here?!"

"You were possessed." Charlotte said, unsure how of the Mayor could've failed to realize that.

"I was what?!"

Every time.

"Psst!" I half-whispered to Charlotte. "They usually gotta realize that on their own."

"I'm sorry but it's true." Barnaby jumped back in. "As hard as it may be to believe."

"How do you think all that black shit got on your face? You puked up a lower demon." It was a detail I thought she needed.

"No. No!" Craine said as she tried to stand. But the strain of the ordeal and the exhaustion of her body brought her right back down to the chair. She shook her head in denial and disbelief. "It was all one long nightmare. It had to be. It was a nightmare! It had to be!"

"You were floating when I got to you." I offered.

"You people are insane!" She threw at us as she started to sob again. She touched the clean rag to her face and recoiled in horror at the black goo now soaked into it. Some part of the Mayor knew what we were saying was true. But the other part of her needed to protect itself from that truth. It's what usually led people to rooms with really soft, cushiony walls after an ordeal like that.

Barnaby always knew just what to say.

"We'll get you back to your family as soon as possible, Mayor Crain. But for the sake of argument, let's assume it was. Let's say it was all just a *really* fuckin' bad dream." He went on. "What do you remember of it?"

She hesitated, knowing that whatever she could say would sound like some bad Vanishing Powder trip on its best day.

"I can't even begin to tell you how important it is that we know." Barnaby insisted.

"I wanna go home!" She finally answered.

"We'll take you right home. We just need you to answer our questions first." Charlotte countered.

"It's a lot to wrap your head around, but please try." Barnaby added.

Craine laid out her terms as she wept.

"Right back to my family."

"You have my word." Barnaby replied earnestly.

"And *he!*" She sneered, pointing a trembling finger at me. "Leaves in chains!"

"I saved you!"

"You kidnapped me as far as I can tell!" She cried as she wiped the tears, snot and demon goo from her face.

"Someone's feeling better." I quipped as I went back to my cot.

"I don't know why it matters to any of you in the first place, but dreamt I was lost in the Gulch, ok?!" She said, not having any other options. "Like I was moving through town but didn't know where I was going or what I was doing. The things I saw, the things I heard...they weren't real! I know that much."

She shut down as she continued to convince herself. Indignant and defiant towards the situation and the outlaw, charlatans and overall lunatics involved.

"Go on." I implored impatiently.

It had been a long day. All I wanted was a drink and my bed after all that bullshit. Yet there I was, still on the clock. She trudged along.

"There was a man! It was so dark every time I was near him. Like there was no light left in the entire world! But I feel like he was someone I knew. He kept telling me that his time was coming."

"The Shepherd?" Barnaby asked.

"No..." Craine started before abruptly changing her mind. "No wait! I think it was! How did you...?"

"Keep going, Mayor." Barnaby pressed intently.

Watching her mind drift back to the thoughts themselves was all I needed to see to know that one part of her was starting to outweigh the other.

"The Shepherd had me drink from his cup. And then I was lost. After that I couldn't see him, just this big...dark...spot! Where he should've been. But I knew it was him. And every time I found him again I felt cold and even more alone. There was this *horrible voice* in my head that kept saying we had to do whatever it took to please him. That the only way home was to do exactly what he said."

"Did that mother fucker tell you to deny my permits?!" Barnaby blurted out before he could restrain himself. But honestly it was a fair question.

Craine stared at him in confusion and disbelief, as we all did, before it dawned on her.

"Yes, yes he did!"

"Son of a bitch, I knew it!" Barnaby shouted as spasms flailed his arms in exasperation.

"He said something about less space for you meaning less standing room in the church!"

"Mother fucker!"

"Wait. What? How? That was...That actually...How do you...?" Craine asked as her mind raced, not really knowing how to proceed but having to choose a path anyway. "He would call to me." She continued with a shudder. "No matter where I was or where he was or what we were doing I'd hear him like he was right in my ear. I would find him and he'd tell me what to do and it's like my body would do it without me telling it to. Really, how do know all this? Were you people involved somehow?! How did you know that it was him?!"

"We call that "possessed", Craine." I educated her as her head sank down with the weight of realization.

Barnaby and Charlotte were thinking the same thing, but Barnaby said it first.

"By a very powerful master."

"He kept talking about the Father!" She said as more mental doors unlocked.

"Did you see him?" Charlotte leaned into her hopefully.

Craine shook her head while it reeled.

"He said he wasn't ready to show himself yet. But the darkness around the Shepherd...it's like it was alive. It moved. It breathed! It knew I was there and knew who I am."

The truth, it seemed, was winning. And that would be her first step towards recovering. If she could be strong enough to accept what happened and learn to toughen her mind against the memories and knowledge she would slowly become the unfortunate owner of, then she would overcome what very few people ever have. And I'd probably vote for her next time around.

"Look." She said with an encouraging firmness. "I need to go home! I don't understand what any of this is or what it means, but I need to be with my family! You promised you'd let me go to them now do it!" And the waterworks started up again like a fountain from under her tired eyes.

Or not.

"Barnaby, you know we can't." I said to him rationally.

"Yeah. Doesn't really look like it, does it?" He asked sympathetically yet rhetorically.

"Sure as fuck does not!"

"What?! You promised!" Craine shouted.

"You were in too—"

A thunderous roar from overhead derailed Barnaby's response and the entire conversation as it shot clean through to our guts. A dense, bellowing kind of roar. Like a lion and a gorilla fucked a bear but turned up a few hundred decibels. We all glared up at the ceiling, wondering what could've possibly made such a noise. Barnaby and Charlotte had their suspicions, Craine had her fears and I had the answer somehow.

"Archer."

"What?!" Barnaby asked, rushing back to my side. "How do you know?"

"Benicio knows! It's like everything he saw just dumped directly into my brain!"

"Who's Benicio?!"

"My little tortoise buddy. He was staking out the church."

"I told you that amulet was good shit." Barnaby said slyly.

"Fuck you, we'll talk about it later! He has Benicio!"

My little guy was in danger! I rushed straight to the secret door but Barnaby grabbed my arm and pulled me back.

"Cyrus! Focus! We'll rescue Benicio later!"

"It's Archer! The Shepherd made him into a gargoyle I think."

And as if to prove my point, his pants-shittingly intense voice quaked through the Blood Moon and the Sanctum as he past by in the air above, unaware that I was mere feet below.

"Cyrus!" He boomed. "Cyrus Stone, I'm callin' you out, coward!"

His laugh rattled our teeth as it continued past us.

"You sure the Shepherd did that to him?" Barnaby pressed.

"Benicio saw it so it's like I did too." I replied confidently. "He told the Shepherd something about trusting him with his soul and having faith in the Father or whatever and then he drank some glowing shit from the magic pimp cup and kinda like...out...grew...his whole body."

"Show yourself, Stone!" Archer added from a distance. "Surrender the Mayor and face me like a *man*!"

His laugh rolled like thunder in the skies all around the Gulch as Archer flew laps over the town. Barnaby and Charlotte slowly made their way to each other, both stepping like they were walking to their ultimate doom. A heavy truth was settling in their minds. They were realizing that their suspicions had been correct. Something bigger was at play here.

"See now that's fucked up." I said, stating the obvious. "You don't get to go from old man to winged monster and start saying shit like that."

11

PARLAY

A heavy chill fell over the Gulch in the hours that passed after the Sheriff's flyby and a standoff ensued. Archer wanted Craine, he wanted me, and I wanted his giant ugly head on a stick. Barnaby refused to let me leave the Sanctum or even get close to the door as I paced the room like a tiger in a cage with my hand on my gun. Almost like he knew "I just wanna look outside! I just wanna see where he is!" was an outright lie. He ever so warmly invited me to:

"Sit your happy ass down and be fucking patient for once in your god damn life! We need a plan of attack!" As his wits began to unravel.

Before long, the aerial taunts and the flapping of heavy wings grew distant until the Gulch stood somewhat peacefully. A long night that didn't seem real or even possible breathed its last. The early morning sun glowed sleepily around the edge of the mountains, spreading its faint light over the tops of the town. On the surface, it appeared to be slumbering peacefully in an unseasonably cool embrace. Underneath the doors and windows were sealed tight, their sleepless owners waiting by them with baited breath for any word on their missing Mayor, determined to pretend they didn't hear what they heard roaring over the town and convince themselves it was a trick of the wind. The Shepherd's flock must've known the truth. Something stirred deep within them, in a place they didn't even know existed. They waited by their doors, at the ready, like good little soldiers without an order.

There was little rest to be found in the Blood Moon Saloon either. Barnaby sat up at his work bench with large circles of gray under his eyes as he studied his old brown leather book, cross-referencing it with a few select grimoires. He had barely looked up, slowed down or even took a breath since.

Charlotte was slumped over at the desk, her face down in hefty brown leather book. Craine, thoroughly unconscious, drooled onto her cot with what was left of Barnaby's post-exorcism bottle of Everclear clutched desperately to her chest. And I laid awake, staring straight up at the ceiling, feet up on my cot, a small minefield of squashed cigarette butts around me. My trigger finger and stabbing hand were set to explode at any moment.

Craine was the first to fall, whining and crying about her family as that bottle fought against her sobering reality. Barnaby had laid out a compelling case for her to stay just a little bit longer.

"Until we're sure you and you're family aren't in danger." He had argued.

Charlotte went down the most recently. I'll give her this, she's a trooper. Despite the pots of coffee her and Barnaby kept running back and forth to the bar to get, the hours upon hours of stress and study pulled her head down to the desk only a couple hours prior.

Barnaby refused to stop. He couldn't. Ever since we had met the responsibilities of the Sanctum had always sat heavily on his head, but tonight they weighed him down to the ground. I refused to sleep as long as Barnaby worked. My responsibilities weren't nearly as heavy, but solidarity, ya know?

"Look," he said as he spun around on the workbench stool, "I'll level with you, man."

"By all means." I answered without moving.

"The writing is kinda on the wall here."

I'll bite.

I looked to the walls. There was nothing. If you didn't count the names of the fallen Le Coeurs bolted to the crypt.

"Ok?"

"There's a possibility that this is a little out of our wheelhouse." He said, an exasperated defeat in his voice that I knew he was only comfortable letting me hear.

"Archer?!" I asked incredulously.

"The whole damn thing! What made him! It's all really similar to something Pappy and the first Hunter dealt with, but I can't be sure."

"What was it?" I asked, sitting up.

"That's the thing. I really can't say it until I know."

Can't? Or won't?

I lit another smoke and exhaled with a sigh.

"You know I like the dark. I just don't like being left in it, Barnaby."

"Yeah, man. I know. I'm sorry. It's just..."

There was a stress in his voice that I couldn't quite place.

"The gargoyle has to go." I said with equal measures of blood lust and cold logic.

Barnaby hesitated, picking his next words as carefully as he could.

"It's not like anything we've gone up against before. So I don't want you to prepare for the wrong thing. And I know that if I tell you before I know for sure, you'll go all balls out and we could just end up making this whole thing a helluva lot worse. If I'm right, it scares me. Because you're not ready."

Fuck, dude.

That stung. But trusting his judgement had gotten us this far, so I saw no other option.

"Alright. I guess." I grumbled as I took a drag from my cigarette, feeling a little bit like the kid who had first asked about the Box of Mystery.

Barnaby took a bit of pity on the dejected teenager he saw sitting across from him.

"Let's work through this." He suggested. "What do we know about the Shepherd?"

"He has a stupid pony tail." I said through a plume of smoke.

"Ok. What else?" Barnaby probed, hoping I'd dig deeper.

"He has a stupid beard."

"Cyrus, come on."

"And he dresses like a jackass."

Barnaby shot me that look that I knew could only mean he needed me to get serious.

"You would know better than me!" I argued. "I haven't even really been around!"

"Yeah." Barnaby started. "That's probably true. Well, no one can say where he came from and I haven't really been able to suss that out. As far as the Gulch is concerned, he just blew in off of the flats."

"After Wright died." I added.

"Not too long after, yeah." He continued. "He preaches doomsday salvation. But gets people possessed."

"And turns them into gargoyles."

"He's got that cup."

"The dagger."

"And the dagger." Barnaby pondered the details. "Do we know what's in his book?"

"Pictures of himself, I imagine."

The truth smacked Barnaby in the face like a slice of wet ham.

"We really don't know shit about him do we?!" He tottered dangerously on the edge of whisper yelling and yell whispering.

The nail had officially been hit on the head. The obvious had been stated. We really didn't know shit about him. It felt like even Benicio would've had a better idea of who we were dealing with we did.

Benicio.

My face lit up with the early rumblings of an idea. Barnaby caught on with equal excitement.

"What are you thinking?" He asked, probably thinking the exact same thing.

I pulled the amulet from my shirt. Barnaby let out a short, sharp, excited laugh that threatened to wake the sleeping Sanctum. I took that as a big thumbs up. Up went my pant leg as I picked at my scab. The amulet drank the few small drops and came to life in my hand. My eyes slammed shut. They re-opened low on a far dirtier and dustier floor than the Sanctum's.

The Church of the Seventh Seal was dim and grimy around me, the lanterns and candles burning their last of the night. A heavy chain was wrapped mercilessly around my shell and kept me from moving much farther than a few inches from the corner. Pools of what was once the Sheriff dried and congealed on the floor between the rows of pews. The altar on the stage stood empty. No dagger. No chalice. No book. No Shepherd. Anywhere. The church was quiet and deserted. Until it wasn't. Out of nowhere he appeared, on all fours and nose to nose with me, a crazed look in his wide eyes and even wider smile.

"Hello, Cyrus." He hissed.

AHJESUSFUCK!

How? How did he know? I willed my reptile vocal chords to say the words but all that came out was:

"Auuurg!"

"Don't worry," he said, "I can understand you."

Ok, first of all, what the fuck?

"I know it might be hard to fathom, but yes, Cyrus. I can understand. The Father has given me many gifts. And I know its you at the wheel in there now."

What are you?

"Aurrg!"

"I am salvation." He answered self-assured as he relaxed and sat on the floor in front of me with his knees tucked into his chest.

My tortoise eyes rolled as hard as they could.

Salvation doesn't go around possessing mayors or turning old men into monsters.

"Agggur!"

The Shepherd chuckled to himself.

"My kind of salvation does! I've done more for the people of the Gulch than you could ever hope to."

You have no idea what I've done for them.

"Rrrraug!"

"Don't I? You're the fabled Hunter of Evil, are you not? Or is that just something you like calling yourself?"

If I had hands I would've punched him square in the kidneys for that.

"Arrrg!"

"The New World is coming, Hunter of Evil. The Father will cleanse this earth for his loyal and there's nothing you can do to stop it." The mere thought clearly made him all warm and fuzzy inside.

Who is your daddy? What does he do?

"Auur!"

"You don't know him? That's funny. He knows you. Cyrus, son of James."

My blood ran cold despite the fact that the body I was in was already cold-blooded. This was a classic trick of evil. The tired old "tell you something they shouldn't know" bit. It was effective regardless.

Who are you??

"Aurrg..."

"I'm the Shepherd!" He answered as his smile stretched slowly across his face again. "Listen, I'm glad you came knocking tonight, honestly. I've been wanting to have this chat and I wasn't sure how to go about this without a direct line to you. What are you terms?"

Benicio's face stared at him blankly.

"For Craine. I assume you want this little guy back." He clarified as he aimed an incredulous finger at my tortoise face. "No one needs to get hurt."

One hostage for another sounds good on paper, but I didn't fall for his charming preacher shit as easily as the rest of the Gulch. If he was willing trade then that just meant he needed the Mayor for a reason I just couldn't put my finger on yet. I had faith in both Benicio's survival skills and my ability to inflict pain until I get what I want. Which meant he could:

Take that trade and shove it right up your ass.

"Rauuuurg!"

"I knew you would say that. Oh well! Don't say I didn't offer!" The Shepherd said with a shrug. A new idea formed in his twisted head. "I knew you would say that! I know all about you, Cyrus. But you seem to know absolutely nothing about me! I mean all this vitriol and distrust and you really don't have a clue, do you?"

I wasn't gonna answer that.

"No. You don't. Obviously! Would you like one though?"

He stared deep into my tortoise eyes, damn well knowing the answer.

"Of course you would. So let's do this. Join me for dinner tonight. Before the sun goes down, if that makes you feel safer. Give me the chance to educate you a little. See if we can't find a mutual understanding here, sort out some of the details."

What mutual understanding could we possibly have?

"Arrrg!"

"You'd be surprised! A little friendly discord never hurt anyone! You can debate your side, I'll debate mine. Let's see if we can find some common ground and a peaceful solution to all of this. Some way for you to get what you want, me to get what I want, everybody goes home happy and no one else needs to get hurt."

You turned Archer into a god damn gargoyle!

"Graaaug!"

"And I'll even call him off! He'll be sleeping off his transformation for hours still. I've already ordered the town on a full lockdown. Nobody will interfere. We need some peace talks before this gets out of hand, I realize that."

You've ordered a lockdown?

"Well I asked Archer to. But yes. How does that sound, Cyrus? You can even bring your man in the saloon if you'd like."

Shit, how does he—

"Barnaby, right? Barnaby Le Coeur? Older brother to Charlotte? Great great grandson of Montgomery Le Coeur? Bring him! You can have your guy but I'll send mine away for the night. Just the three of us. A bit of a parlay will be good for all of us! What do you say?"

My eyes shot open to the welcoming sight of the Sanctum. Barnaby knelt anxiously in front of me.

"Well?" He asked on pins and needles. "Did you learn anything?"

"No." I grimaced, dreading what came next. "But I have a date."

12

SPRUNG

The argument worked its way well into the afternoon and managed to rouse Charlotte from her bed of books. Craine on the other hand continued drooling into her cot as the three of us went round in circles.

"It's a trap!" Charlotte pleaded exasperatedly.

"Exactly why he's not going with me!" I countered as I pointed to Barnaby. "The whole damn thing is a trap! He was waiting for me!"

"You'll need me! Who else can identify what he is?" He argued.

"Well maybe if you'd clue me in on what I'm looking for, I can take them both out at once!"

"You can't strike before we know, Cyrus!" He fired back.

"And we can't risk you out in the open!" I shouted at wits end.

"We can't risk *either* of you!" Charlotte interjected.

"We've never put you on the front lines like this before!" I pleaded with Barnaby, refusing to let him endanger himself.

"Extenuating circumstances, mother fucker!" He shouted back.

"I don't know what that means!"

"Cyrus," Barnaby tried to reason, "you know you can't trust him."

"Oh, I'm well aware! That's why I'm not planning on staying long."

"You can't stay at all!" Charlotte contended. "If he gets you, this will all be over before we even have a chance to start it."

"We're not even sure what *it is*, Charlotte. And I'm pretty sure he already started it." I said from the corners of my eyes. "I have to drink from his cup, right? So I won't. It's that easy! I'll even go so far as to not drink anything he offers me! Even if its like a really cool old bourbon or something. Boom, you keep your Hunter of Evil."

"Pretty sure that's what Pappy was told." Barnaby sniped.

I had no fucking clue what that meant but my mind was made up. I was going and I was going alone.

"If he wants me, then why would he invite you? He wants both of us. And if a fight breaks out, I can't be worrying about you."

"This isn't a murder mission, boy. It's intelligence gathering. I'm going with you." Barnaby put his foot down firmly.

"No. You're not." I put my foot down even firmer.

The elder Le Coeur glared down his nose at me. That look could've gotten the devil himself to buckle. I knew what it meant. It meant the argument was officially over and I'd have to figure out a way to make this work safely. Barnaby had never had to face these things down directly. My hope was that he never would. I got my hands dirty while he did the leg work, that's how it always worked, that's how it was supposed to work!

He was determined to put himself in the line of fire and I had no idea why.

"He'll overplay his hand. They always do." I offered. "Something useful will slip out. But if you go, you need to stay back. You're not going to be out in the open."

"Cyrus—" Barnaby started.

"Field work is my game!" I cut him off. "So if we're in the field, we play by my rules. Understood?"

His death glare refused to waver or break. This date wouldn't be unchaperoned. No matter how badly I wanted the alone time.

"I need to see him." Barnaby pressed.

"See him from a distance." I pushed back as I dug my binoculars from my satchel and thrust them into his hands.

"I'll just observe. The same way you did." He said with a smirk.

And that was that. Barnaby and I left the Blood Moon as the sun started its fresh decent behind the mountains. The Gulch was, indeed, in a full on lockdown. This time of day the streets should've been quieting down. The businesses should've been closing, Gulchers should've been making their way home or to the church or the bar. Barnaby and I were the only souls making our way down the stretch of dirt to the festival grounds.

We made our way down the street at a crawl, my steady hand keeping Barnaby back behind me while the other sat on the butt of my gun. If this was going to go sideways and if Barnaby was determined to be in the middle of it, then I was going to do everything in my power to stand between him and disaster. As much as the Gulch needed someone to hunt evil, it needed someone to name it and strategize against it even more. I scanned the skies as we approached, a hand on my gun, waiting for Archer to make his winged debut. Even the clouds seemed to have run for cover though. My eyes darted, never spending too long in a single place, scanning for any hint of a threat. The Gulch was clear and empty above and below. As we neared the edge of town, the remains of Gulchy Day stood hauntingly next to the cemetery before us. A ghost of celebrations now long gone forgotten despite the fact that they happened only yesterday. I stopped and squared up with my old friend.

"Alright." I said firmly. "Last chance. City Hall's the tallest, it'll give the best vantage point."

I nodded up to the only two story building in the center block of buildings. It didn't need the extra space, it was that tall out of nothing more than a need to convey a sense of importance the local government felt they deserved. Yet the church's steeple was still taller, if only be a few feet.

"But then I won't be able to hear." Barnaby said with a coy smile. "I'll be ok."

He meant because I was there. He didn't have to say it, I could hear it in his casual yet encouraging tone. It felt a little like taking dad to the bar though. When some dude spills his beer on your shirt, you can't just go kicking his ass with your old man and his bum knee sitting right there. Besides, the way I operated, he was bound to see me do and say things he wouldn't like. I smirked at him as I turned and pressed on across the short stretch of emptiness that separated the church, cemetery and festival from the main town.

The festival ground felt even more deserted on the inside than it looked somehow. Canvas tents flapped in the light breeze. Grills had long since smoldered out, leaving their frantically abandoned meat to burn until the heat died. Tin cups and plates littered the ground, left right where they had been dropped when the Gulchers heard me kid-nerpin' the may-er. Flies swarmed everything they could get their grubby little feet-hand things on. The left over food and drink and piles of baked shit hummed with their obnoxious buzz. On the stage, at its center, sat the Shepherd at a table set for three.

"I figured this would help make you both feel a little more comfortable." He said as he stood and motioned to the banner-less back of the stage. "You can keep a better eye on the sunset. I know men like you have reason not to trust the dark."

"How romantic." I sneered as we ascended the stage steps, my hand never leaving my gun.

"I can assure you, that won't be necessary." He snickered as he glanced down at my hip.

He was putting on the mask for Barnaby's sake. The fact that I already seen past it and the fact that he knew that made it feel like an even bigger load of bullshit than it already was. The Shepherd stood and offered a hand to Barnaby as he filed in behind me.

"It's a pleasure, Mr. Le Coeur." He offered.

I swatted his hand away spitefully before Barnaby could shake it. He knew better. But better safe than possessed.

"No." I scolded the Shepherd like he was a dog that had just pissed inside.

He smiled at me, confident if not a little cocky.

"Have it your way, Cyrus." He resigned. "Please! Have a seat."

The Shepherd swung his hand wide over the table invitingly. A full on spread had been gathered on top of it. It would've been tempting if it had looked at all edible. Burnt festival meat, warm festival beer, sweets he had plucked from the dirt and plate of grapes that looked closer to raisins.

Not even sure where he got those.

"Apologies, my friends." He said with a fake embarrassment. "I'm not much of a cook so I had to work with what I had."

Barnaby and I kicked our chairs out and sat.

"But something told me there wouldn't be much dining going on here tonight anyway." He added as he sat.

"You can drop the act. He knows you're full of shit." I growled.

The Shepherd laughed deeply and relieved.

"Thank you!" He exclaimed. "I can't begin to tell you how tiring it gets being so uptight and proper all the damn time. Look, Barnaby, Cyrus, I feel like what we have here is basic disagreement of beliefs."

"You turned. The Sheriff. Into. A. *Gargoyle.*" I snarled as I leaned onto the table.

"I did! I'll admit it! Hell I'll even take full responsibility for it! But would you give me a chance to explain why?"

"Enlighten us." Barnaby said as he too leaned forward onto the table.

Player Two has entered the game.

"It's what you might refer to as a "necessary evil"." He began the verbal diarrhea he called

223

an excuse. "I want what's best for the Gulch, and while we don't see eye-to-eye on what that means or what that looks like, know that it's always their best intentions in my heart. And in the vision of the New World the Father has shown me, turning Archer into a beast like that is something we'll need to protect us from men like you." He punctuated his nonsense with a thrust of his finger in my direction.

"And we need *him* to protect us from things like *you*." Barnaby spat back in my defense.

"Do you though?" The Shepherd asked with a chuckle, hot on Barnaby's heels. "I haven't kidnapped anyone. I haven't killed anyone! Your great protector here has done both! All I did, all the Father did, was help Craine and Archer become their best selves."

"First of all," I said as I geared up, "I didn't kidnap anyone. The preferred term there is "liberated". Secondly, anyone I killed was more of a necessary evil than you could ever know! They were fucking *monsters*, creatures born of evil just like your lap dog."

"They were mine! My brothers and sisters, blood of my blood!" Shep argued passionately but pointlessly.

"You weren't even here for most of them! You're just mad I killed your two-faced janitor!"

"Kimberlin! His name was Terry Kimberlin!"

"His name was Mutant Cannibal Asshole!"

"He was the first to take the Father's covenant! He was special!"

Slip up numero uno.

"Wait, you did that to him?! I thought he cleaned something magical or evil or something!"

"No. He was the first of my flock." The Shepherd hissed with a warm rage brewing behind his eyes. "The covenant elixir was a learning process."

Barnaby studied him carefully.

"So your daddy's special gift for that freak was a second face and a hunger for man-flesh?" I scoffed at the preacher.

"I've gotten better at it." He sneered back.

"Gentlemen," Barnaby interjected, "let's rewind this back a bit. You keep mentioning "the Father"." He continued with his his glare locked on the Shepherd. "Who is that exactly? Maybe if you explain it we can try to find the common ground you want."

The Shepherd laughed a little too mischievously and sat in the moment.

"The Father will reveal himself when the time is right, Barnaby, heir of Montgomery. You just need to have a little faith."

The line sounded so incredibly fucking rehearsed. No doubt it was the one he shoved down the throats of every last person in that church. Regardless, it was maddeningly unsatisfying.

"I'll be honest," he rambled on, "I had higher hopes for this meeting. Can we start over? We all came in a little hot."

"What, did you expect us to say we were wrong and you were right?" I asked, mocking him.

"Never!" The Shepherd said through another deep laugh. "I was hoping I could get you to see reason and at the very least get Delilah back to us. But its all going off the rails a little, isn't it? Let's start over, shall we? Before it becomes a fully lost cause."

"Fuck you." I snarled.

Barnaby leaned back in his seat with his arms crossed as he continued to size up the preacher.

"Our methods differ, I'll give you that." The Shepherd continued. "But we want the same thing here."

"You want me to kick you in the nuts too? That's weird." I grumbled.

"So much hate! But you don't even know me."

"We're listening." Barnaby said casually.

"I'm a simple being! I want to save those people. I need to! Same as the both of you. I'm compelled to because I value their souls above everything else."

He leaned in.

"We don't agree on what that entails, but our goals are the same. You want to murder them in the coldest of blood and I want to lay them at the Father's feet to receive his mercy. Cyrus, I know you've seen how fucked this world is. You've been outside the Gulch, you've seen it first hand! Mankind has been dying a slow, ragged death for a long time now and that time is finally coming to an end. Only the Father can give them purpose in the New World and through his covenant, they'll receive it and more."

"Great. You're a regular Reverend Mercy Flush." I mocked, unimpressed.

Barnaby couldn't help but chuckle. The Shepherd brushed it off.

"He's seen the darkness that will drown you all. And he knows how badly you want to stop him. Yet he'd still gladly welcome you in with hungry arms."

"Weird choice of words, Reverend." Barnaby observed.

"And I know they're wasted." Shep conceded grumpily. "Frankly, I don't give a shit. My work will continue rather you see reason or not. It'd just make my life infinitely easier if you'd stop trying to kill my flock. I want Craine back."

"Not gonna happen." Barnaby asserted.

"You haven't seen how much happier and simpler life has become for them. They have one function. No more struggling for scraps. No more trying to grow crops in the cold hardpack. No more fighting for survival in the shadow of those mountains."

With that my glance flicked over to them. The sun was getting dangerously low behind them. I looked to Barnaby out of the corner of my eyes, confirming that he was noticing that as well.

"All they know is what the Father asks of them." Shep kept going. "And Craine was an important figurehead. Once she joined my cause, she gave the whole thing the legitimacy and credibility it needed to get the rest of the town onboard. Even as slowly as it's been growing, she waters that soil."

"She was possessed!" Barnaby growled through clenched jaws.

"I don't know what you think you did for her," Reverend Mercy Flush dismissed, "but I guarantee you she didn't want it."

"We know what we did for her." I defended. "We pulled a lower demon out of her and I shot it in the god damn head."

"That's so disappointing! That was no demon, that was her true self!"

"Her true self was a mass of black ink in the shape of a skeleton?" Barnaby asked, not buying what he was selling.

"It certainly looks like it! That's what the Father really offers. The chance to take your true form, become your full self. It's the only way they'll get to play a part in the New World. It's only way they'll even make it that far! That's all I've done for Archer. He just became what he was always meant to be, *the* apex predator of Gulchy's Gulch."

"Excuse me?" I asked, more than a little offended.

Barnaby's eyes were glued to the mountains. I could only hope he had observed something useful, because our time was growing short.

"I'm not stupid here. I know men like you will never stop until you've destroyed the thing you fail to understand." The Shepherd admitted.

"Men like us?" Barnaby asked with a cocked eyebrow.

"Yes. Men like you." Our enemy answered. "I've faced them before. Time and time again. Ever since I first came down out of those mountains, I knew you'd be a relentless threat and a constant pain in my ass. So sure of your convictions, so set in your ways that you refuse to yield even an inch. But guess what, boys? I don't give a shit! I really don't. Do you want your turtle-spy back or not?"

"He's a tortoise, dumbass." I corrected him.

"Your terms, name them." He said, gravely serious.

I couldn't speak for Barnaby but I knew what my terms would be at least.

"Well. You could take that creepy ass dagger of yours and stab yourself in the face. That would go a long way here."

The Shepherd looked over his shoulder to the mountains and smiled, satisfied with himself.

"Yeah," he said, "I had a feeling."

"It's time to go." I said forcefully to Barnaby as I stood, "Date's over."

"I agree." He pushed his chair back so hard it nearly flew off the edge of the stage.

"Why do you think I've been stalling and carrying on so much?!" The Shepherd cackled as he too stood and backed away from the table. "I don't care about your stupid tortoise! And if you keep trying to stop the Father, you'll only die screaming!"

The first hints of night spread across the valley in a thin veil of shadow as the sun plummeted behind the mountains.

"Right place. Wrong time." The Shepherd concluded sinisterly.

"Barnaby. Run."

As he turned to bolt for the edge of the stage, it erupted beneath us. The Gargoyle Sheriff shot straight up like a missile. We flew back down to the hard ground as an explosion of wood and old food rained down around him. He roared, wings fully spread, as he hovered over the remains of the evening. I pulled Barnaby to his feet and pushed him out in front of me.

"Go! Run!"

He sprinted away from me as I followed with my gun drawn. I fired blindly behind me as Archer and the Shepherd laughed themselves silly. Glancing over my shoulder, I watched as one shining silver bullet streaked through the air and right past the preacher's crazed face, coming close enough to pluck a few wayward hairs from the side of his head.

"Bring them to me and rally the flock." He snarled to his monster minion. "Their time is at hand."

Archer rocketed away from the stage, claws outstretched in front of him.

"Cover!" I shouted to Barnaby as he continued to pull away from me.

He dove for the first thing he came across that even remotely resembled cover, a meat cart, sliding like a baseball guy under the narrow space between its bottom and the ground. Archer flew right past me in a gust of a speed like a furry bullet train. With one hand he grabbed the cart and easily flipped it over, sending it crashing out into the flatlands.

I did my best to aim as I raced towards them, firing through Archer's wings. He groaned in mild annoyance but his attention didn't break. A clawed hand raised high over Barnaby as he stared down the winged lawman, accepting whatever came next with a hardened resolve. As I stopped next to one of the barely standing canvas tents, an empty one the Gulchers referred to as "the cooler downer", I knew what would get his attention.

"Your wife asked me to honk her boobs before I killed her!"

Archer froze. His hand slowly came down as he turned to face me with a horrible scowl on his illformed face.

There he is.

"It was her last request." I added with a shrug. "Felt wrong not to honor it."

The furry bullet train left the station and flew right for me as I ducked into the tent. He banked hard to try and cut me off but instead crashed right into the old canvas, taking the entire structure with him as he flew into it. The tent pulled away, up and over me, as Archer crashed to the ground tangled in it.

Barnaby knew the order. He was on his feet and quickly closing in on the town's center block. I took off after him, peering over my shoulders to watch the Gargoyle Sheriff wrestle with the tent. The stage was as deserted as the rest of the festival grounds, with no sign of where the Shepherd had run off to. Not that I needed it. The doors of the church clicked closed as I ran past it.

"Head for the alleys!" I yelled to Barnaby as I closed the gap between us, Archer's frustrated growls and roars rumbling not far enough away.

"Got it!" Barnaby confirmed as he made a hard turn between the buildings.

I didn't look back, but the severely pissed off howl I heard behind me let me know that Archer had won his ferocious battle with the old tent. Ducking into the same alley as Barnaby, I pressed myself flat to the wall.

"Not to question your judgement, Cy, but what's the point of this?" Barnaby asked as he panted.

"He had trouble with the alleys when he was a human. I'm betting it won't be any better now that he doesn't really fit." I replied, equally breathless.

"Smart!"

"I have my moments."

Archer slammed down on the roofs above us, a leg on either side and snarled down at us. For the moment at least, it seemed I was right. His newly enlarged frame didn't exactly lend itself to tight spaces.

"Get anything useful?" I asked Barnaby.

He nodded bleakly.

"I think so, yeah."

Archer lunged and clawed above us, his body filling most of the space between the roofs. Drool slopped down in fat globs as he snarled and growled.

"You can't hide forever, Stone!" He thundered down to us.

"Wanna bet, dickhead?!"

"When?" Barnaby asked me.

There was a precise timing I was looking for here. An exact right moment to make our break for the Blood Moon. And as Archer swiped and reached and forced himself down on us, I saw it getting closer. That is until he gave up. With a flap of his wings he launched up and away from the rooftops.

"Shit, didn't see that coming."

"Where did he go?" Barnaby's head spun as he looked around in all directions.

"He's around." I said calmly as I opened one of the trashcans congesting the alley.

Improvisation was a skill I prided myself on. Not like, "Welcome to Make 'Em Ups! I need a suggestion!". But like the ability to change a plan on the fly or just cold straight pull one out of thin air. I was doing a bit of both as I pulled a lidless tin can from the garbage and made my way to the other end of the alley.

Stopping a few feet from the opening back into the street opposite the one we entered through, I tossed the can. A tremor shook as Archer landed directly in front of me, seemingly appearing out of fucking nowhere. He slashed and snatched at the air in front of me, a few inches short from my face. His whole torso became wedged as he forced himself closer to me.

"Move!" I ordered Barnaby sharply.

He ran for the free end of the alley as I chased after him. The walls cracked and crunched as Archer fought against the narrow space. We cleared the alley and burst onto the street. Sheriff Flappymonster pulled and twisted in a furious scramble to free himself. Barnaby and I zeroed in on the doors of the Blood Moon and sped right to them as fast our legs could carry us. A heavy crunch and enraged roar in the alley told me that we'd have to move a little faster than that. I really laid down the gas, sprinting ahead of Barnaby. He did the same as we vied for the lead in a footrace with death. My hand landed on the doors first, if only by a fraction of a second. I ripped them open for him as

Archer rose over the center block. Barnaby scrambled inside and I followed, throwing the locks behind me as Archer bombed straight for us. He smashed right into the doors. Or so it would've looked. He actually made impact with an invisible force about six inches in front of them. Crackling red energy burst from them like a bolts of lightning.

Archer shot back and landed in a plume of dust like he stuck a fork in an electrical socket. I stood behind the windows giving him a heartfelt middle finger as he got up, stunned, and charged straight for me. His face slammed into the Blood Moon's defenses and another burst of energy sent him right back where he started. He growled viciously as he got up again, accepting that he wouldn't make it through. With a powerful push of his wings he shot up into the early night sky.

"Flock!" He bellowed. "Your Shepherd calls you to him!"

Archer started his path around the town, calling out to them as he circled above.

"Fulfill your oaths to the Father!"

Barnaby gave me a sympathetic smile as he opened the Sanctum door. I didn't know what it meant, but I knew I didn't like it. In all the years we had been working together, it wasn't a look he had given me or that I had ever even seen on him before. It was the look a doctor gives to a patient before telling them they're terminal.

13

THE SHEEPENING

Fifty-something men and women marched through the streets of Gulchy's Gulch as the moon started to appear behind the mountains and night made its full entrance. In neat, single file rows they made their way towards the Church of the Seventh Seal, like cholesterol pushing its way to the fatal heart attack. Archer circled high overhead, his laugh still invading the air. The most loyal out of his festival mob and of the Shepherd's entire flock were being herded into the church with Archer acting more like a border collie than a gargoyle. Even with the winged Sheriff circling above them, they kept their eyes on the prize, marching dutifully to the church and up the steps.

"Come to your Shepherd!" Archer boomed down to the Gulchers below. "Serve him now as he has served you!"

At a passing glance it would've seemed that a mass hysteria had gripped the people as they stepped in perfect unison, obeying the Gargoyle Sheriff's commands and following him into the unknown. But a closer inspection would've revealed their milky white eyes, completely devoid of color and character. The most devoted, the ones who had literally drank the spooky Kool-Aid, were being called to their Shepherd.

The sane and rational Gulchers, or at least the ones who hand't sipped from the cup of doom, did what any smart person should've done. They hid. Barricading their homes, killing their lights and shuttering their windows. More than hiding though, they were burying their heads in the sand and doing their best to convince themselves it wasn't happening at all. They weren't locking themselves in, they were locking the truth out.

All the while, the towering wooden Gulchy stood watch over the town. His clumsy, clanky body wreathed in grayish white by the newly risen moon. He stared mindlessly from one end of the Gulch to the other. Offering a useless "HAWDY, FOLKS!" to those in hiding and an uncomfortably welcoming wave to the people making their way into the church. Two old farmers with a huge gap in BMI were the first inside.

The Shepherd stood at his altar like a kid waiting for Santa Clause. Benicio sat in the corner, helplessly and desperately clawing at the thick padlock securing him to the wall as the Shepherd grinned in absolute pleasure at the sheep being herded into their pen. The flock filed through the entrance as rigid and mechanical as wind-up toy soldiers. They filled the front rows of pews slowly and systematically, shuffling their way into them and stacking up against each other shoulder to shoulder. After what felt like a minor eternity, they all sat together, perfectly timed in the hive-mind they were now victim too. In the dim light of the church, their cloudy, pupilless eyes were even more unsettling. Whatever was in the chalice when they drank from it had sealed their fate. Every moment after was just a slow march to this one.

"Fear not, my friends." The Shepherd finally said with a gentle wave to his flock. "The New World is upon on us."

The ground shook as Archer landed outside, the flap of his wings like a small hurricane. His feet thundered down into the dirt, sending a tremor rippling through the church floor. The doors burst open and the Gargoyle Sheriff made his way inside, bent low and at an angle to fit his new frame through. Once inside and upright, he towered over the heads of the seated loyalists. Under normal circumstances, that would've been a sight to see. The crowd would've screamed bloody murder and scattered and ran for their lives. But their lifeless eyes refused to move from the Shepherd as the upgraded Archer made his way to the head of the room to take his place next to his master.

"I will say", Shep continued as he came around to the front of the altar. "I had hoped for more. But you, my friends." He inspected his flock from his perch on the stage, speaking only when he was satisfied with what he saw. "You will do just fine. The great darkness I have always promised you is here! And its name is *Cyrus Stone*!"

"KILL! HIM!" The flock chanted in deafening unison. Archer roared disapprovingly at my name like it was the worst profanity he had ever fucking heard. The Shepherd raised a hand to quiet the rabble, silence falling over them as quickly as their anger had been stirred.

"Yes, my friends, yes you will. And through the Father will we reach the shores of utopia. You see, our valiant Sheriff Archer has simply evolved. Evolved into what the New World and the Father will require him to be. And before the night is through, I will ask the same of you."

"Blood! Of my blood!" The flock responded automatically and mechanically.

"There are those in the Gulch who would fear this moment. Those even among our own congregation who refused to heed their call to action. But you? You are the truly enlightened. With hearts harder and tougher than the land you live off of. You accepted the Father in a stronger, deeper bond through his covenant. I will lead you to him and there you will serve the New World as its chosen few!"

"Blood! Of my blood!"

"Archer is not the monster here." The Shepherd told the nearly zombified Gulchers. "The real monster is the one who kidnapped our Mayor!"

"STONE!"

"Who threatens to kill me and rob you of every gift and service I have to offer!"

"STONE!"

"Who sends his *spies*", he yelled, casting an accusatory finger to Benicio, "to infiltrate and disrupt our great works!"

"Auuuurgh!" Benicio shot back defiantly like the absolute cold-blooded badass he was.

"The great darkness is here and Cyrus Stone is the harbinger of it! Will you let him rob you of paradise?! The Sheriff is merely what he needs to be to help end this threat to the salvation and security of our church!"

"BLOOD! OF MY BLOOD!"

"But tonight, I offer you something more. Who among you has not sought redemption in their lifetimes? Who among you has acted purely out of self-interest, with no regard for their neighbors?"

All fifty-whatever hands shot up with Archer sheepishly following suit. The Shepherd glanced to him out of the corner of his eyes before smirking at his flock.

"I can feel how heavily that debt weighs on your hearts, but you will repay it in the hours to come. Tonight the Father offers you nothing short of what Sheriff Archer has been given. Your next evolution, your full potential in the New World, your great act of selflessness in its name. Before you kill Stone, you must first *save your neighbors* from him."

They stood with a hefty stomp that rattled that church.

"My brave followers, the Father's courageous chosen few, tonight you will march out into the Gulch and rouse your friends, your families, your neighbors! Bring them from their beds to the shelter of our church. Show them what they could be if only they had were as lionhearted as you! Then, and only then, when we know they're safe, will we deal with Stone."

The flock turned on their heels and started moving to the ends of their pews.

"Wait, no, not yet!" The Shepherd called, freezing them instantly. "There's one more matter we must attend to first. Please, sit."

The Gulchers still in range of seats, sat on them. Those who had already cleared the end of their pews sat criss-cross-apple-sauce on the floor.

The Shepherd sighed.

"Fuck's sake. Alright! My flock, do you trust me?"

"With our lives!"

"With your souls?!"

"With our souls!"

"And your faith?"

"Belongs to the Father!"

"And will you do what he asks of you? Will you do what is required of you to secure the prosperity of our New World?!"

"Yes, Shepherd!"

The Shepherd stepped back behind the altar, taking a moment to admire his mindless horde, gleaming with devious pride. He reached down below the altar with both hands and produced a heavy brass cauldron, as old and wicked as his chalice or his dagger. Straining against the weight of it, he hefted it onto the altar with a grunt. The same abysmal black brew Archer drank sloshed within.

"Then step forward. And join us in *oblivion!*"

The flock moved to the altar like a school of fish in perfect synchronization. They waited patiently, each taking turns at the cauldron as the Shepherd bled them, dunked his chalice and poured the elixir down their throats in a grotesque communion. When they were done and potion dripped down their chins, they stood quietly to the side, waiting for something they had no way of knowing would come. The Shepherd gleefully knocked the empty cauldron to the floor. He hopped up on to the altar, using it as a seat, his work with the flock now done. His legs swayed carelessly as he looked to the Gulchers with childlike excitement. Turning to Archer, he said only one thing.

"Enjoy the show."

Archer's lips curled into a wicked toothy grin, the pain of his own transformation still fresh as well as the liberating strength that followed it. The fifty-plus chosen cried out in anguish and fell to the ground. Their bodies writhed and convulsed, their new forms bubbling just beneath the skin. They clawed at their clothes like they were on fire, ripping them off until the mass of screaming followers were naked on the floor of the church, a squirming mass of tortured flesh. If only they had stopped at their clothes. The flock went to work on their skin, scratching and tearing chunks of meat from themselves as their screams drowned the church. The Shepherd watched with wide eyes full of anticipation and excitement.

In the great heap of suffering, it was hard to tell what exactly was happening and even harder to tell what it was transforming into. Heavy hooves burst out from where feet once were, faces split and peeled back as snouts erupted out of them, muscles thickened and bones changed shape. Blood sprayed the walls and pews and flooded the filthy wooden floors. Pounds of raw flesh and fat clumped like pale islands in a dark red sea. Eyeballs shot out of their sockets with sickening pops and bounced and splattered around the room like wet ping pong balls. Blood soaked hands grasped at the pews as the flock began to separate, desperately trying to pull themselves up on the muscular goat-like legs that were tearing themselves into existence beneath them. Thick fingers and heavy, barbed claws replaced their fingers as they shredded into ribbons and pushed themselves up onto their hooves.

The Shepherd looked on, puzzled. Whatever the flock was turning into wasn't the same as Archer. That much was apparent from the chaotic, almost uncoordinated bodies thumping and smashing against the ground and his pews. Their screams became shorter, choppier as the snouts protruding from their faces split their heads and gave birth to entirely new and larger ones.

A chorus of revolting splats and rips fought for dominance over their screams as a noise far deeper and more animalistic started to spew from their throats. What was left of the humanity of the Gulchers burst away from them. Bits of who they once were flew out in all directions like the explosion of some morbid firework. The Shepherd shielded himself from the blast of viscera. Archer barely even seemed to notice as it covered him.

"Auurg!" Benicio groaned in protest as pieces of person splattered his face and shell.

What stood before the Shepherd was no longer human, but still retained their humanoid figure. Taller but not as tall as Archer. Covered in a dense, strong musculature, but not as dense and strong as his. They were missing wings, but what they did have were thick coats of bloody wool from head to toe. Heads with widely set eyes and rectangular pupils. Long, almost goofy ears and even longer snouts tipped by pale pink noses and filled with short, sharp, pointed teeth. Their true selves revealed at last, the most easily swayed, the weakest minds, the Shepherd's flock of *weresheep*. All together they hoisted their heads to the ceiling and let out a guttural "BAAAAAAH!"

Their master got up from his altar and crossed to them as Archer stomped after him. They both took a second, staring at the confusing results of their blood oaths and the Shepherd's magic.

"They're...sheep?" Archer growled as he wiped chunks of the flock from his already matted hair.

"The covenant isn't an exact science." The Shepherd answered with a shrug. "You turned into what the Father needed most of you and I guess so did they. It's ok! Look at them! We can make this work."

The weresheep started to disperse, wandering around the room more like actual sheep than corrupted beasts of the sulfury void.

The Shepherd groaned. He clapped to get their attention. "Hey! Hey! All eyes on me."

The weresheep stopped and looked to him in surprised unison. A few fainted and fell over.

"Do you remember what we were just talking about? Saving your neighbors? Killing Cyrus Stone?"

The weresheep flashed their small fangs as they let out another gut-trembling "BAAAAH!"

"What are you waiting for?! Go!"

The flock turned and ran for the door, bursting out into the night.

"Stay with them." He ordered Archer. "Do _not_ let them kill anyone! We'll need every last one of them. Just let them do whatever damage they need to to draw Stone from the saloon."

"Dead or alive?" The Gargoyle snarled impatiently.

"I could sincerely give a fuck as long as he doesn't get away again." The Shepherd scoffed. "Have your fun."

Archer nodded as he turned and left his master alone in the church covered in blood and body parts. He basked in the moonlight as he stepped through the door. Outside, the scene was already chaotic. The weresheep had scattered. Smashing through the unfortunate doors, windows and walls of buildings in their way on a direct collision course with the neighborhood. The Gargoyle Sheriff took to the skies, surveying the developing mayhem from above.

"Secure the nonbelievers!" He commanded the flock from on high.

The flock stormed the houses, descending on the neighborhood like a swarm of slightly ungraceful and blood thirsty locust. The dumbest of barnyard animals corrupted by evil and malice set loose on the unsuspecting and terrified, bursting through front doors, leaping through windows and easily scaling their way up to the roofs.

"HAWDY, FOLKS!"

The screams of the families within mixed with the warped bleating of the weresheep and rang out into the night. A misshapen smile curled its way too far up Archer's face as he flew overhead, feeling some kind of vindicated. The nonbelievers, the faithless and the disloyal would have their part to play in Daddy's end times whether they liked it or not.

Weresheep chased the Gulchers from their homes, storming around inside them like a wild stampede and destroying everything they touched. Their friends, their neighbors, their own families, as unrecognizable to them as the weresheep were themselves. All the while cementing the trauma of the night with that unnaturally deep and haunting "BAAAAAH!". They forced them from their beds, they forced them from their hiding spots, they grazed on dried grass and dead weeds in their front yards, leaving huge piles of weird balled up sheep shit wherever they went.

The remaining human Gulchers ran in all directions, desperately fleeing for their lives only to be met by wool and teeth at every turn. Children, who were having the time of their lives at the festival games, wept as their parents held them close to their chests. The panic-stricken humans outnumbered their corrupted pursuers but there was no escaping a flock that was seemingly everywhere all at once, moving with no discernible purpose beyond random destruction and mindless chaos. And nowhere left to run with their neighbors crowding and tripping and falling over each other, congesting their own paths to freedom.

Gunshots broke through the pandemonium in vain as the brave few attempted to defend home and hearth. Archer kept an eye on the rampage from the cloudless sky above. He scanned every inch of the Gulch as he circled against the moon like an owl looking for a field mouse that was dressed in black leather and a cowboy hat. With no sign to be seen, he decided it was time to close ranks.

"Surround them!" He ordered the flock.

They did as they were instructed by their winged Lassie. The weresheep broke away from the yards and jumped down from roofs, they burst out of the homes, many forgetting that doors existed and choosing instead to use the walls and windows. Faster than they could realize, the situation went from desperately hopeless to completely fucked for the Gulchers as the weresheep dashed and leapt all around them, trapping them in the neighborhood on all sides and at every opening. Their bulging arms and jagged hands caught anyone foolish enough to make a break past them, tossing the people effortlessly back into the fold. The weresheep bleated and swiped and snapped as they pushed the

Gulchers towards the front row of homes in a tighter and tighter group until they stood in a huddled mass of fear in the open space between the neighborhood and the town. Their screams, cries for help and pleas to higher powers threatened to drown out the calls of the weresheep that were undoubtedly being etched into their memories forever. Archer tossed his hat into the ring, shaking the ground beneath them with a roar as he hovered above.

At his altar, the Shepherd sharpened his dagger, soaking in the sounds of utter bedlam that had drifted down to the other side of town. Benicio shook his head as best as he could, flinging a piece of leg-skin and a wayward nipple from his face. The Shepherd glared at him, smug in his victory.

"I hope you saw that." He sneered at him as he tucked the dagger into his belt.

The Shepherd found a seat, one of the few in the front rows that had made it out of the weresheeps' transformations in one piece. The nightmarish sound of unimaginable evil all around him was music to his ears as he comfortably lounged amongst the carnage of the church.

"I hope you know how fucked you are."

14

DEMONIC DEBATES

Ever since I was an adorable little orphan boy living hand-to-mouth and switchblade-to-pursestrings in the streets of Gulchy's Gulch, Sheriff Archer had a weird hard-on for me. Not, like, a *literal* hard-on. It was more of a strong, unhealthy fixation. Something about that penniless, dirty little teenager really drove him up a wall. I was the only thing in the Gulch that stood out to him. The only one not pulling their weight in his eyes. And with a shortage of any legitimate or serious crime to deal with, he followed my every move. Which, of course, made fucking with him that much easier and that much more fun. Despite the fact that the one crime he should've been investigating way back when, the one that left me orphaned in the first place, he ruled an accident after exactly fifteen minutes of "police work". More than anything, I think he resented me for making him do his god damn job during a time when the newly-appointed Sheriff Archer was more than content Barney Fife-ing it. I had been a turd in his punchbowl for twenty years. Give or take.

As an adult, our cycle didn't break but it did evolve. I would've loved to have lived behind the Blood Moon's kitchen with Barnaby and Charlotte or on my cot in the Sanctum instead of my fake haunted shack, but I was never willing to risk exposing the entire operation because ol' grumble-stache wanted to see me hang. There was the matter of me killing the shit out of his wife in constant play too. He saw the aftermath, but not the actual fight. That is how it always went after all. Regardless, the corpse I left behind definitely wasn't human and even though he thought her demonic deformities were somehow my doing, he refused to ever see reason on the matter. Like how could I have murdered her so good that she grew horns? That's just stupid. He would never stop. And clearly there was no limit to how far he would go to get his hands on me. But tonight he crossed a line and I was well within my right and responsibility to bring it all to the grisly end he so desperately wanted.

Barnaby, of course, knew this. As the first Gulcher to show me any actual, real kindness all those years ago, he understood better than anyone. He knew how deep the Sheriff's hate for me ran and he knew how much I resented the old fucker. He knew how ugly this would have to get before it could well and truly be over. Which is what promoted him to say:

"I know, Cyrus." As he put his hands on my shoulders and locked me in. "But we can't go into this half cocked. There's a stronger magic at play."

"He's a fucking gargoyle now!" I argued heatedly.

"He's a pawn. We need to take out the king." Barnaby countered.

"Or I could go kick the pawn in the dick while you figure out what exactly the king is!" Which honestly sounded like a pretty solid plan to me.

"Trust me, Cyrus. Please. Trust *us*."

The Sanctum had quickly become a mess of old books in the aftermath of Archer's flyover. Nearly every available surface, the floors, the workbench, the cots, they were all littered with cracked spines and yellow pages. Mayor Craine sat on one of the unoccupied cots, a selection of illustrated volumes laid out at her feet, full on shock (and probably an Everclear hangover) having its way with her and preventing her from picking out any of the sketches from what she saw in her dreams. Charlotte, with a book bigger than her head, bounced around the room, doing her best to pour over every page of every book all at once.

"Barnaby, are we right?" She asked nervously, only half paying attention to us.

"I think we are." He said as he left me to return to Charlotte's side.

This had been going on for nearly an hour now. Back and forth and back and forth, books and concerned looks and whispered theories that I apparently wasn't cool enough to be let in on. The Le Coeurs knew something. They knew before I made it back to town but Craine's stories from her time possessed and details from our sunset dinner date were just sending them further down the rabbit hole. The one thing they kept repeating stayed the same.

"Right about what?!" I asked, deciding it was finally time I was included.

He sighed, still not wanting to let me in on the big fucking secret before it was time.

"Kinda feel like I need to know what I could be up against here." I added because it was true.

Barnaby and Charlotte shared a look, that annoying sibling pseudo-telepathy thing at work.

"You do." Barnaby finally said after a frus-tratingly long silence. "We think the Shepherd may be involved with a puppet demon. At the very least he's working for one."

"Like Fozzie Bear?"

"That's a muppet." Charlotte said with an eye roll.

"Right. So the Shepherd's working with a muppet demon. What's that mean? How do I kill it?"

"It's a little more complicated than that." Barnaby clarified. "Puppet demons are old. Very old. One of the most ancient and dangerous orders in hell. This is exactly exactly what we were afraid was happening. If there's a puppet demon in the Gulch, we have to play this right. You can't just run up and shoot him."

"Why not? That strategy has a proven track record!"

"There's a certain magic that we need to really be careful of." He explained.

Charlotte consulted the brown leather book.

"With the blood of the devoted servant forcefully given", she read aloud, "and the souls of the unknowing dishonorably taken, the puppet demon arises to awaken his great champion, calling him to purge the Earth in his name."

"The Shepherd's New World?" I asked, piecing it all together and doing the math.

"That's what I'm sayin'!" He shouted. "And that's not even all of it!"

"What, because purging the world isn't enough?!" It really felt like that should've been enough.

"Kill their body and the soul will just regenerate it over time. We need to make sure you can kill both."

I had never seen him take a threat this seriously before. Usually he'd give me a bunch of bullets or some special weapon and send me on my way, but this time it seemed he had no clear battle plan for me.

"There's something else we need to figure out." Charlotte added.

"Oh come on!"

"How fucked is the preacher?" Barnaby continued. "The puppet demon is defined by its ability to control. Is he in its pocket or is he like Craine was?"

"We'll never get close enough to him to find out with Flappy Bird flying around there!" I snarled.

"I know!" Barnaby admitted as a new look of dire frustration fell over him. "But if we kill the wrong guy first we won't get a chance to kill the right one!"

"Well he's the one making them drink from the evil punchbowl sooo..." I reasoned.

"I'm not sold." Barnaby shook his head. "He kept talking about "the Father". Demons of this caliber don't refer to other beings with that kind of respect. Not even the few superiors they actually have. He could be taking the blood oaths in its name because he's already taken it himself. Archer's change, what happened with Craine, that all coulda been some sorta gift from the Big Boss. Decoys or backup for the real servant! We can't chance killing either one of them without calling out their big guns and sending the world straight to Hell! So before you start shootin' we need to be sure we can destroy the demon's soul too!"

"Well shit. Mayor?! What do you think?" I asked as I turned to the catatonic official. "Is he's holding the strings and working the mouth?"

While her eyes were glued to the floor, her stare was miles away. Craine was lost in the knowledge she had received and the events that were unfolding around her as it all threatened to consume her. She clutched the remains of Barnaby's bottle of Everclear like it was only her tether to reality.

"Craine?!" I said a little louder.

Nothing. I ripped a page out of one of the books I deemed unimportant based on the fact that nobody important was looking at it, balled it up, tossed it and bounced it off her forehead.

"Hey!"

She slowly looked up at me.

"That was uncalled for, Cyrus." Charlotte scolded.

"I-I need to see my family." Craine muttered under her breath.

"Well, you're gonna have to chill." I told her. "I'm not having you go get all possessed again."

"He's right." Barnaby confirmed. "The Shepherd wants you back in the game."

She went right back to staring at her spot on the floor. Super helpful.

"Not to like second guess you guys or anything but how do we know for sure it's actually a muppet demon? Could it be something that's less of a pain in the ass?"

267

Which, to me, made sense. There's a million different orders, classes and choirs of demons in Hell. Some are obviously way easier to kill than others. Maybe we'd get lucky.

"She's sitting right there and he's flying around outside. Everything he said tonight. It fucking has to be." Barnaby answered, exasperated.

"The only thing that explains it is the Covenant of the Puppet. It binds them to the demon, trading their souls for power." Charlotte added.

"The demon fucks 'em though." Barnaby went on.

"Of course it does."

"They only get whatever power that's useful to it and they usually don't get to choose how that power manifests. Craine became a totally empty vessel, kind of the sweet spot for a puppet demon. Archer became a gargoyle."

"Alright." I said not really knowing how to handle that.

"We know what we're doing, Cyrus." Barnaby reminded me.

"Alright!" I never doubted that, I was just wondering, geez.

It wasn't fun seeing Barnaby like this. He wanted to cut to the monster murder as much as I did, but beneath the determination and frustration, there was a mild degree of panic. We had been up against the wall neck deep in bullshit before, but we always found a way. The odds were almost never in our favor. There was something else though, something that Barnaby and Charlotte still weren't telling me. I bought the ticket, I would have to take the ride regardless.

"What do the books say?" I asked the two Le Coeurs.

"That we're shit out of luck." Charlotte replied, more callus than I knew she could be.

"No!" Barnaby corrected sternly before I could even think about saying something snarky. "We'll figure it out! Somewhere in one of these god damn books is a fucking solution. And we'll find it!"

Silence fell over the Sanctum, nothing but the sounds of pages turning feverishly and Craine beginning to gently weep on her cot. Barnaby had never let me down before and Charlotte would get the seal of approval from me sooner or later. Trusting them was easy. Waiting was the hard part.

I should've kept that phone. I bet it had games on it.

My trigger finger and stabbing hand itched something fierce. You couldn't just dangle that much evil in front of me and then tell me I'm not allowed to go kill it! That's just cruel. The monster hunter's equivalent of teasing the tip.

"What about the—" I began to suggest.

"There's nothing in the damn Box of Mystery!" Barnaby fired back.

"Fine!"

"You ain't ready for that shit!"

"I get it! Damn, man."

I decided to take an inventory of every weapon in the Sanctum. They had their way of helping and so did I. Somewhere amongst all those instruments of war, on those shelves of death and damnation, had to be something that could be useful.

While I knew the weapons with an otherworldly bend would probably be most helpful, the ones in Barnaby's collection of relics that were blessed or cursed or enchanted in someway or another, it wasn't up to me to sign off on them. Hell, even the ceremonial tools might've had their applications. But if the answer was buried in between them, Barnaby would've already found it. Nobody knew his collection and their uses better than he did. So I turned my attention to the guns and ammo.

UV grenade down the throat? No. Silver buckshot to the face? No. Super Soaker full of holy water? Meh. UV grenade up the ass! No.

I itemized every single piece on those shelves and ran through how exactly I would use them. But whether they were meant to kill the damned or worked just fine on normal regular-ass people, none of them exactly jumped out at me. None of them screamed "KILL THE MUPPET DEMON!" Even though, in a way, I guess they kind of all did. Like I'm sure if I used *all* of it, all the guns and all the magic shit, something was bound to work. Like betting on everything at the roulette wheel, the ball's gotta land somewhere! Which also happens to be my favorite strategy. It's won me dozens of dollars over the years, so there was always a chance it could work there too.

"Cyrus." Barnaby said. The pleading look on his face told me he was about to ask for something I wouldn't be particularly excited about. "She might know something we don't."

Nope!

"I mean probably. But I can't do it." I told him, laying down the law.

"Do you want to start killing shit or not?!" He asked.

I did. I totally did. More than anything! But it didn't change the fact that:

"I can't! Seriously. If I bug Katrina too much she calls me "needy" and stops talking to me for awhile."

"You kidding me?" Barnaby asked with a cocked eyebrow.

"Yeah..." I said with the closest thing I'm capable of feeling that even remotely resembles shame or regret. "I drunk-summoned her a few times. So I have a one summoning per week thing now."

I wasn't going to go into any further detail than that. He was going to have to take it and learn to live with it as I had. He wasn't going to though.

"I think you can risk it under the circum-stances!"

"No, really! What if she doesn't know anything? Then she'll be all annoyed and I won't be able to summon her if I *really* need her!"

My satchel bounced and shook angrily as the mirror inside protested against being bothered for a second time in so many hours.

"See?!"

Barnaby set his book down in a huff.

"We *really* need her now, Cyrus! What circumstance could seriously be more of a "*really* need her" kind of thing than this?! We can sit here reading all damn night while the puppet gets stronger and stronger or you could..."

His voice trailed off. I was listening, I swear I was! But something was drowning out literally all of my senses. A cold shiver shot up my spine like that time I accidentally sat on a popsicle. Benicio. He chose a hell of a moment to share what he saw with me. Or however our connection worked. I turned to face the wall behind me as the events played out in my head and I saw what the Shepherd wanted me to. Just beyond it, the Gargoyle Sheriff was setting up his big play and the flock was rounding up the town. It was a trap, that was pretty fucking apparent. But innocent lives were at risk. A whole lot of them. And really what *hadn't* been a trap so far? Pure blind instinct took over. My hand landed on my gun and stake. Their cool metals were singing my song and that song was called "Like It Or Not (It's Go Time)".

"Cyrus?!" Barnaby shouted, snapping me out of it.

I blew right by him on my way to the secret door.

Bag check! Gun, bullets, stake, backup stake, NO TIME!

"What are you doing?!" Barnaby called after me as I pulled the release and the wall slid apart.

I looked to him over my shoulder as I stepped through the door.

"I'm going in half cocked."

15

TIME TO PLAY THE MUSIC

The streets of the Gulch were even more eerie than usual. The slow decay of the town was moving just a little faster. At first glance, in one direction, they were as empty and calm as they always were that late at night. But the sounds of hysterical, terrified weeping and ravenous, impatient weresheep drifted ominously throughout them. It wasn't hard to track their source. At the other end of town, right in front of the neighborhood, were fifty-something weresheep holding the rest of the town hostage with a huge fucking gargoyle standing at the head of them.

My pulse quickened as I took a step away from the safety and protection of the Blood Moon and into the street. Archer's eyes glowed in the moonlight as he followed my every move. I squared myself up with him in the middle of the street as I slowly made my way down. My view of him was much clearer and easier now that I wasn't running for my life. The cowering, quivering Gulchers were dwarfed by the Gargoyle Sheriff. Even the weresheep, as bulky and sizable as they were, didn't come close to his intimidating stature.

Shit shit shit shit shit.

Archer's claws clenched and his wings spread wide. A display of dominance, an intimidation tactic if I've ever seen one. I threw my jacket back, flashing my gun and stake as my hands landed on them. The weresheep bleated furiously, barely able to contain their bloodthirsty excitement as they caught sight of their dreaded foe. Their staggered cries got louder and louder with every step I took. Archer growled deeply at them, a command to stay steady. The look on the Gulchers' faces was a win in and of itself. I was the only one who could save them now and they were learning that lesson the hard way.

As I pressed on I scoured through every detail of every fight I've ever been in and every monster I've ever killed. Somewhere within them was the tactic I needed to see this through. From the fiery, piercing glare Archer was giving me, I could tell he wasn't thinking of plans or strategies. His mind was focused on one thing and one thing alone, the details of my disemboweling. His darkest fantasies made possible before him. But I wasn't nine feet tall and super jacked with a massive wingspan. I mean, I was buff! Don't get me wrong. Just not like him. There was an obvious disadvantage. Regardless, I needed a plan. I knew the town like the back of my hand. Where to hide, where to run, where to take cover and, of course, his issues with alleys. That was something. But it wouldn't do much good against something that could just hover over me. And then there was the flock to worry about.

Eh, fingers crossed.

A little bit of the cop Archer once was came through as the gap between us shrank to just a few dozen yards.

"That's far enough, Stone." He said with a clawed hand out.

I stopped. And then took one more step. Because fuck him.

"It's over." He snarled as he flashed his long fangs. "Surrender. No one needs to get hurt here...'cept you."

Something about the big toothy grin he developed as he said that really pushed my buttons. Our cycle evolved yet again. I thumbed back the hammer on my gun as my eyes narrowed. My pulse raced even faster.

"Your time has come. The people have spoken!" He called as he lifted his arms to the flock behind him.

"What people?" I asked. There were no people.

"Us! The Shepherd's flock! The Father's chosen!"

"Those people?!"

The weresheep snarled and bleated like there was even a remote possibility they understood I was insulting them.

"Yes!" The Gargoyle Sheriff shot back offended. "We are what the Father and the New World demand of us!"

"Those are not people." I said, simply pointing out a fact.

Archer seethed as he clenched his claws together even tighter.

"You're a plague on this town, Stone. A menace!" He snapped at me. "Come to the Shepherd and receive the Father's judgement."

"Hard pass." There was no fucking way.

"The flock won't be denied!" He yelled before letting out a hollow roar that rattled windows and threatened to burst every eardrum present. The weresheep joined in, throwing their heads up to the moon with a bellowing "BAAAAAAH!"

"Well. You know what they say." I said as I squeezed the grip of my gun a little tighter. "Mary had a little lamb."

The weresheep worked themselves into a frenzy. Mouthes foaming, teeth gnashing, their eyes began to glow a deep shade of yellow.

Draw them off, away from the people.

The silver of my stake was slick in my hand as my palms began to sweat.

"Whose fleece *ran red with blood!*"

Archer roared a command to the flock and the weresheep charged. Some on all fours, some like the men and women they used to be. Archer shot straight up into the air and out of sight. In a flash, my gun was out of its holster and six silver bullets were sailing through the air. Six bullets, six direct hits on the nearest weresheep. As the silver ripped into them, they did something I would've never expected. They exploded. Like they full on burst like they were giant water balloons filled with blood and covered in wool. The force and violent spray stunned the weresheep nearest to them. Silver, man. It can have a powerful effect on lower beings of evil.

That's something!

I hightailed it away from the flock, running as fast as I could, their hooves pounding after me. I knew exactly where to go. They needed to be funneled and I needed cover. The alley behind the doctor's office could do just that. The building was compromised, but it could serve as my escape route if I needed it to. There was enough room to put some space between me and them, while keeping them coming in tight, close groups directly in front of me.

Archer circled high above, like a vulture, waiting for the right moment to tag in and pick at my carcass. Throwing a look over my shoulder, through the flock, I could just make out the Gulchers running for their lives in all directions. Back into their homes, out towards the flatlands and the mountains, anywhere they thought would be safer than where they were. There was a small comfort in that. No matter what happened, at least they had gotten away.

Good enough.

I dumped the empty shells from my gun and quickly jammed fresh ones in their places as I neared the doctor's alley and the dead exit. A small amount of pride and dread welled up within me as I realized that I was about to redefine that nickname one way or the other. A couple quick rounds shot behind my back as I made the hard turn into the alley. The repulsively wet splat of exploding weresheep and the angry bleating of the ones that had been thrown off by it told me that I didn't need to confirm the kills.

I had seconds to find my place to stage this slaughter. As close to the dead exit as possible seemed like the safest bet. The back door was wide open. The festival mob had managed to actually do something helpful. I made my stand in front of it as the flock flooded the alley with the force and speed of rolling magma, tightly pressed against each other and struggling for the space to move in a clumsy mass of wool and teeth. Their claws swiped, jaws snapped and hooves stamped as they nearly fell over each other. There was no need to be careful with my aim.

BOOM! BOOM! BOOM! BOOM!

I emptied what was left in my gun and bits of weresheep rained down all over the walls. The flock stumbled and staggered from the blasts. With a flick of my wrist, the cylinder opened and dumped its shells. I dug in my satchel for the next batch, expertly dropping them in and flicking the cylinder closed again. Six more shots, six more gory explosions. The alley was painted red and the dirt beneath them was turning into a thick, black mud. Patches of wool and bits of weresheep provided a much needed pop of color.

As I dumped the shells again, the weresheep managed to regroup a little faster. Even as their hooves slid in the mud, they pushed on. Inching closer to me than before by the time I reloaded and killed the next six my gun could find. They were pressing too steadily for that plan to work long-term, using the force of their numbers to roll them onward through the empty space their burst friends left. But I wouldn't pull the ripcord and retreat just yet. I needed to thin the flock a little more before I could do that.

I fired off the shots as quickly as my finger could squeeze the trigger. Blood sprayed my face as the distance between me and the weresheep closed even more. Do you know what weresheep blood tastes like? It's like a nickel covered in garlic salt. Do not recommend. I barely even had time to react and my time to reload was even shorter. So out came my stake.

The stake sliced a platinum streak through the air, stabbing and hacking into the weresheep with a savage accuracy as they slowly enveloped me. Like an extension of my own arm, it moved with ease, plunging into the skulls and chests and guts of the weresheep. They exploded practically on impact, the only thing keeping the inevitable dog pile at bay as they crowded the dead exit. Their strength became apparent as I absorbed the impact of the bursts, like being hit by a guy on a Vespa going kinda slow, as I cleared the space I needed.

Covered head to toe in weresheep blood, my boots slipping through the puddles of bloody mud beneath me, I fell back into the office. With a couple of well placed stab-and-pops, I slammed the door closed, throwing the deadbolt as I leaned all of my weight against it. The walls rocked and the office swayed as the full force of the weresheep slammed against the door, nearly knocking me over. I doubled my efforts and pushed against the door as I quickly dumped the spent rounds from my gun and reloaded, a task made a little more complicated by the blood making my hands slick and clumsy.

The cylinder snapped back into place and I cocked the gun, backing away from the door as quickly as I could. Blood dripped off of me and pooled on the floor like I had just stepped out of a jacuzzi full of it. It stung at my eyes and filled my nostrils but I refused to look away from the door or lower my gun as the weresheep slammed into it again and again. The door began to crack and splinter with each hit. I kept my stake at the ready as wooden shrapnel flew at me.

Come on, you bastards.

The door disintegrated as it burst in and the flock smashed through. The first few fell in a heap on the floor, narrowly avoiding the rounds I sent their way, the weresheep behind them exploded. The beasts on the floor didn't fare much better. Their counterparts trampled them into nothing as they surged through the door. Their numbers were thinning, but not by enough. Not by a long shot.

I backed up past the patient rooms and supply closets into the office as I reloaded, grabbing a cabinet of medical bullshit and pulling it down into the weresheep's path as I did. They stepped right over it.

God damn it!

The gunshots were deafening in the closed space of the office as six more bullets produced six more splatters of blood on the walls. My own blood ran cold as I heard that wretched bleating come in from behind me. I didn't dare take my eyes off of the monsters in front of me, but it was then that I kinda regretted shooting out the office's front window. I gave it the quickest look I could and sure enough, the flock had broken off into two groups. Half of them had come around the building, making their way through the shattered window.

They crawled and jumped clumsily over the broken glass and through the window frame, attacking from two fronts. I reloaded as fast as I could and brought my weapons back up to murder position. One hand stabbed wildly while the other carefully picked shots based on the nearest threat as I ducked and weaved away from claws and jaws. Weresheep blew up to my left and right, threatening to knock me off balance, the force hitting harder on two sides as the flock surrounded me. Like being hit by a guy on a Vespa going kinda fast. The flock wasn't immune either, stumbling and falling where there was room. My ears rang as what I'm sure what was a concussion set in. The taste of blood in my mouth was definitely mine now, usually a sign that something internally was bleeding when it wasn't supposed to be. I weaved and ducked swiftly through swiping claws and snapping jaws, taking up the available space as it emptied. Yet with every burst of blood I somehow ended up with a fresh bite or cut on my arms and back as I fought my way out of the flock.

Through the heavy fog of vicious, uncoordinated wool and spraying blood I saw something I thought would be pretty handy in the corner of the room. Over by the cabinet of medical shit I had knocked over was a rack of three dull gray oxygen tanks no bigger than my arm.

"Smile, you sons of bitches!"

BOOOOOM!

One shot and the entire block shuddered as the tanks exploded. I flew straight the door, taking it clean off its hinges and sliding on it flat on my back to the middle of the street. Now one hundred percent sure I had a concussion and internal bleeding. The smell of burning wool immediately filled the air. Which was honestly miles better than the smell of their blood. I craned my head up and watched as flames engulfed the office, igniting whatever other flammable gasses and solutions Doc Torrance had stored. I knew it wouldn't kill them all but hoped it'd at least reduce their threat level maybe buy me some time. No matter how little it was. I didn't get the chance to enjoy the sight of an office full of burning weresheep for very long before the ones lucky enough to have not been inside turned to me.

I got to my feet and bolted down the street as quickly as I could. By my best estimate, there were maybe twenty remaining weresheep in hot pursuit, counting the ones that looked like overdone marshmallows still near the edge of the medical inferno. A significant dent in their numbers, all things considered, a little more manageable. But still not enough for me to unpucker my butthole quite yet. I flicked open my gun and dumped the empty shells into the dirt. As I reached into my satchel for the reload, a pair of talons that could've only belonged to a big flying dickhead latched down onto my shoulders.

Archer lifted me into the air and over the rooftops as he took off towards the church. The weresheep followed from the ground. Smoke rose from the doctor's office.

Damn it, I'm gonna have to pay for that.

I swung my stake up and buried it deep in Archer's massive leg. He groaned in pain, but his grip didn't loosen. Not even a little bit. His talons pressed deeper into my flesh, threatening to pierce me clean through with a pressure that sent waves of pain across my chest as the bones cracked. I pressed the stake in as deep as I could and for good measure gave it a hard jerk and twist. Archer's pain continued to barely register. If I couldn't hurt him, I could at least annoy the shit out of him. I ripped the stake out and stabbed as fast and hard as I could all over the side of his leg, punching holes up and down it. It wasn't long before the onslaught of wild, aimless stabbing got to him. Archer roared, in what I'm sure was more irritation that actual pain, and tossed me. Head over ass I tumbled through the air.

Wheeee!

The fun was momentary and way too abruptly brought to an end as I smashed through the wooden roof of the building he flung me towards. I fell through something equally hard before hitting the floor with a mighty crunch. Dust and debris fell around me. The white hot telltale pain of broken ribs flooded my torso.

"Dick move, Sheriff." I groaned as I ignored it and pushed myself upright.

The moon shined in like a spotlight through the hole I made in the roof, just enough to brighten the otherwise dark and empty space. A quick scan revealed that he had thrown me through the roof of City Hall. I had fallen directly into the unnecessarily spacious entryway, right through the receptionist's desk. A staircase ran up the wall across from me to a small landing and a narrow walkway that stretched all the way across the building, allowing access to a small collection of offices against its backside. Where the handful of Gulch officials conducted whatever half-assed business they had to conduct. A framed portrait of Craine hung in the center of them.

"I partially blame you for this." I snarled at it as I nursed my rib.

I dug my weapons from the rubble and ran for the door. The remaining weresheep swarmed the front of the building and stopped me dead half way to it, crowding into the two large windows to get a look inside. The extra crispy weresheep with zero wool and severe burns cracking and blistering their skin were even more savagely crazed than their unscathed friends. But they did not strike. Instead, they stayed put. Content to just watch through their frenzy. Archer dropped down like a furry meteorite through the involuntary skylight behind me, his wings folding back behind him as he landed in a flurry of dust.

"Nowhere left to run, you monster." He growled at me behind me.

"You talking to me or them?" I asked seriously with a nod to the windows as I turned to face him.

"You tighten your noose with every one of my brothers and sisters that you destroy!"

This felt like a good time to reload.

"To be fair, you're the one that led them..." I said as I jammed new rounds into my gun.

"Don't say it!"

"Like lambs."

I snapped the gun shut and jerked back the hammer.

"Fuck you!"

"To the slaughter!"

I couldn't resist. The weresheep lost what little patience they had left, throwing themselves into City Hall's face. Archer lunged, launching himself across the room and touching back down in front of me faster than I could react. His claws tore through the air and across my chest, ripping into me like meathooks and opening deep canyons of blood and muscle. Blinding agony overtook my senses. Channeling it, I thrust my stake into his ribs. Bone scraped harshly against its tip. The Gargoyle Sheriff roared in actual pain, rattling my skull and shaking my teeth.

Someone's ticklish there.

With a heavy flap of his wings he hurtled me across the pointlessly spacious building. I'm not sure if it was my skull or the front door but something definitely cracked as I hit. My vision swam and danced. Two or three Archers were calmly making their way towards me. I picked the one in the middle, raised my gun and let the silver fly. Archer's stride broke as he groaned and the bullets landed in a nice, neat, smiley face grouping on his chest. He looked down at the incredibly pleasant arrangement of entry wounds on his chest with a growl.

I snickered as I climbed to my feet, determined to mine as much joy out of this experience as possible. The windows and door burst in behind me. Weresheep spilled over, voraciously forcing their way into City Hall, clawing and crowding and stepping over each other. Empty shells chimed at my feet as I ran for the stairs and the Gargoyle Sheriff retreated, enraged by the happy little holes in his chest and the silver burning within them. The remaining weresheep gathered around him, showing whatever adorable level of concern beasts like them could muster for a beast like him. They crowded around his bleeding chest with a confused curiosity, poking and prodding it to test just how damaged he really was.

"Go!" He barked impatiently. "Don't let him get away!"

The weresheep came in from every angle, running up the stairs and climbing over the creaking wooden rail as I backed my way up to the offices. The smell of burnt wool and blood filled my nose. Their numbers continued to shrink with every pull of the trigger and every step I climbed, forcing the shots that followed to be more precise and thought out. There weren't enough left for me to just fire wildly anymore, as fun as that was. With every splatter of blood on the walls the flock got less and less dense, the survivors gained space to really stretch their unwieldy legs. They came in faster and more aggressively as I dumped my shells and reloaded. An expertly placed crane kick to the face sent the one closet to me tumbling back down the stairs, taking a few of its friends down with it.

I dug in my satchel for the next salvo and my heart dropped down to my ass.

"Oh fuck."

Out of ammo. The last handful of weresheep slowed, too many than I was comfortable counting, savoring the moment before they struck. My fingers danced over my backup stake and I quickly drew it as I holstered my gun. Dual silver spikes and my sheer fucking determination were all I had to see the job through. Also my skill, my strength and my unwillingness to die. But who's counting?

The weresheep sprung forward with an even greater resolve. I blocked an incoming claw with the tip of Stake A while stabbing another in the gut with Stake B. Through the bursts of blood I wrapped my arm around another's throat, using it as a wooly shield while I shanked the shit out of the few behind him. It clawed through my jacket and into my arm as it fought for freedom. I jammed my stake straight up through its jaw, fully anticipating the impact of their bursts now and steeling myself against it. Blood doused the portrait of Craine as I retreated. Out of the back, near the stairs, one of them remembered how well they could jump. It came down hard on my back as I ran, slamming my face down to the walkway. Stake B rolled across the wood as it slid from my hand and Stake A went over the edge, back down the ground floor below. The others surged around us, I was barely able to roll over onto my back before the jumpy douchebag pinned me down with a heavy hoof crushing my chest. I twisted and pulled and fought against them as they dug their claws into my legs. The sharp, searing pain was hard to work with as I threw all of my strength into trying to retrieve Stake A, just beyond my grasp. Archer drifted up, blood matting down the already gross fur on his chest.

"The Shepherd didn't say if he wanted him dead or alive!" He called to his minions. His vile mouth twisted into a devious little smirk that I really didn't care for. "Or how many pieces he should be in."

Shit shit shit shit SHIT!

The weresheep pulled my legs akimbo first as I kicked against them. Next came my arm as it pulled against its socket and they bleated furiously. My other arm ran across the wood frantically. And right as they grabbed it to pull it away or out or off or whatever their plan was, I felt salvation in the form of cool, slippery silver.

The stake came up with lightning speed, diving through the leg of one of the weresheep holding me down. The burst wasn't enough to stun anymore, these sole survivors had endured it enough to be nearly acclimated, but it was enough to work with. The briefest flash of a distraction. I tore free of their grip and pushed myself up, running to the nearest office door and throwing myself through it.

The door flew back into the wall as I burst in. A quick inspection told me that that office was, in fact, Craine's. The nicest desk, the plushest chair, a large window behind them looking out onto the roof of a structure I knew all too well, the Sheriff's office, its rear neighbor. And a metal plaque on the desk that read "Mayor Craine", that was a pretty big giveaway.

I turned in the doorway, as hooves rumbled hurriedly behind me. Holding the stake out in front of me, its tip pointing out of the office, I waited. I gripped the wet silver with both hands, adjusting for impact pressure and the slickness of the blood covering it. The weresheep rounded the door and the stupid, unobservant asshole in front ran straight into my stake. It disappeared from sight as it slid deep into the weresheep's chest, all the way down until my fingers touched wool. The weresheep burst, throwing blood in all directions around Craine's office.

The last three standing made their way in cautiously but menacingly through the cloud of gore as it fell. Separating, two flanked me while one stood guard near the door. They snarled and snapped at me as I backed away closer to the desk to open up the battle-field, but they didn't advance. Archer drifted up and over the railing, the wood of the walkway cracking beneath his feet as he landed. He bent and angled himself through the door, his head scraping the roof as he stood upright inside the office.

"End of the line, Stone." He said smugly, the old Sheriff I remember poking through his new monstrous face. "You're cornered."

He might've been right. But that didn't mean I was out of options. Not yet. I did a quick inventory of the room.

The desk lamp? Hit him in the head with it and run like Hell. No. The chair? Hit him in the head with it and run like Hell. Damn it, no.

The waning moonlight drifted in through the window behind me, my faint shadow reaching out and touching Archer's hideous feet.

Yahtzee!

I grabbed the weresheep nearest to me by the arms, spinning it around and hurling it at Archer. As the two beasts collided, I struck. Driving my stake into the weresheep's belly, it exploded in Archer's face as I made a break for it. Blood erupted up at him and into his eyes. It was temporary, super temporary, but it worked all the same.

Sliding over the desk and kicking the chair aside, I hurled myself through the window. You know in the movies when the hero lands totally unscathed after jumping through glass? Yeah, that would've been cool. I hit the roof of the neighboring building in a heap, my head and shoulders neatly carved by the razor-sharp shards I had just dove through, fresh streams of blood running down all over me.

"Ow." I groaned as I laid there a second, staring up into the night sky and bleeding into the roof of Archer's office, hoping it was seeping through and pooling on his desk.

I'd get no time for rest though. The last two weresheep were in the window, sizing up the jump. With whatever strength I had left, I clambered myself up and limped across the roofs. Two loud crashes came from behind me as the weresheep jumped from the window, came down hard and smashed clean through the Sheriff's roof. My face stung and burned, but the smile I had felt good regardless.

The weresheep shot up and out of the Sheriff's office and landed on the rood. They didn't need to do much more than casually walk after me as I limped away. I needed a new plan. I couldn't hobble over the Gulch forever. I'd run out of roofs sooner or later. I could stand and fight. But blood loss and trauma wouldn't make that very viable for long. Fifty were too slow and clumsy, but two was a problem. The cracking and groaning of the old-ass wood under their hooves was getting closer with every step I took. My body ached all over like I had been put through a meat grinder. The breath in my lungs scorched like I just took a big fat hit of some douchebag's vape pen. And no matter how hard I pushed myself, the hooves just kept getting closer.

"Alright, fuck it." I said as I stopped.

They did the same as I turned to face them, standing a few feet apart, waiting anxiously and excitedly for me to make my next move.

"This is gonna suck." I grimaced. "Could you two just like...move...a little closer together?"

The weresheep looked to each other, lost. I motioned with my hands exactly what I needed from them. Just a couple feet towards each other.

"Tighten up a little, boys, c'mon."

They humored me, moving together until their shoulders were touching.

"Cool. There we go. Thanks."

I flashed back to the warehouse in Louisiana as I threw my stake. The silver danced through the air end over end. It made its way over to the weresheep, impaling itself into the eye socket of the one on the left. My legs gave me what little juice they had left as I ran forward. The weresheep ruptured in a glorious blast of blood. The stake flew back at me like a small silver rocket. I grabbed it out of the air and jumped, closing the gap between me and the last one standing. My hand and the stake came down on top of its head, plunging into its brain. The final weresheep splattered out into the night, leaving me alone on the quiet rooftop. I took a breath and soaked up the stillness that had suddenly fallen over the Gulch. The Shepherd's flock was well and truly vanquished, leaving me alone on the roof.

"Did anybody else see that?! That was cool as fuck!"

"I saw." Archer's voice rumbled in the distance.

The wall of the Mayor's office shattered as the Gargoyle Sheriff flew through it, wings fully spread and arms out ahead of him.

"God damn it!"

His claws wrapped around my throat as he drove me into the wood of the roofs. My stake was ripped from my hand as he pushed, scraping me along the rooftops at top speed.

The wood splintered against my head as Archer used my body to carve a path down to the end of the block. I have no fucking idea what even happened to my hat. It's lost in there somewhere and honestly the fact that it stayed on that long was some kind of minor miracle.

Darkness consumed my vision as I looked up at the Sheriff, a look of demented glee on his face as we neared the end of the roofs. As I reached my breaking point, when the world teetered on the edge of oblivion around me and I thought my head would cave in completely, it stopped. The sharp, barbs of the roof weren't below me anymore. Nothing was. Nothing at all. Archer held me high over the end of the block for the briefest of seconds before tossing me like a rag doll out into the flatlands.

I rolled as I hit the dirt, leaving a trail behind me as I bled from just about everywhere. I wasn't even sure how much of that blood was mine and how much came from the weresheep but as I laid there completely soaked through from head to toe, I was pretty sure that ratio had shifted in my favor.

Getting up was a Herculean task. Beyond the fact that it felt like nearly everything was broken or fractured and I was bleeding from just about everywhere, I just plain ol' didn't want to. But I had to. I couldn't die there. Not at the hands of Sheriff Archer of all people. If you could even still call him that.

My legs quivered weakly beneath me as I stood. The ground trembled as Archer landed in front of me, jolting me back down to my knees.

"I'm gonna enjoy what comes next. I hope you know that." He snarled at me.

"And...what's that?" I asked as I finally managed to will myself up.

"Pulling you apart, limb by limb, and delivering you to the Shepherd as a stump!"

"Right. Right. That."

"No guns. No stakes. Nothing to save you now."

"Hang on, I'm sure I've got something in here." I told him as I reached into my satchel.

"I don't think so!" He roared as my hand swam through all the tools that would've probably been pretty useless in that situation.

Wow, I really did run into this half cocked.

Archer lifted off and rocketed towards me. *Nope!*

I pulled a vial of holy water from my satchel as he bore down on me like a freight train and chucked it at his head. The glass shattered right between his eyes. His sizzling forehead left thin trails of smoke in the air behind him. I ducked as he sailed over me in a gust of foul smelling wind. My hand dove back into the satchel as he crashed to the ground like a downed jet. In the bottom of the bag, my hand found something smooth, metallic and very old. It was risky, but it would have to do. The distance between us wasn't exactly vast, a few dozen feet at most, but I would have to make it work. I limped away as fast as I could. My gargoyle nemesis growled low and deep as he stood. He frantically rubbed the burning holy water from his now bald and bleeding face before he launched his next attack. He shot through the air after me as I pulled Katrina's hand mirror from my satchel.

"Get back here, you little shit!" He shouted as he closed in.

"No, wait! Give me a second!" I yelled back as I stared into the mirror.

He pulled up right before the second of impact. The force of his tail wind nearly blew me over.

"What do you really think you're gonna do here, Stone?! How far do you think you're gonna get?!" He asked through a laugh.

I changed directions and started hobbling off the way I came.

"Leave me alone, asshole!" I yelled at him kinda wishing he just would.

"Face your fate like a man!"

"Hold on! Be right with you!"

It wasn't clear how long my body would allow it, but I was determined to limp as far as I could for as long as I could as I stared at my battered reflection in the hand mirror.

"What, do you want one last look at yourself before you die?!" Archer taunted as he darted around in front of me again.

I couldn't help it. I had to savor my one last chance to piss him off. So as I changed directions again and slowly staggered across the desert, I sang him a little song I like to call:

"You're never gonna caaaatch meeeee!"

He swooped down in front of me, dirt and dust billowing out from underneath him like a small sandstorm as he landed. I turned around and pressed forward.

"Do you have to be such a tool?!"

No. No I did not. But it was fun. And it was buying me precious, valuable seconds apparently.

"I want you to do one thing for me before I eat your goddamn head." He growled.

"And what's that?" I asked as my reflection began to ripple.

"Say her name." Archer said through a scowl.

"Who's name?"

"My wife!" He shouted like a thunder clap. "Eleanor Dingle Archer!"

"Wait, her middle name was Dingle?" I chuckled.

Finally, Katrina appeared.

"I swear to God if you're—" She cut herself short upon seeing my bloody and broken form. "Cyrus!" She exclaimed with genuine horror.

Which I couldn't really blame her for, I looked like total shit. Felt like it too! Archer launched towards me at full speed, claws in front of him and wings spread wide.

"Gargoyle!" I screamed as I turned the mirror to the Sheriff.

A piercing white light, like the sun itself contained in the mirror, shot out. Archer was hit dead on like a monster in the headlights, freezing in place instantly. He hovered for a moment, blinded and stunned by the light. His feet became too heavy to handle and they thudded into the dirt as he shielded his eyes from it. Like dried concrete rising up from his talons, he was slowly covered in thick stone. It hardened all the way up his body as he watched in terror. He clawed at it desperately as it froze his body wherever it touched. Solidifying his legs first then crawling up his chest, across his wings, up his neck and finally his arms. The last I saw of Sheriff Archer were those two cueballs he called eyes, a look of immediate realization and the bitter taste of defeat caked on his face as the stone enveloped his head was encased in rock and he became nothing more than a nine foot tall statue.

The light disappeared as quickly as it had appeared. I turned the mirror to face Katrina.

"You see! I do try to save it for the important shit." I said with a coy and tired smile.

"Sunlight, Cyrus Stone. Gargoyles can't do sunlight, you should've waited until morning." She scolded.

"Thanks, Kat."

"Don't call me that." She said as her image faded away, leaving nothing but my own busted-ass face for me to look at.

I dropped the mirror back into my satchel. My body was running on absolute fumes and I knew I had a long walk back to the Blood Moon. What felt like a billion miles in my current condition, every muscle screaming in angry protest, blood pouring out of me with every slow beat of my heart. But I also had something I needed my strength for just a little bit more. As I started my walk towards town and passed the frozen former Sheriff, I gave him a good hard push. His monolithic body tumbled over, hammering into the earth beneath him. His arm, a wing and the top corner of his burnt head broke away and crumbled into bits in a plume of fresh dust.

Just for good measure.

16

ANCIENT HISTORY

Barnaby stared at the secret Sanctum door. By all accounts, he had been doing so since I left to go get my ass kicked. He knew better than to chase after me once my mind was made up and I was rushing headlong into violence, but it didn't curb his concern. The elder Le Coeur paced the Sanctum, the toll on his knee becoming greater with every step as pain came dangerously close to consuming the stress. Yet he refused to stop or take his eyes off of the door, hoping it'd slide open at any moment and I'd recount him with the tale of Cyrus Stone versus the Weresheep. But right now he couldn't hear a damn thing. No gunshots, no weresheep, no Cyrus Stone.

There was a point that hadn't been crossed quite yet but was quickly approaching. It was what Barnaby dreaded most about nights like that. When it had been too quiet for too long and I had yet to come swaggering through the door triumphantly, a rescue expedition would need to be launched. Only he knew the right timing of it. Too soon and they could be walking into whatever left over mess there was in the streets. Too soon and they could risk exposing the Blood Moon Saloon. Too late and I'd be a pile of bloody uselessness in the streets. Too late and the rescue would become a recovery.

It had been awhile since such a thing was necessary but the memory was still fresh in Barnaby's mind. The night I rode out into battle against a skinwalker that had come down out of the mountains to stalk the neighborhood. He found me two days later pinned under a dead tree, wounded, unconscious and fairly dehydrated, next to the corpse of a creature with the body of a cougar and the head of a man. He carried me back to the Sanctum and nursed me back to health himself. But this was not that. And he wasn't so sure the outcome would be the same.

Charlotte fidgeted nervously at the desk, the thick brown leather tome sprawled open in front of her. Her concern sent her further down the research rabbit hole, absorbing every bit of knowledge she could find regarding the muppet demon. When faced with the prospect of proceeding without Good Ol' Cyrus Stone, she was taking it upon herself to find a solution to the problem that had presented itself. It was a compulsion, really. Despite everything she had been through today, everything she had dealt with, she was still new to the job. And the only move she had was to study the employee handbooks.

In the corner of the Sanctum, still glued to a cot, Mayor Craine rocked back and forth. Sometime between my departure and the chilling stillness that embraced the town, she began showing signs of actual life again. Brought on by the nervous, anxious energy radiating off of the Le Coeurs, the reality of her situation was manifesting itself in the form of panicked whimpering and rocking. But honestly who could blame her? Her introduction to the world as it really was had been rude at best, as it so often was for the exorcised. In fact, it was Craine who broke the silence first.

"M-Mister Le Coeur?" She asked sheepishly as her eyes darted around the walls of the Sanctum.

Barnaby paid her zero attention. He had more pressing matters on his mind. Like the wellbeing of his best buddy.

"Mister Le Coeur?" She asked again as she started to unravel further.

"You can't leave yet. I'm sorry." Barnaby snapped back impatiently without breaking his pace or his glare to the door.

"I...I need to know..."

"You and me both."

"How...how long?"

"Any minute now." He said definitively, trying to will it to be so. But that's not what Craine was worried about.

"No..." Her voice trembled. "How long has all...*this*...been here?"

"It's not really the best time for a fucking history lesson." He barked at her with all the venom he had, his striding unchanging and his gaze unmoving.

It was a question that would have to be answered eventually. For someone that was supposed to know the town backwards and forwards, discovering a secret monster hunting lair in the back of one the oldest standing structures could be a bit of a mindfuck. And with everything else she had learned in the last day or so, focusing on the tangible must've had its allure. Charlotte took the lead.

"Generations, Mayor." She said sympathetically as she looked up from her book.

That was the last answer Craine wanted. Hearing that the Sanctum was new would've been bad enough. At least then she would've just been a negligent elected official, not exactly blazing a new trail in that arena. But hearing that the Sanctum had resided in the same place she grew up, while she was growing up, the same place her parents grew up for that matter, was not an easy truth to settle.

315

Home became a stranger, a place she never really knew at all.

"What?!" She cried hysterically, the little bit of color that had returned to her cheeks vanishing in an instant. "No! That can't...that can't be! It can't! It's not!"

Barnaby sighed, not wanting to get dragged into it, his mind still out and wandering the streets.

"It's grown over the years!" Charlotte said in a too-little-too-late attempt to comfort the Mayor as her chest began to heave and tears started to flow again. "Trust me, it's evolved! It didn't really even look like this when I was a kid!"

"I don't understand! How?! *How?!*" Craine managed through a volley of heavy sobs.

"We're not the first people to fight the puppet demon." Barnaby said authoritatively as his knee finally won. He planted his feet directly in front of the secret door and continued his staring contest with it, keeping his back to the Mayor and his sister. If Craine wanted to know so damn badly, then so be it.

"This saloon has been passed down through my family since the Gulch was built."

"E-everybody knows that." Craine whimpered, trying to convince herself that she still had some expertise.

"But what they don't know is that the responsibility that it comes with has also been passed down. All the way to me and one day to Charlotte."

"It's our great privilege." Charlotte said, unaware of the weight those words should've carried.

"And our burden." Barnaby added.

"Barnaby wanted me to go to NYU." She confessed to Craine with a roll of her eyes.

While the Mayor could've given a shit about this detail, it definitely caught Barnaby's attention.

"You had scholarships! You had better important things to do!" He argued pleadingly as his head snapped away from the door and to his naive little sister.

"Better than saving the world?" His sister questioned with a cocked eyebrow. The world really did lose out on a hell of a prosecutor with Charlotte Le Coeur. She really got him there.

"You really got me there." Barnaby admitted with a small smile. "I just never wanted you to have to make that choice. Your life or this one. Your life or theirs." He threw a nod over to Craine.

"It was an easy call to make." She countered confidently and maybe even a little defiantly.

Barnaby's face relaxed if only a little as it curled into a small smile. You really couldn't help but be proud of the kid. As stupid as she was about the whole thing. He went back to glaring at the door. As interesting as their family drama must've been for the Mayor, Barnaby still had an explanation to get through.

"My great grandpappy helped the first Hunter of Evil fight the puppet demon." He went on. "He made a vow. As long as there's evil in the Gulch and as long as there's a man brave enough to hunt it—"

"There'll be a Le Coeur by his side." Charlotte finished.

"Always."

"And...*Stone*?" Craine asked with an unnecessary amount of disgust coming poking through all of her shock, confusion and frustration. Barnaby gave the thought a chuckle.

"I caught him trying to steal a bottle of whiskey off of my top shelf when he was barely a teenager! I knew it then. Could see it in his eyes. That boy had the look of someone who had just seen something *seriously* fucked up."

"How did I not know?" Craine asked, trying to settle her still-spinning head.

"He doesn't talk about his parents much."

"The demon!" She wailed.

"Would you have believed us if we told you?" Charlotte argued

"Hey, Mayor, we suspect the town's being taken over by an ancient puppet demon! Again." Barnaby tossed over his shoulder. "Shit you were in his inner circle and you still didn't believe it."

"No one's ever seen the demon's true face." Charlotte offered helpfully. "I don't even think the Shepherd has."

"We see it, we're fucked." Barnaby muttered grumpily.

"It signals the apex of the demon's power." Charlotte sighed as she slammed her book closed. "And no record of it exists anywhere."

"How would it have looked if we told you we thought it might be the Shepherd but we were wrong and he turned out to be just like you? You would've run us out of town!" Barnaby grumbled.

"It could be either of you then!" Craine shouted with a new paranoia.

"We took the demon out of you!" He scoffed.

Craine accepted that, but was still nowhere near understanding any of it.

"You said nobody's seen him, but your grandfather..." She tried to rationalize.

"Pappy helped the OG hunter push the demon back down into the hole it came out of, same as I'll do for Cyrus now." Barnaby said defensively. "This party's been on the calendar since before any of us were even born. But *he* never saw it. Only the Hunter did."

Barnaby's face became even more grim and serious than it already was. A small detail was bouncing around his mind now, one that he had been trying to keep at bay since I got back to the Gulch. Craine grasped at the straws in front of her.

"Then the first Hunter of Evil..."

"Didn't made it back."

Barnaby had to say it before anyone else could. He knew it was on the tip of Charlotte's know-it-all tongue and Craine was piecing it all together. What difference it made to her, I'll never know. Either way, I really wish Barnaby had looped me in on all of that before I rushed out guns blazing, instead of way after the fact.

As I limped and stumbled through the streets of the Gulch, leaving a thick trail of blood behind me, blissful in my ignorance, I couldn't help but wonder:

Is that asshole gonna come rescue me or not?!

The Gulch was calm. The waves had broken. What remained of the living Gulchers had long since fled to whatever hiding place or safe haven they knew or could improvise, leaving me alone in streets covered in the night's gore. The tall wooden Gulchy smiled that big, dumb, openmouthed smile down onto all the blood and wool, looking almost morbidly satisfied with it all.

"HAWDY, FOLKS!"

Sick bastard.

One boot in front of the other, I pressed through the alleys and streets in a straight line across the town. Or as straight as it could've been given my condition. My body had gone numb. Never a good sign. As catastrophically bad as all my injuries were, I couldn't feel any of them. I think they call that "going into shock from trauma and blood loss". But what did I know? I'm no doctor. I'm just the guy who blew up his office. The smell of smoke was distant, dwindling. The office had burned itself out. If it hadn't, the entire block would be up in flames and then it wouldn't have mattered how many people I saved. They would've focused on how I burned down the town instead. My thought process wasn't exactly clear, but somehow that felt like I would've been doing them a favor.

Pack up, people. Go start over somewhere not evil.

My vision swam through two tiny pinholes in front of me. Sweat and blood glued my hair to my face and dripped down, stinging my nose and tongue as I panted heavily. If the town was more complex, I would've been completely fucked. I would've had no idea where I even was. There were flashes of beige and hints of buildings, but I couldn't make out anything significant. Thankfully, I could find the Blood Moon Saloon with my eyes closed. Which I nearly had to. As I blinked hard to try to drive the fluids from my eyes, they only got harder to open again. Every time they closed the probability of them not opening again only increased.

A dull crimson forced its way through the fog overtaking me like a lighthouse. Harsh, yet fuzzy, the Blood Moon's sign gave me a landmark to head for. All the years of making this trek hammered told me that it was only twenty steps ahead of me. And as I took my first of twenty, I started to realize just how high that number actually was. The gap before me might as well have been miles as my full steps were reduced to halves and quarters after that. My boots and pants were thick with mud mixed from my own blood as it no doubt washed away whatever was left of the weresheep.

I reached my hand out in front of me as I hit step number eight and three quarters, desperately hoping to feel the cold metal of the Blood Moon doors. Katrina danced in front of me. Like literally. The witch twirled around in a billowing white dress, her eyes looking more inviting than they ever had when she still in the mirror. Benicio materialized behind her, in front of the thick doors. I could've sworn he was smiling at me as he raised one of his scaly feet and gave me a clawed thumbs up. Barnaby and Charlotte appeared too, waving me forward with smiles as wide as the street behind the thick glass of the Blood Moon's window. The dirt beneath my boots stopped crunching. My legs felt lighter and my head clearer. The sun rose and bathed us in warm, welcoming light. Bringing with it all the hopes and promises of a new, better day. Katrina put a guiding hand on my shoulder as I struggled to reach the front of the saloon. Benicio doubled back behind me and nudged my heels with his nose. Two new figures appeared, holding open the Blood Moon's doors for me. They were nothing more than shadows, silhouettes I could barely remember, but I knew who they were and why they were here.

"They need you, Cyrus." A voice said from the door.

"You have to be strong, bud." Echoed the silhouette next to it.

Katrina and Benicio pushed me forward. My body trembled and shook as I reached for the two silhouettes. The shapes of their face became more defined but still unrecognizable, their details lost somewhere in my whiskey drenched memory. The sunlight vanished like a giant switch had been flipped in the sky and the street was once again filled with the utter darkness of a moonless Gulch. Katrina dissolved, Benicio vanished and the silhouette's faded from existence, leaving me alone as my hand fell to the latch. The Blood Moon Saloon stood empty as the secret door behind the bar slid open inside. I gripped the handle and fell through the door as it slid open. Barnaby and Charlotte rushed back from behind the bar to me.

"Charlotte! Get the elixirs and some gauze!" Barnaby shouted as he gripped the reins. "Cyrus! Cyrus can you hear me!"

I was safe. I was home. But all I could muster in response was:

"NUUUH!"

Barnaby hooked his arms under mine and dragged me back to the Sanctuary, leaving rivers of red twisting and turning across the dusty brown floor. Charlotte rushed ahead of us, frantically pulling everything she thought might've been useful from the shelves. The white light of the secret door nearly convinced me that I had died as it overwhelmed me.

The familiar walls burst in and out of reality around me as Barnaby hoisted me onto my cot.

"Is he ok?! Did he get them?!" I heard Craine ask impatiently.

"Fuck...you..." I said as I raised a solitary and rebellious finger in the general direction of the woman I now fully blamed.

And why not?! She let the Shepherd get this far! She let Archer keep his job well past the mandatory retirement age! And worst of all, she drank from that damn cup without even asking what kind of evil was in it. Just like the rest of the Gulchers that were exploded all over the town with no hope of ever seeing home again, she fell for the half-assed promises of a man she shouldn't have trusted simply because she was too stupid to see through his neatly groomed bullshit and too lazy to think for herself.

"Be still, Cyrus." Barnaby ordered as he pulled my satchel off and gingerly placed it next to the cot. He ripped open my clothes. The buttons of my shirt flew out in all directions, bouncing off the walls and floors. The weresheep had left my pants in tatters, he barely had to pull at the weak threads holding them together. Charlotte's horrified gasps told me everything I needed to know about how gruesome the injuries were and what a sorry state I was actually in. She crossed to me with even more urgency, her arms loaded to capacity with medicinal items from all over the supernatural spectrum, dumping it all out in a pile next to the cot.

Barnaby dove right in, working as quickly and precisely as he could, pulling out a wad of particularly pungent herbs. Like sage had a baby with some stankin'-ass bunk weed. He stuffed a fistful into his mouth and chewed them into a course green paste as Charlotte followed his lead and did the same. They moved as one, packing it into each of my gaping wounds. The blood immediately changed course, soaking back into my cuts, gashes, tears and bites rather than pouring freely from them. Barnaby went back into the pile, pulling out a small black bottle with a shining metal cap.

"Cyrus?" He said as he knelt down to my ears. "You know what's next, man. I'm sorry."

If I could've grimaced or protested, I would've. That black bottle meant nothing fun or pleasant was coming. It meant my body was about to be purged of any lingering effects evil-inflicted wounds might've had and the healing process was about to kick into high gear. My eyes closed as I heard the cap clink across the floor as Barnaby spun it from the bottle. I weakly gripped the sides of the cot, bracing myself. Barnaby dumped his own proprietary cleansing elixir, brewed from generations of Le Coeur family research into such things, directly into my wounds. Every nerve in my body jolted awake as searing, thundering waves of agony rage across my body. Every one of my mighty muscles clenched and tightened as I wailed out into the Sanctum.

"Hang on. Hang on! Just one more." He told me firmly with a steadying hand on my bloody chest.

The next tonic was the most important. It would tell my wounds that nature was a bitch and take its slow regenerative pace personally. Another Le Coeur special straight from the R&D table. He uncorked a large blue glass vessel and poured its shimmering green contents over me. The wounds began to sizzle as a thick gray foam gurgled up from within them. I'd say it felt like my entire body was on fire, but I've been on fire before and honestly magically encouraged healing was way worse. I only had one option left here and I took it, passing right the fuck out into the deepest sleep or lightest coma I would ever know.

I didn't need to be awake to know where it went from there. Barnaby had patched me up enough times and Charlotte had studied the manuals and texts enough to know what to do. They wrapped my wounds tenderly, sealing them in with the bubbling gray foam and encasing me in gauze. What I wish I had been awake for was what I was told happened after they stood up and stepped away from me.

"What now?" Charlotte asked, both concerned and trying to remember the process she was still learning.

"The herbs and potions act fast," Barnaby replied, "but he'll still need all the time we can give him."

"Are...are we safe? Is it over?" Craine asked meekly from the cot she apparently now lived on. "Can I leave?"

Barnaby had the answer, but he didn't have to give it. Charlotte had her suspicions, but she didn't get the chance to voice them. The Gulch did that for them. The shelves and their contents swayed and rocked. The ground began to rumble and shake like an apocalyptic earthquake was set on ripping the town in two. Barnaby and Charlotte steadied themselves as Craine wept inconsolably.

17

TIME TO LIGHT THE LIGHTS

Out in the flatlands, as Barnaby and Charlotte patched me up, a petrified gargoyle laid motionless in the dirt. A gentle wind blew dirt over his frozen form, the misery of defeat cemented onto its cold, rocky face. A knock on its body would've revealed that it was completely hollow, though the shallow outlining crater in the dirt under it would've suggested the opposite. If you had gotten close to it, like really close, like if you pressed an ear to its chest, I'm sure you would've heard the smallest, yet most frantic, scratching noises. Like a rat trying to claw its way out. The vermin trapped inside the stone corpse was scared and desperate, tearing its fingernails against the rock.

The gargoyle's body had only three imperfections. A hole in its back where a wing once was, a similar one where there used to be an arm and a chunk of its oversized head big enough to jam a softball through. A human hand erupted from the hole in the gargoyle's back, slick with sweat and red with blood. It pawed at the stone around it, pulling pieces off in a mad claw to freedom. The gargoyle's back crumbled in on itself and Sheriff Archer slowly emerged, drenched in sweat and blood and naked as the day he was born. Human again, but not quite as he once was. A gash deep and wide enough to stick your fist in ran from his shoulder down to the small of his elderly back, pearly white bones and the fibers of his muscles were laid bare. His right arm abruptly ended mid-bicep, a ragged mass of torn flesh and exposed veins dripped blood on the frozen husk below him. And his forehead on the same side, from just above his eyebrow, all the way up to his crown and clear around to the back, was missing. His exposed brain pulsed as the wind blew against it. His exposed dick was smaller than I ever imagined it would be.

Only a force of terrible evil could've kept such a being alive. And it was a force of terrible evil that Archer was determined to get back to. His eyes rolled independently and against each other in their sockets as he stood up in his shell, dazed and half alive. With the will he had left, he forced his eyes straight and fixated on the Church of the Seventh Seal. It was far but he could still see its dark steeple looming over the town. The control he had over his vocal chords and speech center was weak. A longing, gurgling grunt was the best he could do.

Archer slurped up a string of mindless drool as it plunged from his lips and down his revoltingly wet mustache. With whatever focus he had in his three quarters of a head, he lifted a leg and took a labored step out of his gargoyle remains. As he slowly lifted the other to free himself from it entirely, he tripped on the edge and tumbled over. Archer cried in braindead anguish as his stump of an arm and gaping head wound dug into the dirt. He reached his good arm forward, clawing at the earth, and began to crawl, moaning deeply and mournfully with every inch he gained. It would've been a sorrowful, pitiful display if he hadn't been such a raging a piece of shit. People would've been begging for him to be put out of his misery, if anything just so they didn't have to look at his mangled form or hear his morbid wails. But no one left alive in town would shed a tear for their favorite lawman's fall from grace. Even if the remaining Gulchers hadn't taken to hiding, fleeing and battening down the hatches, there would've been no sympathy for him now. Holding the town hostage with a small army of monsters was the kind of thing Gulchers tended not to forgive super easily. His tormented howls yawned unnoticed from one end of Gulchy's Gulch to the other.

The former Sheriff's trip through town was much more difficult than my own. First of all, I could still walk for the most part. Secondly, I had my whole head. He crawled until he was out of the flatlands and used the side of the bank to pull himself up. His legs were shaky beneath him. He took two or three strained and labored steps before collapsing again. All evidence pointed to him repeating this process all the way to the church. Up, down, crawl, repeat. Like a man at the end of a week long bender, he clumsily stumbled and crawled his way across the town and up the steps of the church, completely devoid of any coordination or greater brain function.

Archer fell through the doors of the church and wailed as he hit the floor like a zombie stuck on a chainlink fence. The Shepherd sat on the edge of the stage in front of his altar, utter disgust written all over him, as he picked at his finger nails with the tip of his knife. His book sat peacefully on his lap. The blood and chunks of weresheep birth on his clothes had begun to dry. While Barnaby feared the silence that had fallen over the Gulch, Shep knew exactly what it meant. And yet, he wasn't the least bit surprised.

"Shame." He said calmly. "You did better than I thought you would." He grumbled over his shoulder to Benicio, still chained in the far corner behind him and clawing furiously at the wall he was anchored to, leaving a hole in the wood barely big enough to fit his head through.

"AURRG!" He shot back at him with pure hate and rage.

"Oh calm down!" The Shepherd groaned back with a roll of his eyes. "You're not going anywhere."

"Auurg!" He went back to his Shawshank escape hole, testing its width with his face before clawing at it again.

Archer crawled up the center of the church, moaning sickeningly with every drag of his broken, cursed body. The Shepherd shook his head and sighed. He slid the knife into the back of his belt and approached the remainder of the Sheriff with the book under his arm.

"The flock?" He asked as he glared down at him.

"D-d-d-deaaaa..." Archer forced himself to say.

The Shepherd seethed, running his spindly fingers through his greasy and blood-crusted hair. Archer cowered as Daddy seemed poised to rip off his belt and give him the beating of a lifetime. His faithful were reduced to just one. And that one was honestly more like one half now. It was a blow to the preacher's ego, but nothing more. He exhaled slowly, reminding himself of that and regaining his composure.

"It's fine! We'll rebuild." He took a deep breath, hoping for better news with his next question. "And Stone?"

Archer grunted and groaned as he tried to shake his head. It jerked from side to side in a ragged confirmation of complete and total failure. This was a harder pill for the Shepherd to swallow. The death of the flock wounded his ego, my survival wounded his odds. His jaw clenched and his teeth ground as he tried to keep a lid on the fury bubbling up in his gut. What was left of the Sheriff gripped the Shepherd's ankle, groveling and leaking drool and brain juice all over his shoes. Master knelt down to servant and ever so gingerly lifted his chin in his hands.

"You failed us in life, Sheriff." The Shepherd said gently as Archer stared up at him with wide, pleading eyes. In one swift motion the Shepherd hoisted him by the chin up to his feet and gripped his throat tightly in his fist, bringing their faces within inches of each other.

"But the Father still has use for you in death." He added with a sick grin.

Benicio pulled at his chains with all his sluggish might as he forced his head through the hole. Archer's feet dropped out from under him as the Shepherd dragged him to the door by the throat. He swung it open with such force that the hinges pulled and cracked against their frame. The cool night air hit the Shepherd as they emerged, dark storm clouds gathered menacingly over the church and nowhere else.

The Shepherd's eyes shined with ghoulish determination. Archer grabbed his wrist and held on for whatever dear life he had left as he was dragged through the dirt. They went out and around the church, Archer's limp legs leaving two long trails straight into the cemetery. The Shepherd dragged him past all the graves, over all the headstones, locked in on one in particular.

"My most *fearsome ally*." He hissed down at the Sheriff without looking at him. "You led my flock to its destruction. The Father would've liked to have had them by his side in the New World. And I would've liked to have found another way but it's become increasingly more apparent that it's time for you to serve your real purpose. Thankfully. Since you couldn't even do the only other thing he asked you to! I can't help but wonder? Are you disappointed with your life, Archer? Are you disappointed in how it all turned out for you?"

He glared down to the dead weight hanging from his arm. Archer moaned helplessly at his side.

"Well I am! And that's the worst part. I'm not mad. I wish I was mad! I'm disappointed. I knew it'd come to this eventually, and trust me it's not really how I saw my day going, but I just would've liked that you had a little more usefulness than this. A little more bang for the Father's buck, you know?! Such promise! Such potential! Such a complete fucking waste."

The Shepherd effortlessly tossed Archer the final few feet to their destination, the largest headstone in the cemetery. The one in the dead center, made from a boulder taken out of the side of the mountains and carved in the shape of a four foot tall pickax.

"HAWDY, FOLKS!"

Archer groaned as he collapsed onto the grave. The Shepherd kicked him into place, laying flat directly over the spot where Gulchy himself was buried, and stood over him.

"I tried to make you into something you're clearly not. See I thought you were a weapon, a blunt object for me to throw at any problem I had. But that's not what the Father needed. What you are, what you always were, what you meant to be...is a *key*. Sheriff Archer?"

"Sh-sheeeepheeeeerd!" He cried up at the preacher miserably.

"Go to Hell."

The Shepherd pulled his dagger from his back in a flash. The cold metal of the blade twinkled as thunder boomed angrily above. He held it high over his head as lightning cut the sky and dropped to his knees, burying the knife into the Sheriff's chest all the way down to the handle. Archer cried out in pain and betrayed terror.

The Shepherd's eyes rolled to white as he opened his book and recited whatever wicked incantations it contained. Latin. Because of course it was. As far as I could hear through Benicio's ears and as best as I remember it sounded something like:

"Sangria pieplate pompadour!"

Archer's blood leaked from his chest as the earth quaked briefly and suddenly. The Shepherd tore the blade from his body as blood sprayed and flooded from the wound. Thunder growled more intensely. The pages of the book burst into flames, but the Shepherd didn't give any indication that he even noticed. His hand plunged deep into Archer's chest cavity as the Sheriff screamed in torment and torture. Whatever humanity he had left was feeling every last thing the Shepherd was doing to him. He ripped Archer's heart out through the hole in chest, a mass of still beating muscle and blood, and held it up to the sky.

"For the Father." He hissed. "Condom accord chalupasauce!"

And brought it down to his mouth and took a massive bite. The beating stopped as the Shepherd chewed half of the heart and blood dribbled down his chin. Life finally left the Sheriff as his body quickly lost all color, turning a sickly gray. Decay and rot rocketed through him faster than nature intended. Lightning cracked and lit up the cemetery in all its macabre detail. The Shepherd crushed the rest of the heart in his hand and tossed it aside before kneeling down over the Sheriff. He placed a hand on his lifeless head as his eyes sunk in and the skin and muscles sagged.

"Obtuse, rubber goose, green moose, guava juice!"

The earth shook more violently. And this time it refused to stop. The tombstones swayed over their departed as the ground convulsed around them. The Shepherd sprung to his feet and backed away as a crack formed beneath Archer's nearly skeletal corpse. His book fully incinerated, turning to ash in his hand. The ground crumbled beneath him and swallowed Archer's body as Gulchy's grave sank into a deep pit that only got deeper and deeper with each rumble of the earth. Archer fell away into the darkness, fading from sight entirely as it claimed him.

I may be shit with Latin, but somethings have a way of coming through so clearly that they engrave themselves into your memory.

And those memories replay randomly through the rest of your life, no matter how much you try to drink them into submission. What the Shepherd said next, I'll never forget.

"Vindicem renascentis!"

I spent the painstaking time and considerable effort necessary to have the words Google translated. I needed to know. Vindicem renascentis. A champion reborn.

"Finis inceperat!"

The end begins.

The pit that was Gulchy's grave hungrily grew outwards. The pickax tombstone plummeted in. Graves and ground crumbled and fell as the Shepherd retreated from them and the pit claimed the cemetery as its own. He landed near the back wall of the church, his previous addition to the Gulch, as he laughed triumphantly if not a little deranged.

The pit grew into a sinkhole. And the sinkhole cracked and stretched into a chasm. The ground settled as it reached its full potential, spanning back clear across the flatlands, teasing at the idea of swallowing the mountains themselves. Though it left plenty of headroom with the church. Almost like it knew better. The bottom of it was impossible to see. It seemed to go down, down, down all the way through the planet and into space on the other side in a never-ending expanse of blackness. Fire exploded straight up into the sky like an erupting volcano, lighting up the town like the sun had risen orange and early. Flames broke up the storm clouds as lightning cracked around them. The inferno curled and retreated back into the chasm, leaving it smoldering and burning like it was filled with hot coals.

Tears of joy ran down the Shepherd's face as he cackled and marveled at what he had created. A hole straight to Hell. His second addition to the Gulch. The chasm howled as it started to inhale like a massive vacuum. A swirling tornado of glowing blue energy formed in the center, roaring across the Gulch from end to end and echoing off of the mountains.

All over the town and the valley, wherever they where Gulchers froze in place. Hiding in the woods, in their closets, under their tables, under their beds, their rigid bodies lifted into their air. Their eyes glowed white. Their mouths dropped open wider than they had any earthly right to. A familiar moaning fog horn sound bellowed out of them and their souls were sucked from their bodies. Ripped away from them aggressively in a ghostly burst of fog from their mouths. The detached souls flew towards the chasm as their bodies dropped lifelessly back to the ground in deflated piles like somebody let all the air out of a bunch of people balloons.

From all angles stolen souls flew into the vortex spinning in the chasm as its howls and the scattered, horrid moans of the Gulchers overtook the valley. Souls plunged into the mouth of the vortex and funneled down into the chasm. Electricity crackled through the air as if the souls were powering some kind of infernal battery deep within the abyss they flew into.

"Rise! Destroyer! In the name of the Father, rise!" The Shepherd boomed into the chasm as his victorious laughing swelled.

The festival Gulchy trembled. At first glance, you would've thought it was from the violent acts of evil happening in the ground under his hefty wooden feet. Or maybe that the tremors the chasm created were too much strain on its rusted cogs and its rickety body was finally giving out. And for a second, as Benicio locked onto it with his head through his makeshift escape hole and fear flooded his shell, I thought that might've been the case. That the old clockwork harbinger of Gulchy Day cheer was finally about to collapse into a splintered pile of gears and timber. But then it's eyes began to glow red. It's body creaked as it strained to move. A tendril of blue energy shot from the vortex and landed square in the towering Gulchy's back. The mechanisms in its body sparked with power and life. A trade was happening. The stolen souls of the Gulchers for the recovered soul of the muppet demon's big bad behemoth. The figure shuddered as it came to life.

18

SOUL VACUUM

The Sanctum rocked and vibrated as the chasm opened on the other side of town. Barnaby and Charlotte braced themselves against the walls, doing their best not to let the precious contents of the shelves fall. Craine, in the fetal position on her cot, bawled into her knees. The intense seismic shifts of the Gulch rattled through their bones.

"What is that?!" Charlotte called to Barnaby from the opposite side of the Sanctum, over the rumbling of the town.

"Nothing good." He responded gravely under his breath. Because of course Barnaby knew before he knew.

The quaking hammered away at the Sanctum. Craine cried even louder as if she thought there was a chance that her persistent wails could drown out what was happening to the Gulch.

"Barnaby!" Charlotte yelled desperately to her brother again.

"Just hold on!"

The earth calmed under them. The Sanctum stood still. I stirred on my cot as Benicio downloaded our doom into my brain. Barnaby was the first to snap back into the struggle. He ran for the secret door as quickly as his bum knee and the toll the last couple days had taken on it would allow. Charlotte barely had time to compose herself before he was through the secret door and behind the bar. The moaning of the Gulchers and the howling of the vortex began. Barnaby reached the heavy saloon windows just in time to see the first of the wayward souls sailing past. The glow of the chasm spread far and wide, wreathing the church in orange and yellow in front of it. The top of its blue soul-stealing vortex peaked out from behind it. And for the first time through everything that had happened in the last few hours, real fear and dread crept in on him. His mouth hung stunned as Charlotte reached him.

If it hadn't been for the handful of mystic protections in place over the Sanctum, we would've been deflated skin-balloons the same as the other Gulchers. While I was too unconscious to recognize it, I was grateful for Barnaby's great grandpappy. And sincerely hoped the night wouldn't end with me getting the chance to tell him that in person. Or in spirit. Whatever the hell you wanna call it.

"What's happening?" Charlotte asked, feeling the first sting of fear for her soul.

A lump had formed in Barnaby's throat but he refused to let his voice tremble.

"If I was a bettin' man, and I am, I'd say that the Shepherd just opened a chasm."

"What?!" Charlotte asked in shock and bewilderment as Barnaby made his way back into the Sanctum in a hurry.

"We're out of time. It's coming."

He turned to run back to the Sanctum but paused a beat, crossing to the door and throwing the numerous heavy locks on it before damn near sprinting back to me. Barnaby was doing everything in his power to swallow the panic he felt rising up. But there's a heavy mental fog that comes with the Le Coeur healing practices. The body shuts down completely as it puts itself back together, focusing all of its efforts on making itself whole again at the strong encouragement of whatever was in those bottles and balms. So getting me back online and ready to save the day was gonna take some effort. And luck.

"Cyrus!" He shouted as he grabbed me by the shoulders and tried to shake the life back into me. "Cyrus, come on, man!"

I wanted to answer him. I wanted to wake up and rejoin the battle. I wanted to get up off of that cot, head straight down to the church and beat the Shepherd to death with my barehands. But in my heavily sedated and magically medicated state, all I could manage was a groan and a slurry not-even-semi-conscious:

"Fuck off...sleeping..."

"Damn it!" Barnaby spat as he shook me even more violently. "We have to get him on his feet before anything else goes down or something worse shows up!"

The Mayor spewed tears and mucus into her knees as the howls and moans of the town seeped through the walls of the Sanctum.

"What is that?!" She whined hysterically to nobody in particular.

Charlotte stood by, struggling to form a thought or an idea for once.

"W-what will wake him up?" She asked Barnaby helplessly.

"The mezcal!" He answered without hesitation. He wasn't wrong. He just didn't realize that it wasn't behind the bar anymore.

Charlotte ran out to the bar, frantically searching the rows and rows of bottles, top shelf, bottom and well. But she wouldn't find the one she was after. It was still tucked away safely in my satchel, a few feet away from me. I knew it had survived the night, the battle with the Sheriff and the Flock. That satchel was special. It had a way of keeping fragile things in tact under the most extreme conditions. Sixty-two dollars, REI. Bought it with a gift card. Regardless, I had no way of telling the Le Coeurs that their best hope at reviving me wasn't in the bar.

"You hear that, Cy? Your bottle's coming!" Barnaby whispered to me reassuringly. He clearly didn't take me seriously when I said I was going to steal it. So that was kinda on him.

"I don't see a mezcal!" Charlotte called from the bar as the howls and moans grew even louder. As did Craine's whimpers and wails.

I fought through the fog filling my head and numbing my body and forced another four words from my mouth.

"Already...stole it...fucker."

"Shit! Go for the whiskeys, Charlotte!" Barnaby hollered to the bar. "Something Irish!"

"THAT NOISE!!" Craine bawled as she buried her head in her hands.

"How is getting him hammered gonna help?!" Charlotte asked super judgmentally as she popped her head back into the Sanctum.

"Damn it, Charlotte, I know this man!"

"Wh...whiskey?"

"See?!"

Charlotte hastily disappeared into the bar again. The steady sounds of stolen souls and the unrelenting roar of the chasm vortex surrounded the Sanctum in a flurry like a monsoon right outside our door.

"WHAT IS GOING ON?!" Craine shrieked.

"The Shepherd opened a portal to Hell and it's swallowing every soul in town!" Barnaby snapped at her, because fuck bedside manner.

The Mayor screamed and cried until her throat was raw, guilt finally finding its place in her growing collection of negative emotions.

"THIS IS ALL MY FAULT!"

Kinda.

"You gotta get your shit together, Craine!". Barnaby shouted, officially over her nonsense.

Charlotte poked her head back in, just double checking.

"There isn't like a potion we should give him or something?"

"Yes! There is! Now go get it!" Barnaby barked back, knowing that there was only one potion that could bring me back to the land of the living. And it was copper pot distilled with an oaky finish.

"I welcomed him in! I handed the town over to him!" Craine lamented with wide, bloodshot eyes. The reality of just how badly she had fucked up finally nailing her in her stupid face.

"You were possessed! You get a pass on this one." Barnaby said, not wanting to continue this conversation anymore than he knew Craine was already going to.

"I let him take over the old church! I let him damn us all to Hell!"

"B-Barnaby?" I strained.

"Reverend Wright! It all just happened so fast! The people needed somebody to help them! I didn't know! I DIDN'T KNOW!" Craine continued in a frenzy, throwing a full on guilty pity party that nobody else was attending.

"I'm here, Cyrus! Can you hear me?" Barnaby asked as he studied me with an anxious concern. I had something important to tell him and was determined to do it. A small detail that I knew both he and Charlotte had overlooked in all the newly devolved pandemonium. Something that I knew deep down, despite how out of it I was, would be our salvation. I poured all my strength, focus and grit into forming the words.

"N-no...ice...neat."

"Charlotte! The whiskey!" He shouted.

"I'm working on it!" She shouted back.

"My family! What about my family?!" Craine whined, turning her regret outwards. I couldn't say what had become of them. But if I had to guess I'd say they were probably a pile of deflated skin in whatever house was theirs. So what good was all her crying and hysterics really gonna do?

Charlotte hurried back into the Sanctum, a bottle of black label hope grasped firmly in her hand, the sounds of damnation reaching their apex outside.

"I can't be here! My family! I can't be here!" Craine screamed, crazed, her voice cracking. The hellscape outside and her role in our doom finally broke her completely. "I have to get out of here!"

She darted up from the cot and took off straight for the secret door in a frantic dash to freedom as Charlotte hurried towards me. Their shoulders collided and Charlotte spun around. The whiskey slipped through her fingers and plummeted to the floor. The bottle exploded into a million pieces, sending daggers of glass and drops of optimism flying in all directions. My mind and body responded how years of training had conditioned them to. I sat straight up with a righteous fury in my wide open eyes.

"Be careful with that god damn it!" I scolded fiercely.

"Cyrus?!" Barnaby allowed himself the smallest breath of relief, as hope returned to him.

"The whole town's going to Hell." I groaned, the effort of yelling at Charlotte and the Mayor exhausting me.

"More than you know! The Shepherd opened—" Barnaby started.

"A chasm." We both said simultaneously.

"Benicio's still alive?" He asked.

"You know it, baby."

Craine fled, running straight to the saloon's heavy doors. She pulled on them wildly, only to find the heavy locks firmly in place. Charlotte and her bleeding heart chased after her.

"Let me out! Let me out!" The Mayor howled at the doors like she expected them to magically open if she was stern and loud enough.

"It's not safe out there!" Charlotte argued as she landed next to her, putting a hand on the door to steady it.

"I wanna go home! I need to be with my family!"

"You *need* to stay *here*! This is the only place you'll be safe!"

"Then I'll get them and bring them here!" Craine countered, unaware of what a stupid idea actually that was.

"Absolutely fucking not!" I yelled from the Sanctum.

Barnaby steadied me as I slowly slung my legs over the side of the cot.

"Easy, Cy. The tonics haven't had a chance to fully run their course." He advised.

He really didn't need to point that out. I discovered that just fine on my own. My body ached and throbbed from head to toe like I had just been pulled from one of those sausage making machines. There was no strength left in my muscles, only sharp stings of dissent as they moved. The world around me, as frantic and chaotic as it was, moved at a snail's pace.

"He used Archer to open it." I grunted. "What was left of him anyway."

"Then we gotta move." Barnaby said with a new resolve. "You have to kill him and close the chasm before—"

"The behemoth. He's already working on that."

"Shit!" Barnaby took a breath, processing all the new tortoise recon. "Are you up for a fight?"

"Do I have a choice?"

"Not really. Gotta get to work."

"And we better step on it." I added gravely. "It's waking up."

I tried to stand but my legs said "fuck no!" And I dropped right back down to the cot. My eyelids flickered, wanting more than anything to just stay closed again.

"I'll check the books." Barnaby said. "Maybe if we kill the Shepherd, the behemoth will fuck off before their boss shows his face. We can't just send you out and hope for the best."

"Why not? It kinda worked the last time."

Mostly.

He crossed to the desk and the heavy leather-bound book Charlotte had left sitting there, just in time to see her through the secret door, struggling with the Mayor.

"Charlotte?!" He yelled over to her.

But Charlotte didn't look up. She didn't even move. She stayed at the door, pressing her weight into and arguing a case for Craine's soul as her doughy fingers fumbled with the locks.

"Nowhere is safe!" She protested.

"We can fix this! Please!" Charlotte begged.

"NO!" Craine shouted.

"You need to stay inside!"

"I'm! Going! HOME!"

She threw all of her weight behind three pulls at the door. With her last the door flew free, narrowly clearing its locks. Charlotte stumbled back as it caught her in the chin, but barely skipped a beat.

"No!" She yelled after the Mayor as she ran recklessly through and into the night.

Charlotte sprinted after her, knowing better but with zero regard for own wellbeing. Barnaby broke from the workbench and raced to the door, his worst fears being realized in front of him. His little sister in real, immortal danger of the greater evils of Gulchy's Gulch.

"Charlotte! Get back in here!" He commanded as he crossed through the secret door.

"Barnaby!" I shouted after him. "We gotta figure out the muppet thing!"

I took a step off of the cot and hit the ground with a thud that felt like I fell from the roof instead. My legs were stiff and heavy like they were filled with slowly drying concrete. I growled as I forced myself up and onto them. Steading myself on whatever I could, trunks, boxes, shelves, the frame of the secret door, as I chased after Barnaby.

Craine charged ahead into the street with Charlotte in hot pursuit. She latched onto the Mayor's wrist as she froze in the middle. All at once, the Gulch calmed down. Like whatever horrors they had been hearing had simply been switched off. The vortex was silent. The souls drifting by overhead vanished. If it hadn't been for the eerie orange glow behind the church, it all might've seemed like nothing more than a trick of the wind. No howls. No foghorn moans. There was something else in the air though. Like some great beast in the sky had caught the scent of a valuable prey. The two women surveyed their surroundings, totally puzzled.

"Wh-what? I don't understand?" She stammered.

Charlotte tugged forcefully at her wrist.

"Mayor Craine. Delilah. Please." She pleaded fearfully. "We need to go back inside. It's not safe."

Charlotte fought with all her weight and strength against the immovably sturdy Mayor.

"Charlotte, let her go. Get back inside." Barnaby said calmly, as he inched closer to the door.

"Is it over?" She asked him, hoping he would respond positively but not wanting to get her hopes up.

"You know it's not! Get back inside." He begged her.

I crossed the threshold into the saloon as Barnaby got within centimeters of the doorframe and the dangers of the Gulch outside.

"Barnaby, get away from the door! The enchantments!" I barked. He knew better, same as Charlotte, but was getting way too close to showing the same reckless amount of care she had.

"I know!" He spat back at me. "Charlotte! Come on!"

"We can't just leave her out here on her own!" Charlotte insisted.

"Lesson one, Char! Not everyone can be saved every time."

Craine began to cry anew. Gentle tears ran down her puffy cheeks as she gave up trying to break free from Charlotte's grip.

"Thank you for helping me. All of you. Really." She offered the Le Coeurs, her mind made up. "Goodbye."

Charlotte's hold on Craine's wrist loosened as she realized she had lost the fight. The Mayor pulled her arm back and took a step away from her, turning to head off to the neighborhoods. She took another step and her body went rigid. As did Charlotte's. A deep cackle drifted faintly on the air. The howl of the vortex exploded across the valley. Charlotte and Craine lifted into the air, perfectly petrified. Their mouths dropped open wide and the foghorns returned, trumpeting out of their own mouths.

"Charlotte!" Barnaby screamed desperately.

He ran through the door, arms outreached, total terror flooding his higher reasoning, determined to save the sister he knew was well beyond saving.

"Barnaby no!" I cried out as I hobbled away from the bar.

He too floated up into the air, that same gut wrenching moan erupting out of his inhumanly agape mouth. All three souls were ripped from their respective bodies together in bursts of gray steam. The souls hung in the air for a moment, taunting me. As if the Shepherd or the muppet demon or whatever the fuck was showing me just how powerful he had become and the level of damage he could inflict regardless of my intervention. Regardless of *our* intervention. They glowed a little as they finally whipped away towards the chasm and the swirling vortex of doomy evil within it. Their bodies collapsed into deflated piles in the street.

I watched from the door as they crested the church, closed in on the vortex and disappeared from sight into its swirling maw. The souls of the other remaining Gulchers continued to pass over the town on their way to their final destination. Barnaby, Charlotte and the pain in the ass Mayor laid in fleshy heaps a few feet away from me. They deserved better. Well, Barnaby and Charlotte deserved better. But there was no way I was going out there to get them. The Blood Moon was safe and the streets were a trap, one I was seriously not willing to spring. So I closed the door. And latched the locks. And slid down against the door until I was flat on the floor as a feeling so foreign it almost felt new crept its way up my spine. But I recognized it quickly enough. It was dread.

19

DEPRESSION SHOPPING

I have no idea how much time had passed.
How long it took me to get up and make my
way into the Sanctum for my satchel and back
to the bar or how long I had been sitting
there. The darkness outside had an unholy
thickness to it as smoke billowed from the
chasm like a foundry and blacked out the
sky. The sun was starting to rise but there
was no way of telling beyond the deep orange
glow fighting for recognition behind the
infernal veil shrouding the Gulch. The sharp
glow of the chasm on the other end of town
penetrated the unearthly blackness around
it. The silence was worse. The moans

stopped, but I had no idea how long it had been since they had. The vortex had even retreated. Yet the behemoth hadn't gone tearing through town. It was waiting. And what it was waiting for was posted up at the bar in the Blood Moon Saloon. Nursing a bottle of mezcal.

Instead of going bottoms up with all I had left, I actually used a glass for once. Pouring it neat the way Barnaby would've and taking my time with it. I didn't want to blackout or erase this night or ignore it, I wanted to feel its burn. I wanted to let the liquor punish me as intended.

The closed Sanctum door left the Blood Moon dark. Nobody had the time to turn on the lights in the chaos and confusion of the night and I refused to. I didn't want to look up and see all the work the Le Coeurs had done over the generations gone to waste. I sloshed the mezcal around my glass. Without Barnaby behind the bar, the place just felt wrong. Unnatural. Hopeless. And that was a reality I was in no way ready to face.

Is this my fault? It feels like my fault.

The what-ifs, maybes and should'ves fought the mezcal for control of my remaining sober brain cells. I didn't kill Archer properly. I was too confident, too wounded, too tired to check that he was completely dead. I let him get back to the church. If Barnaby hadn't been so worried about me, he could've stopped Charlotte from running outside. If I had more strength I could've stopped him from doing the same. I didn't listen. I didn't care. Big Bad Cyrus Stone, the Hunter of Evil, just had to go on his glorious killing spree. He just had to be the hero and save the day and doom us all just the same. But none of that was any use now. It was done. And I had done it. Or hadn't done it. Either or, same thing.

How do I do this job without you, Barnaby?

The muppet demon felt way beyond my pay grade now. Everything Barnaby had taught me in the last few decades and everything we had done together, all the vampires, succubi and possibly possessed cattle farmers didn't quite scratch the surface of something that ancient and apparently hard to kill for good. There was no plan.

No strategy. No super specific weapon. No Le Coeurs in the Gulch for the first time since it spawned. Just a miserable drunk with no support and even fewer friends. If I went out there, if I faced the Shepherd and the demon and it went sideways, there'd be no one to patch me up and send me back out with a smack on the back. No one to say "Try shooting him here and with this." No one to help me clean up my mess. No one left to save.

Seriously. I have no idea what I'm doing here.

Barnaby had every right to kick my ass the night we met. I was just some shithead kid. Lost in the Gulch and stealing his booze, covered in soot and my parents' blood. But he sat me down and listened to me. Listened to every gory detail of that miserable night. What Archer should've done but was too lazy and too arrogant to do. Instead of brushing me off as insane as I told him the story of how the house spontaneously combusted and smoke ate mom and dad, he let me keep the bottle and took me back into the Sanctum for the very first time. He showed me the world as it was instead of what I thought and rather than cower away from like Craine had, I ran full steam ahead, balls out, straight down the rabbit hole.

I'd come and go as I pleased in those early days. Bumming around the Gulch before coming back to the Blood Moon for more stories, more training, more instruction. I lusted after it. I wanted to know everything I could about the workings of evil. I wanted to know how to kill every damn thing that ever bumped in the night. The only thing Barnaby never gave me was a place to live.

"Man, what would people say if they found out I had a little white boy living with me in my bar?!" He'd say.

And he wasn't wrong. It would've looked super weird. Even though everyone in town knew I was an orphan and had nowhere else to go. They would've judged the fuck out of us. Like all the people in Gotham that thought something fishy was going on in Robin's tights. In a way I was grateful for it though and always kinda wondered if that was just Barnaby's way of toughening me up in a hurry.

It wasn't until I was way older that that invite finally got extended. But by then I was too infamous for our association to be known as anything other than bartender and bartendee. He showed me humanity. He showed me patience. He showed me how to hunt and how to kill and how to save the souls of the innocent from the darkness that lurked behind every corner.

And now your soul is stuck in some big hole with all those other people who's names escape me.

I glared out of the corner of my eyes to the windows. The town outside wasn't just dead, it was soulless. Gulchy's Gulch wouldn't become one of those old abandoned ghost towns. It was missing the departed souls that become ghosts in the first place.

This is how it ends I guess.

I dumped the mezcal down my throat and refilled my glass.

The fearsome Hunter of Evil died alone in a bar in a place remembered by no one while the world died a slow death.

The mezcal went down again.

"Actually that sounds kinda badass." I slurred to myself, the mezcal serving its purpose.

But if I'm going to die, I'm not going to die sober like some nerd!

I picked up the mezcal to refill my glass. The bottle tipped as the half that was left inside rolled towards the mouth. Before it could leave and spill down to its penultimate destination, I stopped. Had I known it'd be the last recommendation Barnaby would ever give me, I would've nursed it a little more. I decided to cap it off. That bottle needed to be special, held in higher esteem than every other bottle.

Special occasions. In his memory.

I swung my satchel up from the barstool next to me and tucked the bottle back inside where I knew it'd be safe until the time was right again. That left me staring at the wall of other bottles in Barnaby's old territory behind the bar. As my eyes poured over the labels and my memory drifted away to all the nights Barnaby would suggest something because he knew I'd like it or that my night

371

needed it, I couldn't stop myself from saying:

"Why couldn't he ever just get the name brands?! I don't know what half this shit is!"

That's what Barnaby was for! Alright. Alright, calm your ass. What follows mezcal? What would Barnaby say? Mezcal is followed by what? Byyyyy what? I'm sure I've got some Vanishing Powder I could— no, no, bad idea, I'm too sad. What would Barnaby say? What would Barnaby say?! . . .

"What would Barnaby say?"

I could almost hear him and I did my best to listen. His disembodied voice filled the Blood Moon the same as my head.

"GET OFF YOUR DRUNK ASS AND SAVE THE WORLD, CYRUS STONE!"

"I just don't know!" I cried as I threw my glass into the bottles that sat there mocking me.

A heavy crash broke the silence of the saloon as they shattered in unison and liquor of all colors dripped onto the floor. I shot up from my barstool in a huff, my legs mostly back online but loose from the booze.

The Shepherd.

I didn't really care if he was just another errand boy or not, he did this and he would suffer and die all the same. And when his boss showed his face, he would feel my wrath too. This was their fault. Raw fury coursed through my body like a controlled explosion as my eyes narrowed.

"You don't *fuck* with a man's bartender!" I roared as I slammed my fists down onto the bar, cracking the age-old wood.

That's a step too far! That's a low blow! There's a special circle of Hell reserved for people who do that kind of shit...

"And I hope you like it there! You! Do NOT! FUCK! With a man's bartender!" The incredible clarity that the fancier cousin to tequila and unbridled rage and pain provided.

Whatever happened to me didn't matter. Support system or no, the Shepherd and the muppet demon had a world of pain coming their way and I needed to be the one to deliver it. I stormed back behind the bar and grabbed the Le Coeur Special. With a mighty pull I ripped it down off the wall as the Sanctum revealed itself. The weight in my hand was a relief. It was full.

You'll do.

The wax tore free as I gripped the cork in my teeth. I ripped it out, spit it into the the light of the Sanctum and took a swig. No idea what it was! But it tasted like nutsack. Like some past Le Coeur mixed scotch with skunky beer and said "Yeah that's the good stuff!" Beggars and choosers though, right?

I burst into the Sanctum, liquor dribbling down my face and over the crisscrossed scars and dirty bandages on my chest. If I couldn't put the muppet down for good, then maybe, at the very least I could slow it down. Buy the world some time. Throw a wrench in its plans. Kick the preacher's ass proper for Barnaby and Charlotte before I cash it all in. Kill the preacher, kill the behemoth, draw out the Father. Hope for a fight, expect all out war. And I knew just how to start that dance. My head cocked over to the workbench and the thick brown leather book sitting on it.

"Yeah, like I'm gonna read!" I cringed as I took another drink.

I went straight for the wall of weapons and relics and reached for the very first thing I saw. My hand froze inches away from a horned skull made of frosted glass and filled with sand.

"Oh shit, what do I actually need here?"

It hovered in the air as I remembered a simple fact. You could study under Barnaby and listen to everything he had to say all day, everyday, for a lifetime and never even get past the tip of the iceberg that was his knowledge and expertise. My hand dropped. I poured over all the weapons, row upon row of guns, ammo, specialty ammo, knick-knacks and trinkets older than the dirt they were found in. Tapping into the vast reserve of wisdom Barnaby has given me, remembering everything I had learned from the oldest of the Le Coeur line or even heard him mention, I made the most educated decision I could.

"Fuck it. Better take it all."

What I had thought yesterday was dead on accurate. Something in here was bound to kill that son of bitch right when the time came.

I'll throw every last thing we have at him until I find the one that sticks.

I raced around the room as quickly as my buzzed and freshly mended legs would allow, digging out old canvas duffle bags and whatever other empty receptacles I could find. Before long a pile of bags, sacks, totes and boxes formed in front of the weapons and relics. There was even an old bucket and a faded *Sanford and Son* lunchbox.

I was ready to go shopping. Starting with my satchel, with sweeping arms, I dumped everything off of the shelves to fill out my final arsenal. First the stuff I knew. Silver bullets, lots of them. Guns? Even more of them in every caliber and capacity imaginable. Silver stakes, holy water, salt. An old pack of Chesterfields. Those were for me. A collection of sacred daggers Barnaby once said would kill the Anti-Christ if the time ever came.

I mean he feels pretty Anti-Christy. Maybe?

A ring that rather made you fireproof or more flammable, I couldn't remember which. Slipped that bad boy right on my thumb and hoped for the best. An anklet meant for spiritual protection.

Huh. Barnaby really should've worn this. No, rose gold isn't his color.

Garlic cloves! White oak shavings! UV light grenades, an all-time favorite. Then I moved to the more confusing objects. The glass skull full of sand?

Sure.

A shrunken foot?

Why the hell not?!

A porcelain doll with bloodshot human eyes?

Get in the bag, little lady, we're going to war!

No matter how weird, creepy or seemingly useless it was, I packed it up. My satchel swelled, testing the tensile strength of whatever mythical material REI made it out of. The boxes and bags on the floor were at capacity, stuffed to their absolute limits. I was taking everything in the Sanctum minus the books with me.

At least they'll know Cyrus Stone tried.

I approached the Le Coeur family crypt with all the respect and reverence it deserved, placing a hand on the nameplates of the Le

Coeurs of old. Something I needed to do before I could go out in a blaze of glory.

"I'll avenge him." I whispered to them. "Both of them. No matter what, you have my word. I won't go down until they know just how badly they *fucked up*."

The toes of my boots grazed something titillating below the names.

"When you're ready." Barnaby told me when I was a kid, the first time I had asked to open the great Box of Mystery, making sure to give the words the weight they needed while blowing right past them. Each time I asked after that only earned a less patient response. And I asked a lot. Like a couple times a year, every year, at minimum. It felt like the time had finally come rather Barnaby signed off on it or not. Seeing as I didn't know if I'd even live to see it again. And there was no one around to stop me.

Decades of waiting and wondering would be put to rest. As I carried the blackened steel to the work bunch, I couldn't help but get a little excited. A lifetime of theories ran wild through my mind.

I hope it's Ninja Turtles!

The trunk rattled the table with a heavy slam as I dropped it. The lock and latch were imposing, as old as any of the relics now geared up and ready for battle. The gravity of it spun around the Sanctum. This was the moment every little boy dreamed of. When their best friend had his soul sucked out by a vortex of evil before he could tell him he was ready for the Only-When-You're-Ready Box and decided to open it anyway. I gave the lock a pull. Unsurprisingly, it didn't budge. The keyhole was long and wide, like only an old pirate key would fit inside it. And I was fresh out of old pirate keys. Thankfully, over the years, I had developed an affinity for picking locks. There wasn't a single one ever made that could keep me from what I wanted. So I grabbed a hammer from the pegboard of tools and smashed the bejesus out of it. Four good whacks was all it took and the lock burst into pieces and fell from the trunk.

The lid came up slowly as I savored the anticipation of the moment. The darkness of the trunk's interior did nothing to betray its contents. I snapped it shut as a horrible thought crossed my mind, a possibility I hadn't entertained.

What if this is one of those stupid-ass "the strength was in you all along" type things?

"I swear to god if it's just like a mirror in here I'm just gonna go back to the bar!"

I threw the lid back. The pegboard jolted as it slammed against it. A rush of nerves passed through my gut as I peered over the edge and inside. A cowboy hat with a silver studded band around the center, a thermal hunting shirt and a pair of cargo pants. All in black.

"The fuck?! I had to be ready for an outfit?!"

The hat was cool, sure, but c'mon. I pulled the clothes out and looked underneath them, hoping I'd find some kind of special gun or stake or mint-in-package Raphael.

"How does he even know these will fit?!"

But no. There was just a coat. An old leather duster, like the battle worn one I had on, but worse. It was thicker, heavier, dustier. Mine had a collar that I could pull up whenever I wanted to look mysterious, and this one had two big leathery flap things that ran down the shoulders. I dropped it all onto the bench and looked to see if there was anything cooler. But there was only a postcard. I recognized Barnaby's handwriting immediately.

Cyrus,

First of all, calm your shit. I know you were expecting more. But this is all I've got for you and yeah, I made you wait for it. The shirt and the pants are whatever, the shirt will keep you warmer and conceal your scent and all that and the pants will let you carry more tools and ammo and keep you loose, sure. As for the hat, that's just an idea I'm rolling with. Keep some damn silver on your head, see if that helps with anything! They were late additions. I could've given them to you at anytime, but I wanted to keep it all together. The jacket is the important thing here. You had to earn that mother fucker! Prove you deserved it, you know? It's all that's left of the original Hunter of Evil. He rode off on a horse to save the Gulch and this was all Pappy found of him after the dust settled. Every Hunter to come after him wore it as a way to honor him and passed it on when their time came. They never had to face the kind of evil the OG did and with any luck you won't either.

"Missed the mark on that one, bud." I scoffed. "Way to twist the knife."

But if you have this jacket then it means you're ready for it regardless. Whether you think you are or not. You're part of a long legacy, Cyrus Stone. We both are. And we have to do our best to live up to it. For better or worse, you are the Hunter of Evil. Don't let us down.

B.

Turning the postcard over, I discovered it wasn't a postcard at all. Barnaby's note was written on the back of an old sepia tone photograph of his Pappy and the Hunter of Evil who's jacket I was now expected to wear. The resemblance in the Le Coeur line was impossible to ignore. It was like looking into a different time where Barnaby was standing with a different man, on the exact same mission we've always had. His Pappy grinned cheerfully, a feat that could not have been easy in a time when you had to stand still for a full day and a half to get your picture taken. The old Hunter had a look I recognized the second I saw it. His thousand yard stare and thick growth of stubble were like looking into every hungover mirror I had ever faced. I had been calling myself the Hunter of Evil my entire adult life, but only then did the full weight of that title land on my shoulders.

"Huh. Alright." I said as I accepted what I could only assume was fate.

Barnaby was definitely onto something. As I looked down at myself, it started to seem like maybe I actually was ready. I mean I looked like absolute shit. I hadn't really gotten a chance to check myself since getting off the cot but now that I had I realized that I didn't really have that "Hunter of Evil's Last Stand" kind of look I had hoped for. It was more of a

"Crazed Homeless Man Robbed a Pawn Shop" type thing. The new wounds were on their way to becoming just another part of my collection of scars but the buttons from my shirt were all over the floor, my pants were ripped open from belt to ankle and what was left of my jacket dangled off of me in ribbons. Not to mention the blood and mud caked over it all.

I peeled off the old clothes and tossed it all onto my cot like a python shedding its skin. Piece by piece I took up the mantle of my predecessor with Barnaby's additions. The pants fit just right. Room for gear and room to move, blossoming out as I tucked them into my same old boots. The shirt was snug, insulating, showing off every ripple of my heroic musculature. The jacket hung from me like a leathery suit of armor. The silver studs of the new hat twinkled against the black felt like stars in the sky. If I was going to die, if tonight was the last night, then I was going to go out as I lived. As the Hunter of Evil. On a mission of justice and terrible vengeance against the nightmares that threatened mankind. And also kinda buzzed. I took one last drink from the Le

Coeur special. A healthy amount remained inside. I placed the bottle softly at the foot of the Le Coeur crypt, where the trunk holding my new superhero uniform had once been.

"One for the road." I said as I tipped my new hat. "Even if it does taste like sweaty butthole."

I turned to face the Sanctum door across from me. Darkness lie waiting on the other side. The time had come. Someone somewhere was tolling a bell. There was just one last thing I needed.

Back up.

20

THE MUPPET SHOW

The impenetrably thick smoke swirled and billowed in the sky with the faint glow of daylight imprisoned behind it. I stood in the street in front of the saloon, Barnaby, Charlotte and Craine's skin balloons were moved safely inside, my satchel, belt and cargo pockets were loaded for the end times. Behind me stood an army of one hundred full grown, battle ready desert tortoises. Packed up with the Sanctum armory in bags and boxes tied to their shells like my own slow moving war sherpas. I lit a Chesterfield. The cherry red ember spread a gentle glow across my face as I glared from under my hat at the Church of the Seventh Seal on the apocalyptic horizon.

We marched forward as one, the tortoises doing their best to keep my pace and me trying my hardest to accommodate theirs. The added weight couldn't have been easy for my desert infantry, but they powered on with all their might. The Shepherd had one of their own. It was as personal for them as it was me. Have you ever seen a tortoise snarl? It's way more threatening than you'd think. My parade of death filed down the streets. Passed the drying residual gore of the weresheep, passed the destruction they caused, passed the buildings Archer damaged dragging me across their roofs, passed a town that needed its Hunter more than it ever had.

You were dicks. And mindless rednecks. But I'll avenge you too all the same.

As the church grew closer, my desire to do just that only grew. Like a coal in my gut burning hotter and brighter with each breath I took until a inferno of hate and rage ravaged my core. Sticking with the tortoises allowed me plenty of time to mentally play out every option for every terrible thing I would do to him once I got my hands on him. It gave me time to run through all my options for once his demon daddy showed his ugly mug, the limitless uses for the wide array of weapons and relics I had packed onto me and that inched along behind me. And for the life of me I couldn't remember what the hell it was the tortoises were carrying past the guns and ammo.

There was like a doll or something? Shit.

I resolved to keep it simple, straight forward, barbaric.

Start with what you know and work your way out. Find the thing that hurts the most and then keep hurting him with it until rather I die or he does.

As I got closer to the church, I also got closer to the behemoth. The animated Gulchy stood still on the edge of the chasm. I would've rather he was moving honestly. Just standing there, gazing down into the fires of Hell with that stupid Gulchy smile was unnerving.

Did he power down or something?

I knew I couldn't (*shouldn't*) bet on that. I'd have to deal with it too. But one fire at a time. I wanted, needed, preacher blood on my hands before behemoth splinters. The church doors stood but a few feet ahead of me. There was no sign of the Shepherd though. No laughs, no yells, no cheers, no defenses. But I didn't need to see what Benicio saw to know exactly where he was and what he was doing.

The Shepherd stood at his altar, patiently waiting with ravenous eyes fixed on the door. He had taken his jacket off and rolled up his sleeves neatly, expecting to have to get his hands even dirtier before the day was through. What he was saving them for, I had no idea. Even his shirt was crusted to the seams with dried chunks of weresheep and Sheriff blood. He spun his dagger in leisurely circles, the tip carving a divot in the top of the altar.

Good. Keep your eyes where they are, bitch.

With a powerful kick I sent the doors flying from their hinges and tumbling into the church, followed closely by two UV light grenades.

"Close your eyes, boys!" I yelled to my tortoise legion as the grenades bounced off the floor and burst in the heart of the room.

I turned away as blinding white and yellow light exploded through the church, as powerful and radiant as the sun itself. For the briefest second, the world around the church shifted to high noon before returning to low midnight. The Shepherd barely seemed to notice. He rubbed his eyes, irritated when his retinas should've been seared to a crisp, and smiled as wide as the Gulchy behemoth when he saw me standing in the broken doorway. Weapons at the ready, tortoises at my six.

"And so the Hunter of Evil comes to witness the depth of his failure." He taunted as I took a determined step inside.

"My friends souls. I'm gonna need those back." I snarled, my voice full of malice. For a second I hope I'd be intimidating enough that he'd just be like "Oh shit, yeah, here you go. Sorry for the trouble, bro." But no.

The Shepherd let out a deep and confident rolling belly laugh.

"You're too late, Stone! They've moved on! They feed my glorious purpose."

"What purpose is that exactly? Being a douchebag?" Got him.

"No." He said as he shook his head like a parent correcting their endearingly stupid child.

The church trembled. Outside, directly behind the servant of muppet dickheadedness, the vortex reawakened. The heaving howl of it blasted into the night around us followed by a series of groans and creaks that signaled the arrival of nothing particularly fun or positive. The Shepherd's face lit up with pure, unadulterated joy. The corners of the room cracked and snapped and the roof tore off in one clean piece. It went spinning and flying off into the desert like the vortex itself tossed it somewhere far off with a thunderous crash. Wooden fingers curled around the edges of the church, where the walls would've met the roof and the behemoth pulled himself forward out of the darkness, glaring down at me with that haunting Gulchy glee.

"Awakening THE BEHEMOTH!" The Shepherd called up to it triumphantly.

Keep your cool, Cyrus. Don't let him know how close to pants shitting territory you are.

"Right. Your whole big evil plan is to make Gulchy a real boy." I said, as cooly as possible under the circumstances.

"Once the destroyer of worlds reaches his full might, *nothing* will stand in our way! The Father will claim this world as his own!" He shouted over the roar of the vortex. "He just needs one. More. Soul."

I had a solid guess as to who's soul he was talking about.

The Shepherd ran the blade of his dagger up his shirt, slicing it open. He tore it from his body, revealing a form more muscular than his usual uniform would've suggested.

"That's excessive." I said because it was. You didn't see me cutting me clothes off to prove how buff and hardcore I was. I'm not that insecure. "What, are we gonna fuck first?"

"Joke all you want, Stone." He said as he made his way down from his altar and to the head of the room, standing amongst the wreckage of his front pews. "I can smell your fear! Practically taste it."

"Gross. You wanna taste me?"

"I'll take the greatest pleasure in harvesting your soul for him myself." He sneered at me as he brandished his curved blade of condemnation menacingly.

Keep it simple. Start with what you know.

I drew my stake and held it at the ready, my grip like a vise around it. My eyes narrowed. As did the Shepherd's. We sized each other up, planning our first strikes while guessing where the other's would fall. My heart jackhammered in my chest as a bead of anxious sweat rolled down my brow. My stomach lurched and my muscles tensed, like a rattlesnake about to strike.

For the Le Coeurs.

"Let's dance, hot pants."

We charged at each other full speed. The church blurred around me as my vision focused on him and only him. We crashed together in the center of the room with titanic force.

His dagger went high, my stake rose to meet it. His dagger went low, I sidestepped and plunged the stake forward. His arm deflected it. He was fast. Faster than I expected. Almost faster than me. The shining platinum of his dagger was everywhere all at once, whizzing past my flesh and missing by inches as I blocked and dodged his strikes. But I was no slouch either. My stake cut through the air furiously, desperate to find its target but met with his blade at every point of entry. Sparks flew from our weapons as they clashed and glanced off each other.

We independently but simultaneously agreed to mix it up. In came the fists and feet. A right hook to my jaw, a jab to his solar plexus, and uppercut to my nose, a knee to his gut. An absolute haymaker came down on my face, I caught it mid air and responded with a left cross to his. We traded blows and stabs, equally skilled in the killing arts and too equally matched for either of us to gain the upper hand. We fought like two sides of the same coin. He knew my moves before I did and I matched his perfectly as they came.

Block this, mother fucker.

I leaped up and tucked my knees in. My legs shot out like a cannonball in front of me and straight into his chest. The Shepherd flew back to the altar, smashing into it as I hit the ground with a hard bang. He slowly got to his feet, brushing splinters and shards of the wooden altar from his shoulder.

"Enough of this. The time has come." He snarled at me as he split blood onto the floor. Thick, black blood. Like he was full of printer ink.

"For you to die?" I shot back. "You're right. Thought you'd put up more of a fight honestly. I brought all this shit with me." I said as I glanced back to the tortoises, stalling to give myself time to catch my breath.

"No." The Shepherd said as he raised his arms at his sides. "The Father approaches."

Flames burst from the floor under him. A rolling tornado of fire spun its way up to the exposed sky as it engulfed him. I pulled my hat low to shield my eyes from the impossibly bright burn.

His voice boomed through the fire, filling the church.

"See, Stone, Gulchy has *always* been a real boy! And much closer than you've ever known."

The flames climbed higher and higher, out through the open roof and towards the clouds of smoke above us. They spread out, consuming what was left of the altar and the front rows of pews, scorching the floor to embers. I took a step back, then another as the violent firestorm clawed at the church around it. A hand reached out from within it. Larger than the Shepherd's, larger than the Gargoyle Sheriff's, with long, yellow hooked nails on the ends of its sausage-shaped fingers. The rest of the muppet demon came into view as he stepped through the fire. Hulking, like literally he was as big as the Hulk. Ten feet tall at least with muscles on his muscles and skin like granite. Taking it all in at once threatened to shatter my hold on reality so I chose to itemize. Thick, heavy hooves. Tall, pointed bat-like ears. A mouth that had once been full of teeth that was now just a collection of stray and wayward fangs under a long white beard. Big, almost welcoming and oddly friendly eyes and crazy Doc Brown hair. The most monumental, sinister and unsettling demon I had ever laid eyes on. With the face of Gulchy E. Gulcherson and a vampire bat's nose.

"Hawdy, folks!" He said with an ominous smile that mirrored the behemoth as the flames flared out behind him. His voice high and borderline cartoonish.

"The fuck is this?!"

"When I done founded this dip durn town, it was for a reason, I tell ya what!"

"What...what the hell is going on here?!" I seriously needed clarification. I looked to my tortoises and I swear I saw them shrug, just as lost as I was.

"I was the preacher!" He roared in that goofy Gulchy voice. "Me! Your ol' puppet demon pal Gulchy Gulcherson!"

"Are you kidding me?! *You're* the muppet demon?!"

"Gulchy got no daddy but his-self! I tell ya, this here Gulch is on the perfect intersection of demonic ley lines! A place for all the evils of Hell to converge into one spot. That's whys I builts the town here! But I wasn't strong enough to control it back yonder. Hads to be patient like a buck hunter in the bush and wait for my influence to grow! And now that that fleshy meat sack has helped me become strong enough to show my true hootin' hollerin' form again, the big guy and I will use the Gulch's power to reduce yer world to ashes!"

"HAWDY, FOLKS!" The behemoth rumbled, its voice now deeper like the grinding of the gears inside it as it stepped around the church.

"Hawdy, folks!" The real Gulchy hollered back up at him.

"HAWDY, FOLKS!"

"Hawdy, folks!"

"Alright!" I yelled over them. "This is weird. I'm over it. Tortoises!" I barked over my shoulder. They straightened up and raised their heads in a majestic display of intimidation. "The guns!"

The front line crept towards me as fast as they could. But I mean, they were tortoises, it was still gonna take a minute. Gulchy cackled fiendishly.

"You're turtle magic can't save you now, Hunter of Evil!"

A gargantuan wooden fist came smashing down into the tortoises like an asteroid, crushing the middle lines and sweeping away the survivors behind them. The behemoth wiped out the majority of my infantry with a single strike and swat. Their bodies and my gear flew like boulders back into the town. I dove for the front line as they made their way into the church, barely escaping the behemoth's wrath. The first two tortoises, the head of my slow charge, twin 12-gauge Winchester 1901 lever-action repeating shotguns and a whole fuckload of silver buckshot. I hit the ground with a roll in front of them and retrieved my deadly payload in a flash.

"He's not quite there yet but he's still handy in a pinch, ain't he?!" Gulchy yelled smugly.

I jammed in as many shells as the shotguns could handle.

"He'll get there though, that's fer sure!" He went on. "Right after I SWALLOW YER SOUL!"

I wheeled around to face my foe, the twins raised at eye level.

BOOM! BOOM!

The shotguns exploded as fiery molten silver burst from their mouths. They kicked violently in my hands like they were making a break to freedom, but I refused to let them go. Gulchy let out an animalistic cry as the silver peppered his chest. As far as his body was concerned, the buckshot might as well have been bird. But the look of anguish on his face was all the motivation I needed to keep going.

"Watchit fella! That really hurt!"

A satisfied smile curled my lips as the pleasure of his pain washed over me. With a snap of my wrists I quickly spun the twins by their levers, cocking them like a stone cold killing machine. Two fresh shells racked in, ready to fly.

"Good."

The thunder of the shotguns overlapped as I fired. There would be no quarter for Gulchy Gulcherson. I wouldn't allow it now that I knew he wasn't a fan of silver shells. I fell into a pretty fun rhythm.

Shoot one, spin the other, shoot, advance, rinse and repeat. BOOM! Forward. Spin. BOOM! Forward. Spin. BOOM! He whined and cried as the silver ripped into him in sequence and I closed the space between us. Each volley hammered into his body and knocked him a little closer to the back wall. The unnecessarily loud CLICK of two empty shotguns stopped my heart for a beat as Gulchy dropped to the floor and doubled over in pain.

"Aw! Ow! Ah! Ya got me! Ya got me! I'm dyin'! I'm dead." He wailed unconvincingly. My smile died immediately.

"Well that smells like bull—"

Before I could reload or even finish my sentence, Gulchy sprang from the floor with blistering demonic speed, my throat clutched in his hand under enough pressure to make my eyes bulge as he lifted me off my feet.

"Gotcha, friend!" He sneered in my face, breath like the burning flesh of a million damned.

"That's about right." I gurgled.

Gulchy effortlessly tossed me across the church. I flailed through the air, no more than a rag doll's worth of weight to him, and smashed into the pews. He was toying with me. Enjoying the kill and taking it slow, comfortable in the knowledge that he was in control.

The pain barely even had time to register before he was on me again, grabbing my whole head in a single hand like it was a baseball. His skin was course on my face and reeked of sulfur. I felt my body rocket as he threw me again. The interior of the church ripped away from me as I slammed through the front wall and out into the night.

I hit the ground and rolled through the dirt limply. Gulchy's wretched cackle screeched from out of the church. My eyes spun as they landed on the crushed corpses of dozens of fallen tortoises warriors. There was no time to mourn them though. Gulchy was on me again in the blink of an eye. He gripped me tightly by the ankle and squeezed. The bones in my leg crunched and cracked as he swung me high over his head and and down through the church steps, hammering me into a shallow crater of splintered wood and dirt.

"Ow." I grunted plainly despite the fact that it felt like my whole ass was broken, refusing to let him know how badly that hurt.

The demon Gulcherson loomed over me. His eyes glowed a deep, hateful shade of crimson like they were made of magma. I winced as he cocked his leg back and kicked me with a casual indifference like I was an annoying Chihuahua. I flew through the broken church entryway likc a silver bullet and smashed cleanly through the back wall.

Sliding through the dirt as I landed, I came to a stop inches from the edge of the chasm. The heat was greater than anything man could've ever produced. Burning souls in an infernal bonfire set in the earth's crust. The flames licked up at me from deep down like greedy hands that couldn't wait to pull me in.

"Ah! Ah! Fire!" I shouted as I clambered to my feet and backed away from the rim of oblivion.

"HAWDY, FOLKS!" The behemoth roared from above.

A giant clockwork hand closed crushingly around me. It raised me slowly, high over the chasm and the remains of the worst Gulchy Day the town had ever known. He held me up to its face to meet its gaze. A deep red glow from his eyes that matched his boss's bathed me as I struggled against his clockwork fingers. It gave me a strong squeeze. Snapping and popping around my lungs signaled every one of my ribs breaking. I ignored the pain as I pushed and pulled and wriggled until I worked my revolver free. The behemoth let out a quaking, moaning growl from its un-moving mouth. It rattled my teeth and shook my brain, but I wrestled my arm free from its grip all the same. I raised the revolver and emptied it right into the bright red orb it called an eye. It ex-ploded into a thick black slime, leaving an empty socket where no actual eye had been. It oozed and spurted black tar down the behemoth's face like he was full of the stuff as I tucked the revolver away.

The abominable Pincchio groaned as it swayed and sprayed slime from its face. He covered his new eye hole with one sprawling hand and the other flailed rigidly yet frenzied as it stumbled, dangling me over the dead center of the burning chasm and the vortex. His stiff body teetered and tottered and threatened to tip over into the abyss beside it.

"No! No! Go back the other way! Fall the other way!" I shouted at it.

With a slow, mechanical shake of its head the behemoth regained its composure and steadied itself. A low growl rumbled up from its gears and cogs as it realized where it was still dangling me. The demon Gulchy cackled below us. He stepped through the hole I left in the back wall of the church as it burst violently around his imposing form.

"It's a helluva a thang, Stone! Holdin' all that ya need in the palm of yer hand!" He yelled up to me. "Why I'd give anythang to be in his shoes right naw!"

The behemoth centered me over the mouth of the vortex. The aggressive soul vacuum pulled at my feet. One of the massive fingers binding me creaked as its mechanisms strained. It's pinky sprang free with a metallic clang and my legs hung freely.

"Oh shit." I muttered.

"Oops! Don't look like he'll be holdin' it fer much longer!"

Gulchy laughed madly on the ground as I fought to dig my hand to my satchel.

"Hold on! I know I've got something in here!"

Its ring finger shot free. Gulchy howled in demented delight. My hand worked its way to its target, the heavy leather of my predecessor protecting me from the jagged splinters and sharp slivers digging into my arm. The side of the satchel teased my fingertips. The behemoth's middle finger began to creak and moan. I wormed my hand into the satchel and grabbed the first thing it landed on. Barnaby's mezcal. The middle finger jolted outward with another loud clang of its inner workings. I held onto the pointer finger with everything I had, the only one now holding me beyond its thumb. It was a mixed bag. One more finger and I'd be in serious trouble. But for now it meant I had room to work. I pulled the mezcal from my satchel and tossed it underhanded up the behemoth's arm. It shattered against the wood, leaving a dark, wet spot a few feet from the hand. I dove back into my satchel and found the old pack of Chesterfields.

The index finger flew away from the thumb like the behemoth was flicking a gigantic bug. My grip and core strength were put to their ultimate test as I wrapped it and hung on. I slammed into the rest of the fingers, nearly slipping off. My feet scrambled to gain purchase between them as I fumbled with the pack of cigarettes. The top flipped open. I pulled one of the long, stale smokes from the pack with my mouth as it slipped through my grasp and drifted down into the chasm.

One for the boys.

The behemoth swung its arm back and forth in a wide swipe in front of it. Slow and creaky at first but quickly gaining momentum. I pulled myself up on the finger and wrapped an arm around it, squeezing as tightly as I could. My free arm dove into the jacket to the inside pocket. Jackets change, where I keep my lighter doesn't. Shit I'll *make* an inside pocket if I have to! That's where the lighter goes. I clicked it to life and brought it to the cigarette, taking a few healthy drags and hoping they wouldn't be my last. Especially since old cigarettes taste like shit. And I don't even think they make Chesterfields anymore.

It got harder to hang on as the behemoth's arm gained speed and the threat of being shaken off became even more real. My aim would have to be precise.

Work with the wind, not against it.

I flicked the old, stale smoke. It's cherry glowed brightly as it went end over end through the air, landing right on the wet mezcal on the behemoth's arm. A fire, insignificant to the beast, ignited. Gulchy's laughter below reached near gut-busting levels.

"Ya tried, Cyrus Stone! Ya can always tell folks that!"

My thoughts exactly.

A wrench in his plans.

If I didn't make it, at least I'd take Gulchy's big buddy with me. I slid that fire ring I couldn't remember the purpose of off my finger.

"Let's see what you do."

With all of my strength and determination to do damage, I slammed the ring down into the weathered joints of the behemoth's fingers, burying it deep. Absolutely nothing happened.

"Seriously?!"

The behemoth didn't even seem to notice. But then, starting at the small fire on its arm and working its way up to its head, a scorching blaze spread over the body made out of dry kindling. The behemoth moaned in shocked misery as its chest and head burned. The obnoxious evil laughing from the ground stopped as the fire shot down the behemoth's legs. It staggered as it rocked back and forth over the chasm, desperate to find a way to save its self and put out the blaze. Its hands came up to its face swat the flames. Seeing my one opportunity, I let go. Plunging helplessly to relative safety below. I slammed down hard on the edge of the chasm, most definitely breaking my ass. Even so, it was better than the alternative.

The behemoth's moans got louder and more crazed as every inch of its body was covered in a fire it'd never be able to put out. Its wooden legs lifted and stomped as it tried to will itself to run. Instead, it only managed to trip over itself. Apparently my soul would've been the one to help it really nail its fine motor skills. It fell face first into the chasm. Hell itself greedily reclaimed it. An eruption of flame and embers shot into the sky as I backed away and the behemoth burned to nothing.

The vortex spun more aggressively as I pushed myself to my feet. A powerful wind pushed me back and howls of intake became the blast of release as it reversed direction. In a blast of gray fog like a steam engine, stolen souls exploded from the mouth of the vortex. Flying off in every direction, knowing their way back to their respective owners. No longer bound to the incinerated behemoth. A deep pride overcame me. Pride and pain from the amount of blunt force trauma and broken bones I had. But that's neither here nor there. I smiled up at the souls as they darted for home.

A force like a freight train hit square in the back and threw me off my feet. I touched down with a skid inches from falling into the chasm. A cloven hoof hammered down onto my chest before I could react, shattering sternum into a dozen jagged shards. Gulchy leaned down to me.

"Ya think you've won, Hunter of Evil?!" He screamed in my face. "Ya think killing my best friend in the whole wide world will stop me?! All you've done is slow me down! I was gonna give your kind a quick death but without my dad gum champion, I'm just gonna have ta do it *nice* and *slow*. One by one!"

I reached for my gun, stealthily drawing it from its holster and angling it towards Gulchy's head. The click of the hammer as I squeezed the trigger reminded me that it was empty. But that didn't matter to the pissed off Gulchy. He swatted the gun from hand, snapping the bones holding it like twigs.

"Clearly," I grunted as I struggled breath as my chest cavity collapsed, "I've struck some sort of nerve here."

"Oh, don't worry, fella!" Gulchy growled as he straightened up and glared down at me. "You and yer pals will be down thar sooner than a pinecone on a porcupine!"

"What does that even mean?"

"Ya can tell them all about how ya died!" He yelled vengefully as he raised a clawed hand high.

I closed my eyes, accepting whatever came next. Comfortable in the knowledge that I had, in fact, slowed him down and made his wretched life more difficult. And more than a little satisfied in knowing that the pain of losing his champion seemed to be far worse than anything I had done to him physically. My work was done. My mission accomplished. And so would end the Hunter of Evil.

Gulchy screamed, deeply and anguished. He fell over, landing the dirt next to me. He writhed in excruciating pain and clutched his leg, a torrent of blood flooded from under his hand. Something hard and sharped scraped against my boot. I looked up and there was Benicio, Gulchy's Achilles Tendon hanging from his fearsome little mouth in a mass of bloody demon flesh.

"I owe you one, little buddy." I said to him with a nod and a tip of my hat. I owed him more than that honestly. This whole thing would've gone tits up if it wasn't for my brave tortoise.

"Auuurg!" He totally knew that.

Getting up was difficult, painful and borderline impossible. But I did it anyway. I stood over Gulchy as he rolled around in tormenting pain.

"How 'bout this instead?" I asked him rhetorically. "I go back to my friends. . .and tell them all about how you got your ass kicked by me?!"

"AUUUG!"

"Right, sorry, bud. And a tortoise! I'll tell the whole world how you got your ass kicked by me *and* a tortoise!"

I pulled a vial of holy water from my satchel, sticking to what I know, and smashed it on Gulchy's face. His dark gray skin sizzled and burned as his hands shot from his mangled leg to his melting face. His cries boomed around us as his skin fell between his fingers, revealing a jet black skull underneath. I calmly drew my stake and let out a mighty, barbaric holler. The stake went up and right back down harder than was measurable and faster than the eye could perceive, burying itself deep into Gulchy's skull. His screams and cries were cut off, red eyes full of fiery hate stared up at me.

"Y'all. . .come back. . .now..." He strained to get out against his dying breath. His eyes cooled and faded, two dark coals in his face.

I knelt down and got my hands under his massive body. The weight was impossible, but I was determined. Refusing to give into the toll on my very broken body and with a powerful push, I rolled him over the edge of the chasm. His body fell down into Hell, taking my stake with it. A warning to everything else down there of what happens when you fuck with Cyrus Stone. When you cross the Hunter of Evil.

The chasm erupted as it had at its formation. Flames reached high into the sky, breaking up the clouds of smoke and letting sunlight finally break through. The ground rose up within it, snuffing the eruption and healing the earth like it was moving backwards in time. The graves of the past Gulchers returned, their headstones shooting up out of the ground all around. The walls of the church crumbled inward. What was left of the structure imploded in on itself, leaving a pile of condemned rubble and debris.

The clouds dissipated over the town and the warm high noon sun beat down. I raised my face to it and welcomed its warmth, having never realized just how nice the middle of the day could feel or how serene the valley could be. But it was time for my body to shut down whether I liked it or not. I weakly dropped to my knees, damn near every important bone broken and what I could only guess was a considerable amount of internal bleeding. Darkness flooded my vision as blood leaked from my mouth and I fell face first into the dirt.

21

AFTER

"Charlotte, he's awake!" A familiar voice exclaimed excitedly in the darkness.

Footsteps rushed around me as I fought through what felt like twenty pounds of concrete encasing my body. Slowly, sluggishly, I fluttered my eyes open. A blur of light forced them into a tightly pinched squint. The figures around me came into view as out of focus as old Sasquatch footage. I blinked hard, pushing out some of the grogginess and blur. Barnaby and Charlotte smiled down on me in a sea of peaceful light.

"Aw shit, I'm dead."

"No!" Barnaby said with a laugh. "Buddy, you are very much alive."

"And so are we thanks to you." Charlotte beamed at me.

I blinked again. The light around them dulled and the Sanctum came into view. Benicio clawed playfully at the foot of my cot.

"Are you sure?" It's always a good idea to double check.

"Positive." Barnaby said.

"Like totally sure?! You checked that time is working right and you can touch shit and all that?" There was also a strong chance that we were all ghosts.

"Yes!" Charlotte said with an obnoxious but slightly endearing smirk.

"Good." I grunted as I sat up on my cot. "The behemoth...?"

"Released our souls when you killed it." Barnaby confirmed.

"Totally knew that would happen." I rubbed the coma from my eyes. "Called it!"

I threw my legs over the edge and my boots clunked down on the very real floor.

"Take it easy, Cy." Barnaby said as he steadied me.

"I'm good. I'm good." I protested.

"That's because you're fully healed! Minor miracle that your gargoyle wounds held up as well as they did. Sealed is not healed!" He scoffed.

"I could barely even feel them." I shrugged.

"Yeah, no shit." Barnaby replied with a glance over to the crypt, the bottle of Le Coeur Special still resting in front of the names of the fallen. "Nice touch, by the way."

"Thanks. I thought so too."

The Sanctum was much more organized since the last time I was in here. The boxes and trunks were neatly stacked. The weapons and relics were looking a little light, but I guess that was on me. The books had been returned to their shelves, except for one.

"I, uh, missed you guys." I forced myself to say, uncomfortable with that level of intimacy but determined to power through it anyway.

"We could tell!" Charlotte said playfully.

"You did good." Barnaby offered with a smile.

"Did I really?" I needed to know.

"You tell me." Barnaby said as he crouched next to the cot to meet my eye.

"Well." I started as I took a deep breath. "I lit the behemoth thing on fire and it fell into the chasm and then the chasm, like, ate him. So that was that."

Barnaby nodded, acknowledging a job well done.

"And then I stabbed Gulchy in the head with my stake and kicked his ass back into Hell."

Barnaby looked to the floor as Charlotte tried her hardest to wrap her mind around what I had just said.

"Auurrg!"

"Right, yeah, Benicio helped."

"AUUUR!"

"Alright, Benicio helped *a lot!*" Credit where credit was due.

"Wait, Gulchy?!" Charlotte asked, need-ing to verify that I said what she thought I said.

"The Shepherd." Saying his name left a bad taste in my mouth, like licking a lemon filled with battery acid. "He turned into a big demon Gulchy and tossed me around for awhile. The behemoth too! They were both Gulchy and Gulchy was the muppet demon, somethin' like that."

"The First Form?!" Barnaby shouted as he shot up to his feet.

"I guess! He might've mentioned that. Gave me this whole monologue about needing to grow and how he built the town on the perfect intersection of evil blahblahblah or something like that. I don't know, I'm a little foggy."

"That tracks!" Barnaby said as his mind connected the dots. "Build the town, build power, build influence, wake up the big guy."

"Yeah, we should probably go ahead and cancel Gulchy Day next year. Feels a little triggery now." I suggested.

That concerned shared look came back to Barnaby and Charlotte as they stared at each other.

"Oh fuck me, what now?"

"His soul. Did you kill it?" Barnaby asked, a little afraid of the answer.

I poured through my memories on a desperate search for the answer, but nothing I recalled really looked like soul murder to me.

"I mean, I kicked him back into Hell. Does that count?"

"Alright." Barnaby said as he nodded. I could tell though. It wasn't alright. "That jacket looked good on you by the way."

Barnaby broke away and headed for the workbench, where the thick brown leather book Charlotte was attached to was still resting. My new jacket was draped carefully over the stool. Barnaby retrieved the book and returned to Charlotte and I.

"It's time I told you some things. I've put them off long enough." He said with the weight of generations on his shoulders.

"I like stories." I said because I did.

Barnaby sat next to me on the edge of the cot and opened the book to its first page. In a scrawling, flowing, cursive it read "The Testament of Montgomery Le Coeur".

"Your—" I started.

"Great great grandpappy." Barnaby finished with a prideful smirk.

He turned the page, the same handwritten cursive covered every square inch of the ones that followed.

"And the original Hunter, the man who's jacket you now wear." He went on as he searched for a particular entry. "I've waited a long time to show this all to you. And I'm sorry it didn't come sooner."

After a few moments of pregnant silence, Barnaby found the pages he was looking for. He took another, shorter beat to prepare himself and then read aloud:

"And so he left. No instruction and no idea what he was getting himself into. He loaded that old black mare, Enrique, down with guns and was gone before I could stop him. That was the man I had come to know. His wife and son begged same as I, but there was a wrong in the Gulch and he had to be the one to correct it. By far the stupidest and most courageous man I'd ever seen, the Hunter of Evil. A damned fool and a hero if I've ever seen one. There's comfort in knowing that I did all I could. This Sanctum and its collection of books and weapons. All we've become since my suspicions first reared their ugly heads and that unwavering determination set deep in his heart. It was still not enough. I knew that destroying the demon's body would be one matter, while his soul was another entirely. Somewhere in one of those books was the answer to the riddle that was dooming the beast. He needed me and I failed him."

Barnaby paused, a tear in his eye for the repetition of history.

"When the town went quiet, I knew what it meant. I ran as fast as I could to the chasm on the edge of town. Like a great coal fire set deep in a hole in reality itself. There's no knowing what went on before, but when I came upon the scene it was but the aftermath of a great and terrible battle for sure. Discarded guns and bullet casings covered the ground, blood in deep puddles both human, equine and damned. Enrique lay dead, ripped clean in half from head to toe. I watched him fall into the pit and out of existence with the villainous hand of the beast wrapped tightly around his leg.

Leaving only his jacket, tossed aside in the dirt, as a reminder of the man who had given all for our young town. The chasm closed and that was that. Any sign of the demon vanished with it. I made a vow, right there and then. One our children would be wise to keep up with. As long as there is a Hunter of Evil, there will always be a Le Coeur by his side. Our fight was over it seemed, but while the demon's soul lives we will never be truly safe. An evil like that won't leave well enough alone. The end of our troubles, but the beginning for those still to come. The end of Hershel Stone but the beginning of the legend that will be the Hunter of Evil."

Barnaby held the book in his lap as he looked at me, brimming with admiration and relief.

"I'm sorry, could you repeat all that? I'm having a really hard time paying attention."

"Damn it, Cyrus!" Barnaby snapped as he shut the book. "My great great grandpappy helped the first Hunter of Evil and the first Hunter of Evil was *yours!*"

"Whoa." I said as that sunk in.

"That coat and title have passed down your line same as the saloon and Sanctum have ours." He explained with a nod to Charlotte. "I tell you this because it's time you knew. Your parents, that was no random attack! Your father was the Hunter before you."

"Oh fuck." Was all I could manage to say as that hit me square in the chest like a sledgehammer. "Why didn't you tell me?"

"He never wanted you to know. His daddy told him because his daddy told *him* and his daddy told him before that! He wanted to keep you from this life same as I tried with Charlotte. Or at the very least make it your choice."

"How did that work out?" She chimed in.

"Exactly!" Barnaby continued. "When you broke in that night, I knew there'd be no avoiding. You were drawn here by something greater than yourself. I knew someday I'd have to tell you. There's no escaping fate. But not before you were ready to hear it. These facts would've destroyed a child. This story was suppose to come with the jacket you decided to steal."

"My old one was all fucked up!" I shot back in my defense. "I mean you could've put it in the letter, that would've been cool too."

"Man, it was supposed to be this whole big moment! Tell you the story, give you the trunk, you read the letter, start your journey towards fate, all that shit!"

"Who's got the time for that?" I groaned. *Seriously.*

"We sure didn't!" Charlotte argued.

"No, we did not." Barnaby agreed. "That was my bad. So I'm glad it played out like this. But still. Did you catch the details in the story?"

Wait, did I?

"Nope!"

Barnaby sighed.

"Try to keep up, man."

"You're dumping a lot of information on me! I've been awake for like six minutes!"

"Fair. Alright." Barnaby breathed out his frustration. "Hershel Stone was dragged into Hell with the Puppet Demon—"

"Lame."

"But all the blood and shit implies that he had killed, or at least mostly killed his body."

"Great. I'm following."

"You better be! This is important. You did the same thing. Killed his body and kicked him back down, right?"

"Unless he could survive a vial of holy water to the face and a stake in his brain."

"Not likely. But he's back in Hell now, you sent him home. With his soul in tact."

"Not really sure what to do about that."

"He'll do what he did last time. He'll wait. And get stronger. And be back."

"Nothing like a little job security."

"But there's time again now." Charlotte added. "And we'll be ready when he does."

"We better be." I growled, seriously not wanting to go through all that again.

"We will!" Barnaby said as he stood and placed an arm around Charlotte. "The Sanctum will be in good hands."

I stared at the two of them confused as they smiled down at me like some happy monster hunting graduation photo.

"Wait, what?"

"I'm going to be scaling my hours back." Barnaby said, his voice full of pride.

"Why?!" I asked incredulously. "Where are you going?!"

"I've got something else to do now." He said simply.

"That's super vague and unhelpful." I grumbled back.

Charlotte left us to grab a stray piece of paper from the workbench. As she handed it to me, I could read the big bold block letters at the top of it. "Le Coeur for Mayor". I took the campaign flier from her and examined it. Set against the blood moon from the saloon's wooden sign, it read "Le Coeur Le Cares."

Who the fuck came up with that? That's stupid.

"Well shit. I'd vote for you." I conceded.

"I'll be in a better position to spot trouble coming." Barnaby explained.

"I like that." I nodded as a smile crawled its way up my face. It was a solid idea. "Mayor Le Coeur."

"Craine got impeached." Charlotte said probably a little too sympathetically.

"That's what happens when you let a demon take over the damn town!" Barnaby shouted.

I could tell. It wasn't entirely about the muppet demon. If I had to guess, I'd say the saloon would have a patio before long.

"Hold on. How long have I been out?!" I asked as all these new developments wrapped around me.

"Two and a half weeks." Charlotte answered like it was no big deal that I apparently slept for the better part of a month. In my boots. And pants.

"God damn it." I groaned as I stood up. "I've got shit to do."

"We know." She said.

I grabbed my hat and satchel from the floor next to the cot and put them on, making sure to give Benicio a pat on the head first.

"I'll come back as soon as I can." I said as I crossed to the workbench and my jacket.

"You always do." Barnaby added as I threw the old duster on, my gun and a fresh silver stake on the stool under it. "Oh wait! There's one more thing."

I holstered my weapons and turned back to him.

"The Gulchers. They know what you did for them. Most of it anyway. They wanted to thank you for the whole weresheep thing so they gave you a gift. A reward, I guess."

"What, like money?"

Money would be great.

"No, they all came together and agreed to give you this."

Barnaby pulled a set of old, black steel keys on a heavy ring from his pocket. They jangled across the Sanctum as he tossed them to me. I snatched them from the air and examined them with a curious eye. They looked like the old pirate keys that would've fit the lock I had so expertly picked to get to my new jacket and the prologue to Barnaby's history lesson.

"The keys to Gulchy Manor." Barnaby said. "I hear its haunted."

God damn it.

"They found out about the hunting shack?" I asked.

"They found out about the hunting shack." He answered.

"Alright. I'll check it out."

I stashed the keys in my satchel and released the Sanctum door, the bright white light fading to the dim glow of the bar on the other side. It was early still. The sun was dipping low outside. No doubt patrons would be returning to the stools soon now that they had no church to go to. Or at least I hoped. I grabbed a bottle of whatever was closest to me, just in case.

Pushing through the heavy door, I emerged onto the street. The sun was a little more unusual than it had been in the past. To my eyes, it looked like it was taking just a little longer with its retreat behind the mountains. Almost like it knew that Gulchy's Gulch deserved just a little more light now. The streets were quiet and I could feel the normal curious eyes on me as I made my way across the town. But for the first time, it didn't feel like they were keeping tabs on me. Everyone wanted to catch a glimpse of the heroic Hunter of Evil. The man who saved them. And who was right all along.

I lit a smoke as I hit the road in and out of town. A gentle wind blew my coat open as I turned my hat against it. The mountains stood tall and ominous ahead of me, same as they always had. There was work to do elsewhere. There always was. And nothing on earth or in Hell would stop me from doing it. I'd climb my way up them and walk through the pass with my hat low, my eyes sharp, and a hand on my gun. As I had many times before and would many more times still to come. Now more than ever, as the sun made its exit and the moon crested the mountains, I had no fear of whatever lurked in their cursed shadows. Whatever horrors they contained within and beyond would tremble and cower before me. My name is Cyrus Stone. And I hunt evil.

An Uber would be great right now.

Cyrus Stone will return.

Acknowledgments

This book wouldn't have happened at all without Ari Stidham. "I think it's a book" is perhaps his greatest contribution among the many that he gave to Cyrus Stone. Not even to mention all the ideas and silly-ass pitches that made their way into the final text. Suggesting I call it "Gulchy's Gulch" opened a demonic can of worms I never want to close! Thank you, dude. Really. This doesn't exist without you.

Blake, if it wasn't for your constant support, belief and all the hours of listening to me ramble on about these stories, there's no way I would've finished. You kept the faith when I didn't have it myself! Thank you.

And to my family for always believing that I would figure my shit out sooner or later! Sorry it took me so long!

CPSIA information can be obtained
at www.ICGtesting.com
Printed in the USA
BVHW042344050723
666811BV00001B/3

9 798218 221584